DEEP GOLD

SOME WILL DIVE FOR IT.
SOME MUST DIE FOR IT.

ALTMAN: The specialist. He fought—and survived—in the waters off Vietnam. Now, for the first time, he's in over his head.

HARRINGTON: England's man. He tries to keep the operation from exploding in their faces—and for his failure pays a brutal price.

JONES: The captain. No superpower on earth will stop him from bringing up the gold.

PETROSKY: Russia's man. A master diplomatic troubleshooter, he can be both careful and quick on the trigger.

GREY: The President's man. He serves his boss far better than he serves his country.

DEEP GOLD

JAY AMBERG

WARNER BOOKS

A Time Warner Company

WARNER BOOKS EDITION

Copyright © 1991 by Jay Amberg
All rights reserved.

Cover design and illustration by Paul Bacon

Warner Books, Inc.
666 Fifth Avenue
New York, N.Y. 10103

W A Time Warner Company

Printed in the United States of America

First Printing: September, 1991

10 9 8 7 6 5 4 3 2 1

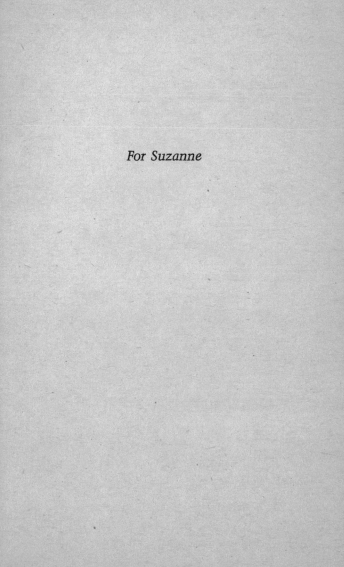

For Suzanne

Thanks and appreciation to Andrew H. Zack for his editorial advice and guidance.

▽ **Prologue** ▽

Murmansk, Russia
May, 1942

In the gray twilight of the arctic night, sleet swept across the deck of a Soviet motor launch approaching the British heavy cruiser HMS *Edinburgh* in Kola Inlet. A tall, broad-shouldered American wearing a long gray overcoat stood on the launch's bow. He pulled the brim of his hat lower over his eyes and, one hand braced against the launch's tarpaulin-covered cargo, stared at the British cruiser. Six hundred and thirteen feet long, the *Edinburgh* boasted four triple turrets of six-inch guns and a dozen four-inch guns. Amidships, sleek tubes housed torpedoes with 750-pound warheads. Four Walrus biplanes stood in the hangars by her launching catapult and recovery cranes. Radar disks on her mastheads scanned the sky.

As the motor launch anchored along the *Edinburgh*'s starboard side shortly after midnight, the cruiser's bugler sounded the call: Both watches on duty fall in. The crew, pulling on duffel coats and balaclava helmets, piled on deck. While thirty Soviet marines lined the launch's railing, an officer marched stiffly out of the wheelhouse. As he spoke

to the American, the launch's searchlights played across the
Edinburgh, temporarily blinding the ship's crew and casting
a dazzling glow in the sleet. A sea ladder was lowered from
the *Edinburgh*'s quarterdeck; the launch's two 47-millimeter
guns were swung around and trained on the cruiser. The
American nodded to the Soviet officer, pointed to the cargo,
climbed the ladder, and met a contingent of Royal Marines
that escorted him to the cruiser's bridge.

A short time later, as the sleet turned to snow, Frank
Swanson, the *Edinburgh*'s chief petty officer on duty, received the order to load the cargo. A squad of British sailors
descended to the barge tied alongside the *Edinburgh* and,
uncovering the tarpaulin, found 135 wooden ammunition
boxes. Each box was bound with copper wire and sealed at
the top; each had rope handles and thick red stenciling.
Although not large, the boxes were so heavy—almost two
hundred pounds apiece—that it took two men to lift them.
As the sailors made their way across the icy deck of the
barge and up the ladder to the cruiser's deck, the rumors
began to spread—the cargo was gold, more than twelve tons
of Russian gold.

Petty Officer Swanson ordered the sailors to carry the
boxes all the way to the flight deck and then to lower them
by ropes through a trunk shaft to the bomb room in the
bowels of the ship. As Swanson supervised the loading of
the cargo, the American joined him on the flight deck. Sleet
and snow clinging to the crown of his hat, the American
greeted Swanson, nodding and saying in a voice with a
slight twang, "A fine night in hell's kitchen, isn't it." He
stuffed his hands into his pockets and silently watched the
cargo serpentine from the launch to the shaft. Swanson was
unsure if he should salute or even speak to the American
who, though obviously a civilian, seemed to wield power
over both the Soviet and British officers.

Swanson heard the contradictory rumors circulate, build,
and take on a life of their own: The gold had been the

czar's, accumulated from foreign wheat sales before the revolution. . . . It was Stalin's personal stockpile, the evil residue of his purges. . . . It had just been mined by slave laborers in Siberia. The gold was headed for Washington, D.C., to pay the war debt. . . . It was bound for the United States to purchase the ultimate weapon in the struggle against the Nazis. The gold had been hidden in Murmansk for a year. . . . It had only recently made the perilous thousand-mile journey by rail from Moscow, just ahead of the advancing German army. The presence of the gold was top secret. . . . The Nazis had learned that the gold was being loaded aboard the *Edinburgh* and would do anything to capture it—or destroy it.

The American alone knew where the cargo had been mined, by what tortuous route it had reached Murmansk, why it was being loaded aboard the *Edinburgh*, and where it was ultimately headed. But he turned his coat collar up under his hat and, hunching his shoulders against the wind, continued to stare impassively into the snow, as though he heard none of the sailor's bantering.

When eighty-seven of the boxes had been lowered down the shaft, the ship's air-raid sirens blasted. As gun crews scurried to their pom-pom and boffin antiaircraft guns, the sailors continued to load the boxes. The 47-millimeter guns on the Russian launch were swung around and pointed skyward, but only a distant rumble echoed through the snow as the German bombers passed high overhead toward other targets.

The snow turned again to sleet and freezing rain, and the red stenciling on the wooden boxes began to run. Thick red drops fell to the *Edinburgh*'s decks, leaving a crimson trail in the trampled snow. Shortly after 2:00 A.M., Swanson checked off the last eight boxes, their stenciling smeared and dripping. As the boxes were lashed and lowered, he signed the inventory list and handed it to the American. They shook hands, but neither man spoke. Though Swanson could not see the American's eyes under the wide brim of the hat, he noticed that the man was clean-shaven and young, almost boyish; his large, soft hands were pink from the cold.

Nineteen hours after the gold was loaded aboard the *Edinburgh*, the thirteen ships of convoy QP11 and their escort sailed from Kola Inlet. The cargo ships steamed northward toward the pack ice in single file at six knots while the six British destroyers and four corvettes ran back and forth around them. The *Edinburgh*, her sonar plumbing the depths for submarines, stayed somewhat astern the convoy. By evening, when the light had faded to a dull gray, an arctic northeaster whipped the water around the ships and dumped snow on them. The empty cargo ships began to yaw in the heavy seas; the decks of the escorts froze with a veneer of icy spray. On board the *Edinburgh*, the crew, bracing themselves against the wind, constantly chipped ice from the gun turrets and torpedo tubes.

Shortly after eight o'clock the following morning, lookouts spotted a Junkers 88 reconnaissance plane circling well out of range on the horizon. The sea was far too rough for the *Edinburgh* to launch her Walrus biplanes, so the crew had to stand by their action stations knowing the convoy was being shadowed and that its course, speed, and direction were being constantly monitored. Already, the U-boats would be positioning themselves; the German Arctic Destroyer Group, three Z-class destroyers led by the *Hermann Schoemann*, would be leaving their home base in Norway.

As the convoy turned westward, the *Edinburgh*, her turbines cranking out eighty thousand horsepower, surged ahead at thirty-three knots, almost her top speed. She passed in front of the convoy, slowing to nineteen knots, and began a zigzag course at regular intervals ranging from under a minute to just more than two minutes. Word came by radio that both the U-boats and the German destroyers were closing in on the convoy. The *Edinburgh*'s lookouts warily scanned the horizon all that day and evening. Through the dim arctic night, the crew stood at battle stations. Snow squalls blew repeatedly across her decks. Finally, just before six o'clock in the morning, the German destroyers, their guns flashing, emerged from behind a snowbank to the northwest.

Bolting in and out of smoke screens, the British and German ships shelled each other. The *Edinburgh* circled to port and fired two salvos that overshot the *Hermann Schoemann*. The Germans returned the fire, and three 5.9-inch shells wracked the destroyer *Foresight*, obliterating her boiler room and killing her stokers. Soon, a cloud of smoke and escaping steam hung over her. The *Edinburgh*'s second salvo devastated the *Hermann Schoemann*. In a sheet of flame the German flagship's superstructure crumbled and her engines exploded. She stopped dead in the water, oily smoke billowing above her. As the German destroyer *Z25* came alongside the sinking *Hermann Schoemann* to pick up survivors, a shell ripped through her bridge and demolished her radio office.

In all the bedlam, no one aboard the *Edinburgh*, not even the lookouts on the platform and in the tower, saw the wakes of the two torpedoes fired from the U-boat lurking to the southwest. The first explosion, admidships on the cruiser's starboard side, opened a fifty-foot hole, destroyed the forward boiler room, and wrecked compartments almost to her port side. The second blast tore off the ship's stern, smashing the quarterdeck upward and over the rear gun turret. The rudder and two of the four propeller shafts were blown away; the armor plating of the hull was bent downward at an acute angle. The *Edinburgh* listed twenty degrees to starboard.

Below decks, bulkheads collapsed, steam pipes burst, and storage tanks ruptured. Petty Officer Swanson, who at the

moment of the first explosion was in the bomb room
supervising the transporting of armaments to the airplane
hangars on deck, was hurled sideways, his head striking the
corner of the bomb rack. Still stunned after the second
explosion, he knelt for a moment in the darkness. All power
was cut; the air was acrid. A warm wetness trickled down
the left side of his neck beneath his antiflash mask. He
grappled for the flashlight clipped to his uniform belt.
Someone near him moaned; steam hissed in the gangway.
Farther away, arctic water thundered through the blast hole
amidships.

Leaning against the tilting bulkhead, Swanson got hold of
the flashlight and switched it on. The decking was strewn
with high-explosive shells and twisted steel racks. Smashed
ammunition boxes were scattered in the debris. One sailor,
pinned under a toppled bomb rack, had his arm almost
severed above the elbow. Another man lay unconscious
against the hatch, but no one else was seriously wounded.
The reinforced, armor-plated bulkheads that had saved them
from the torpedo blast creaked noisily.

Swanson held the flashlight as his mates strapped the
wounded men into Robinson stretchers, and then, because
frigid water had begun to slosh through the hatchway, he
ordered everyone up to the cruiser's deck. Before leaving
the bomb room himself, Swanson panned the flashlight
across the chaotic mess of shells and twisted steel and
tangled wiring. Long golden bars protruded from the shattered
ammunition boxes; the smeared red lettering glared in the
arc of his light. Near the decking, where splintered wood
floated in the rising water, a steel post had carved a deep
gouge in one of the bars. He rubbed his eyes with his
uniform sleeve and stared. A pale, almost ghastly, smoke
seemed to curl above the bar. The strained bulkheads groaned
eerily. Farther away, heavy machinery crashed as it broke
adrift. He was only able to draw his gaze from the bright

smoking bar when he felt the ship suddenly list more steeply.

He shut and bolted the bomb-room hatch and then made his way along the dark and sloping gangway. The water rose above his knees. Two sailors carrying a submersible pump rushed by him. On the platform deck near the forward boiler room, he came across a seaman slumped against the bulkhead. Covered with fuel oil and burned by escaping steam, the man mumbled incoherently. The skin on his neck and both his arms had peeled away. Swanson lifted him up, and together they climbed to the ship's forecastle.

Later, Swanson, one of the last men to be taken off the *Edinburgh*, stood at the railing of the minesweeper *Harrier*. A band of dried blood trailed down his neck from his injured left ear. He squinted through the sleet and spray at the sinking cruiser. White flame shot skyward from the wounded ship, followed by a swirling mass of black smoke. The roar of the explosion rang in his right ear. The *Edinburgh* rolled over on her side. Her stern sank quickly, but her bow rose for a moment before disappearing in the raging sea. The foul stench of fuel oil lingered in the air. Swanson stood rigidly in the wind and, staring at the roiling white water and the dark cloud of smoke where the *Edinburgh* had gone down, wondered if he was going out of his mind.

News of the *Edinburgh*'s sinking reached the young American at the naval operations office in Reykjavík, Iceland, where he had flown from Murmansk. Wearing a dark suit, he sat at a large oak desk separated by a partition from the other desks occupied by uniformed officers. He read the radio dispatch twice, ran his left hand through his thick brown hair, folded the message carefully, and put it in his coat pocket. He then stood, walked over to the window, and gazed out for some time at the brown, stunted grass, the gray patches of melting snow, and the glinting green sea beyond. The window panes rattled in the wind, and he could feel a cold draft on his neck. Although his expression was stolid, he ground his knuckles against the window's hard wooden sill. Almost a year of his life had been lost with the *Edinburgh*'s cargo. He felt a mixture of frustration and anger and, though he could not quite account for it, relief.

▽ One ▽

Drumming his fingers on his desk at the U.S. Office of Undersea Research in Rockville, Maryland, Will Altman pored over photographs and schematic diagrams of a portable decompression chamber. When his phone rang, he rubbed his face with his hand, glanced at the antique brass ship's clock next to the phone, and frowned. His face was broad and expressive, his skin leathery from his years working on boats and in the water. Crow's feet spread from the corners of his eyes, and his dark hair was cut short. Without answering the phone, he loosened his tie, unbuttoned the collar of his blue shirt, and continued to examine the diagrams. The position of the decompression chamber's ventilation system was flawed, and the task of solving the problem under an impossibly tight deadline had, as usual, fallen to him.

Altman grabbed one of the diagrams of the chamber, went over to the lightboard beyond the conference table at the other end of his office, hung the diagram, and switched on the board. Stroking his chin, he wondered how anyone could have designed something quite so maddeningly intricate. He yearned for his thirty-two-foot sloop, *Halcyon*, a fresh breeze, and a clearing sky.

A knock on his office door brought Altman back from his reverie of wind and water. "Come in," he shouted as he switched off the lightboard and returned to his desk.

Altman's supervisor, a stooped, balding career bureaucrat only nine months from his pension, escorted a trim, light-haired man into the office. "Will, this is Richard Grey," the supervisor said, "a special assistant to the President on the National Security Council."

Grey extended his hand, and Altman shook it.

"Mr. Grey would like to speak with you, uh, alone," added Altman's supervisor as he backed toward the doorway.

As his supervisor left, Altman motioned Grey to the conference table and, following him, sized up the man. Grey was, at six feet and about 170 pounds, an inch shorter and twenty pounds lighter than Altman. He was lean, less sturdy and muscular than Altman, but he looked to be in superb shape. Although he was probably in his late forties—a few years older than Altman—his gait was youthful, brash, and fluid. His hair was razor cut and his suit tailored.

Seating himself with his back to the wall, Grey said, "I hear that you are a Cornell man."

"A Cornell graduate, yes." Altman scratched his nose, smiled, and added, "And what exactly does the President's special assistant on the NSC do?"

Ignoring the question, Grey said, "Princeton, myself, class of '65. And you graduated in . . . ?"

Altman looked Grey in the eye. "It was 1968—as I'm sure you know." Having dealt with more "special assistants" and "security officials" than he cared to recall, Altman assumed that, whatever the purpose of Grey's visit, he had already been fully briefed.

"And then a hitch in the navy?"

Altman gazed at his hands, inspecting the assortment of small scars, more vestiges of his years working underwater, and said, "Mr. Grey, I have a deadline to meet. Why don't you state your business."

Grey's smile was less than friendly as he said, "I had been told you were a little rough around the edges. . . ."

Altman rubbed the gnarled knuckles of his left hand and said nothing.

Grey stood up and meandered around the office gazing at the framed photographs Altman had taken of submersibles and other strangely shaped undersea vehicles. He then sauntered over to Altman's desk, scanned the photographs and diagrams of the decompression chamber, and picked up a piece of whale-tooth scrimshaw depicting the bark *Charles W. Morgan*, the last of the great Yankee whaling ships. "Very nice," he said. "Are you a collector?"

Altman realized that, if he wanted to get back to his work, he was going to have to first play Grey's game. "I have a few pieces," he answered. "And I cut a bit myself— or at least I did whenever I shipped out."

Grey brought the scrimshaw over and placed it on the conference table. "Have you ever heard of the HMS *Edinburgh*?" he asked.

Altman shook his head.

"She was a British cruiser sunk in the Arctic Ocean during World War Two. Torpedoed on convoy duty in May of '42."

"Almost exactly a year after the *Bismarck* was sunk."

"Ah, yes. Less famous than the Nazi battle cruiser, perhaps." Grey patted the whale's tooth, his university ring clicking against the ivory. "But the *Edinburgh* is rumored to have had almost thirteen tons of Russian gold aboard her."

Making a quick calculation in his head, Altman whistled. "Even at only $400 an ounce," he said, "that's over a $160 million."

"Well over."

"And?" Altman leaned forward and folded his arms on the table.

"An international consortium plans to attempt to salvage her."

Altman picked up the scrimshaw and, polishing it with the cuff of his shirt, waited for Grey to continue.

"It's actually created quite a headache for us. The gold was owed to Uncle Sam, but the Soviets are now insisting we received payment in full later." Grey waved his hand as if to dismiss as absurd the possibility that the Russians had made good on the deal. "If it exists at all," he went on, "it's aboard a British ship, and naturally, the Brits want a cut, too." He straightened the knot of his dark club tie. "And then there's the cantankerous Cornish bastard who, as head of the salvage consortium, assumes that if he brings the gold up most of it should be his."

"And the National Security Council is involved?" Altman asked.

"Only as a representative of the President. The Old Man designated the NSC the American negotiating partner. I've just returned from London, where the arrangements are being hammered out."

Altman put down the scrimshaw and stared across the table. The "Old Man," as his closest advisers called him, was Edward P. Hartnett, a career politician and the last of the Cold Warriors. Four years earlier he had finally, at age seventy-two, manuevered his way into the White House on a platform of economic conservatism and veiled mistrust of the Soviet's *glasnost* and *perestroika*. Hartnett's views had mirrored the mood of the country, and his subsequent popularity as President had risen and fallen not only with the economy but also with the unpredictable cycle of repression and freedom in China and the Communist Bloc nations. "And what brings you here, Mr. Grey?" Altman asked.

Grey straightened up in his chair and, without hesitating, answered, "If the deal is cut, the Old Man would like you to represent the United States on the salvage mission."

For a moment, Altman was taken aback. "Why me?" he asked.

Grey again smiled coldly. "Because, despite your note-worthy lack of tact, you are the man best qualified for the job."

Wary of Grey's smile, Altman asked, "And what exactly are the qualifications needed for the job?"

"A thorough knowledge of undersea technology."

Altman brushed the table with his hand. "There are half a dozen men as knowledgeable."

Grey waved his hand toward Altman's desk. "None of them knows more about deep dives. None of them was part of both the *Titanic* and *Bismarck* teams." Grey looked at his digital watch and then glanced at the framed photographs on the wall. "And none contributes photos and articles to *Dive* and *National Geographic*. The salvage may well have historical significance, and the Old Man wants a record of what happens. Your reputation as a photo-journalist *and* dive specialist tipped the scales in your favor."

"Who wants the record?" Altman asked. "The President—or his NSC operatives?"

"Look, Altman. . . ." For a moment, anger flashed in Grey's pale eyes. "Save this hard-ass act for someone else." Pausing, he leaned forward to emphasize his point. "You'd never be my choice because you're not always a team player. But a decision has been made—and you're it."

"And what if I say no?"

Grey leaned back in his chair and folded his hands behind his head. "Then you'll be finished in government service. You can pretty much kiss your career good-bye." The ire began to fade from Grey's eyes. "Look," he added, "I'm offering you a chance to be part of the salvage of the century. If it goes, you'll spend a summer at sea, and you'll pull your regular salary plus the equivalent in a bonus when the job's done." He paused, licked his lips, and said, "And

you'll be doing something for your country—if that matters
to you.''

Altman's palms sweated; the back of his neck prickled.
''Don't lay that pseudo-patriotic crap on me,'' he said. ''I
haven't said I wouldn't do it. I just need to know what the
job is and who I'm really working for.''

Grey smiled again. ''You'll represent the President, you'll
offer technical advice when necessary, and you'll make a
written and photographic record of what occurs aboard the
salvage vessel.''

''And that's it?'' Altman's neck still prickled.

''That's it,'' Grey answered, impatiently tapping his
university ring on the table.

''My experience in Vietnam has nothing to do with this?''

Grey slid back his chair and stood up. ''What experience
is that?'' he asked. He walked to the door, and, turning
back toward Altman, nodded. ''You'll hear from me if and
when the deal is cut,'' he said as he left.

Altman sat at the conference table, slowly spinning the
whale's tooth. Although there was something about the deal
that seemed too easy, a summer at sea at double his salary
was hard to ignore. Perhaps the President, making one last
ride under the banner of anticommunism in the coming
fall's election, simply needed a public relations coup like
the salvage of the *Edinburgh*'s cargo to demonstrate that
when the United States benefited economically, he would
gladly work with the Soviets. Altman picked up the scrimshaw, turned it over in his hand, and traced with his
forefinger the *Charles W. Morgan*'s square-rigged main
mast.

▽ TWO ▽

Altman cleared customs at Heathrow International Airport, wound his way through the milling crowd of tourists changing money and waiting for transportation, and headed out the door. The sun broke between high running clouds. The wind, gusting out of the northwest, blew through his sportshirt and disheveled his hair. When Grey had finally contacted him the last week in June, six weeks after their first meeting, Altman had agreed—as he had known that day in his office that he would—to be the President's representative in the attempt to salvage the *Edinburgh*'s cargo. The third week in July, he had received cryptic instructions to fly to London for what Grey called "preliminary planning sessions."

Squinting in the sunlight, Altman strolled toward the row of double-decker buses parked to his left. As he was about to board one marked *City of London*, a green sedan pulled over to the curb, its door swung open, and Grey beckoned him in. The driver placed Altman's camera bag and suitcase into the truck, and the sedan, darting among cars and buses, drove quickly away.

Altman smiled wryly and said, "The service is excellent."

Grey, wearing a light cotton suit and a white shirt, sat

back and said, "Welcome to London. Have you been here before?"

"Only once," answered Altman. "One college summer when I trained aboard a navy clipper." He laughed. "I did most of my traveling in Southeast Asia."

"You'll like it. Very civilized." The tension of their first meeting was gone from Grey's voice. "Do you still sail?" he asked.

"Not much. I've got a small sloop moored out in the Chesapeake, but I've had to lease it."

"Too much upkeep?"

"That, and too little time." As the sedan sped along the highway, Altman gazed out the window at the rows of small houses with fenced backyards and tiny gardens. He caught a glimpse of one overweight woman wearing only shorts and a bra while she cut her lawn.

Grey reached into the front seat next to the driver and lifted up a dark leather briefcase. He opened the briefcase and, drawing out a file folder, said, "I received information this morning that on only its fourth pass, the search ship located a large vessel at approximately the location the *Edinburgh* is believed to have sunk."

"That's a terrific bit of luck," Altman answered.

"Perhaps, but it leaves us too little time to plan strategy." Grey shuffled the papers in the folder. "I've had to reschedule tomorrow's first meeting for this afternoon as soon as you arrive at the hotel. You'll have to shake off any jet lag you're feeling."

Altman nodded and waited for Grey to continue. "Two Russian trawlers are already shadowing the search vessel in the Arctic Ocean," Grey said.

"Why?"

Grey picked a piece of lint from the sleeve of his suit coast. "We don't know, but our intelligence sources suggest something important is going on."

Altman scratched his neck. "Is there a problem with the final agreement?"

Grey shook his head. "There shouldn't be. But the negotiations have been antagonistic at times. The final agreement calls for each of the governments and the salvage consortium to receive twenty-five percent of the claim. After expenses, of course."

"Sounds fair."

"It is equitable. But our information, which in the past has been quite reliable, suggests that there is excessive activity in certain Kremlin offices." Grey gazed at Altman, as if to make sure that his words had been understood. "We have to stay abreast of the situation."

The sedan screeched by a yellow station wagon and, descending a ramp, merged with traffic heading into central London.

Grey placed the folder back in the briefcase and began to fiddle with his university ring. "All of this is confidential, of course," he said. "The Brits need not know about it." Grey glanced at Altman. "The point is that the Russians may already be aware of our meeting." He snapped the lock shut on the briefcase.

"Why the secrecy?" Altman asked.

"Because the Soviets are up to something," Grey answered, the glib smoothness gone from his voice. "Keep your eyes open. Report anything irregular to me. Anything at all."

Altman poured a scotch on the rocks and walked over to the conference table in Grey's suite. The walls of the suite were painted off-white, and the upholstered furniture was pale blue. Grey introduced him to the other two men seated at the conference table. Trevor Harrington nodded and leaned across the table to shake hands. He wore a seersucker sport coat, a white shirt, and a burgundy tie with small images of golden retrievers on it. He was trim for a man in his mid-sixties; his fair hair was receding, and his clear eyes were shining.

Mick Jones stood up, shook Altman's hand, and said, "Welcome aboard, mate." Jones was shorter than Altman, heavyset, and muscular. A wide scar ran from the back of his hand up under the sleeve of his blue blazer. His blue cotton shirt was open at the collar.

Grey said, "Trevor is an administrator in the Defense Ministry in London. Because the *Edinburgh* is designated a British war grave, he'll serve as the titular head of the salvage."

Harrington, who was filling a dark pipe with tobacco, did not respond to the statement.

"Mick," Grey continued, "is the ship's captain and will oversee the diving operation."

"Isn't there a dive master?" Altman asked.   Grey looked over at Jones, who took a long sip of his dark rum. "I've gone after the *Edinburgh* before and missed 'er," Jones said. He looked Altman in the eye. "This is my salvage, and I don't want anybody to mess it up this time."

Harrington, who was taking a stick match from a small box, seemed to pay no attention to the statement. Grey studied the detail of his university ring.

Altman leaned back in his chair and said, "That's fine by me. I'm surprised, though, that as captain you would want to take on the responsibility of the dive, too."

"I want it, and I'll 'andle it."

Altman shrugged and turned to Grey, asking, "How does the Russian rep fit into the cabin of command?"

"Like you," Grey answered, "they are aboard to protect the interests of their government."

"They?" Altman asked.

"The Kremlin," Grey answered, "is sending two representatives."

Altman wondered why Grey had not told him that fact during the ride to the hotel.

Jones laughed. "The bloody commies don't even trust each other," he said. "I'll 'ave a pair of 'em aboard, but we 'aven't even got their names."

Harrington lit his pipe, took two deep puffs, and gazed out the window. "Why haven't we received this information?" he asked.

"I don't know," Grey said quickly, "but the Soviets are never aboveboard in this sort of thing."

"They want all the gold," Jones said.

"I'm not sure that's it," Harrington answered.

"If they knew how to get at the gold, they would 'ave already gone after it," Jones said. He took another long swig of his rum.

"Perhaps," Harrington said. He leaned his pipe against the ashtray in front of him, turned to Grey, and asked, "Is there any other information that suggests the Russians aren't playing cricket?"

"Not really, no," Grey answered. He then glanced at Altman and added, "There are reports of Russian trawlers shadowing the search vessel, but that's pretty standard for the Arctic Ocean." He lifted a cardboard tube from under the table and said, "I think we need to review the dive site once more, so that Will is clear about it." He slid a rolled sheet of paper from the tube and spread the paper on the conference table. "Here is the quadrant of the Barents Sea in which the search vessel has located the wreck. It hasn't been positively identified as the *Edinburgh* yet, but . . ."

"It's the *Edinburgh*, all right," Jones interrupted.

"Assuming that it is her . . ." Grey smiled, his tone condescending. "It looks like an exceptionally deep dive."

Altman asked Jones, "What's your estimate of the depth?"

Jones shrugged. "Maybe 1350 feet."

"The search vessel has the located wreck at 1394 feet," Grey said.

"At either depth," Altman said, "it would be hundreds of feet deeper than any salvage dive ever attempted."

Looking at Altman, Harrington asked, "How dangerous is the dive?"

Jones snorted and finished his rum.

"All dives are potentially dangerous," Altman answered. "Accidents happen. But at great depth the danger increases dramatically." He lifted his glass and swirled the ice in it. "The gases used for saturation are volatile, hot water has to be pumped constantly to the divers, and the fatigue a diver feels is something you can't imagine. The deeper you go, the greater the hazards. And nobody has ever gone this deep, except in controlled experiments."

"Are the risks mortal?" Harrington asked.

"If a diver is badly injured, there's no way to decompress him fast," Altman answered. He turned to Jones and asked, "Is there at least a Diving Medical Officer for the mission?"

Jones nodded. "Of course. I've got a dive doctor in the deck chamber and a German medic in the ship's infirmary."

"What will the weather be like?" Altman asked.

Jones glared at Grey for a moment and then answered, "It would 'ave been a 'ell of a lot better four weeks ago. If the meetings . . ."

"We all understand that, Mick," Harrington said evenly. He picked up his pipe and pointed the stem toward Jones. "But Mr. Altman needs to know what the weather will be like now."

"Fair to middling. Sometimes a gale'll blow in August, but the weather'll be all right. It'll 'old at least till August."

Harrington dragged thoughtfully on his pipe and then asked, "Does that give you enough time to . . ."

"I'll make it enough," Jones answered.

"What I am really asking," Harrington said, his voice calm, "is if the risks are worth it."

Jones scooped a piece of ice from his glass and cracked it between his teeth.

"That depends on your point of view," Altman answered. "The risks are very real, but from what I hear," he nodded toward Jones, "there are tons of gold down there. The payoff'll be enormous."

Grey said, "The entire salvage operation has been dubious from the beginning. The White House has had serious reservations . . ."

"Dubious, 'ell," Jones interrupted. "You dragged your ass from the start. You're worse than the bloody Russians."

His voice controlled, Grey said, "Mr. Jones, the United States wants to find the *Edinburgh* as much as you do, but . . ." He waved his hand around the table. "This group represents only three-fourths of the salvage partnership."

"You, not the Russians, tried to torpedo the talks," Jones said.

Altman was surprised to hear this, and waited for Grey to answer the accusation.

"You aren't looking at the big picture, at the international situation," Grey said. "You don't understand the Soviets the way we do."

Jones clenched his fist, the scar bright white, and answered, "To 'ell with the international situation. The *Edinburgh* is the salvage of the goddamned century. And nobody, Russian *or* American, is going to stop me from bringing up that gold."

▽ **Three** ▽

Altman buttoned his collar, straightened his tie, and put on his sport coat as he walked up the curved driveway of the Bermuda Inn, a restored Georgian great house to which Harrington had invited him for dinner. Opening the door of the restaurant, he saw Harrington standing with an attractive young woman at the other end of the anteroom. The young woman leaned up, kissed Harrington on the cheek, and headed down the hallway. Altman came up to the older man, clapped him on the shoulder, and said, "I see you're already sampling some of the more exotic delicacies."

Confused for a moment, Harrington said, "Oh, hello, Altman. Yes, the Island cuisine here is the best in London."

"Actually, I was referring to your friend."

Harrington smiled. "Oh, Elizabeth is my daughter."

Altman laughed. "That's a time-honored line on both sides of the Atlantic."

Harrington's smile broadened. "But," he said, "in this case, it's true. I hope you don't mind my inviting her to join us for dinner."

Turning, Altman saw the young woman strolling toward them. She was dressed in a light linen suit that did not quite hide a superb figure. Her shoulder-length hair was blond-

22

brown, and her face was tan. "No," Altman answered, "I don't mind at all."

Touching his daughter's arm, Harrington said, "Elizabeth, this is William Altman, my American counterpart on the *Edinburgh* salvage."

She smiled and nodded. She was in her middle thirties; her green eyes were bright and clear like her father's.

They were seated at a table in an alcove off the main dining room. The stone walls gave it the feel of a side chapel in an old church. The light from the two candles on the table reflected off the crystal glasses and the silverware.

When they received their drinks, Altman raised his scotch and said, "Well, we survived the first meeting. Here's to the success of the mission."

Harrington raised his glass only a little. "Of course," he said. After he sipped his sherry, he added, "Apparently, you haven't heard."

"Heard what?" Altman looked first at Harrington and then at Elizabeth. "I left the hotel shortly after the meeting."

"Around six," Harrington answered, "we received news that the wreck the survey vessel discovered has been identified. It's the *Hermann Schoemann*."

Altman exhaled. He looked into the candlelight playing through his water glass. "How did Mick take the news?"

"Predictably." Harrington glanced at his daughter. "He went on a bit again about the Americans dragging their, ah, tails. The survey vessel, being American, earned the brunt of his wrath."

Altman cleared his throat. "I've been aboard the *Twain*. Both its side-scan sonar and sub-bottom sonar produced remarkably high-resolution images. If the *Edinburgh*'s going to be found, the *Twain*'ll find her."

"Of course," Harrington answered. "The *Edinburgh* has to lie close to the German ship. It will likely cause only a few days' delay. Jones has been champing at the bit. He leads with his mouth, that chap."

"I noticed," Altman said. "But he seems to know his stuff."

"He has the reputation for being the best in the British Isles. He's been at it since he was a boy. In fact, he first made his name with a phenomenal find along the coast of Cornwall when he was only twenty-two." Grey took another sip of his sherry. "Still, despite all of his experience, he knows little about international relations—as your Mr. Grey so persistently pointed out this afternoon."

Altman drank his scotch, put the glass down, and said, "You have to understand something. I barely know Grey."

The waiter approached them and took their orders. When he had left again, Harrington said, "I had assumed that you had been apprised of the negotiations all along."

"Not at all. I had one meeting with Grey before my arrival here. I probably know less about the negotiations and about the entire salvage operation, for that matter, than anyone else involved."

"It sounds as though you were a last-minute choice," Elizabeth said.

Altman nodded. "I guess I was."

Harrington took out his pipe and began to fiddle with it. After a moment, he said, "Did Mr. Grey select you for the mission?" He tapped the pipe against the heel of his palm.

"I'm not really sure, but he has been my only contact. Why?"

Harrington shrugged. "No reason. Just wondering."

"Why were you selected?" Elizabeth asked.

"I suppose," Altman answered, "because I'm familiar with the dive technology and I've done some troubleshooting on other deep dives." He turned to Harrington. "The White House wants a complete record of the salvage attempt." Out of the corner of his eye, he saw that Elizabeth was still gazing at him. "I'm a proficient photographer, and I've written quite a few magazine pieces on deep-sea diving."

"So, you're not exactly one of Washington's career bureaucrats?" Elizabeth asked.

"Not really. No." Altman looked into her eyes. "I was a navy diver. Served in Vietnam."

The waiter arrived with mussels for Altman, escargot for Harrington, and a seafood crepe for Elizabeth. As they were eating the appetizers, Elizabeth said to Altman, "You mentioned that you left the hotel after the meeting. Where did you go?"

"For a walk along the Thames. Westminster Abbey. I needed to clear my head."

"Did you take any photographs?" Elizabeth asked.

"No, and I think I was about the only one within a mile of Big Ben who didn't."

"Hyde Park is especially photogenic this time of year," she said.

Altman nodded. "Maybe I'll head over there after the morning meeting tomorrow," he said. "That is, if you'll be my tour guide."

"I'd like that," she answered.

During dinner, they talked mostly about Elizabeth's work as an appraiser for Sotheby's in London. Her specialty was eighteenth-century furniture, particularly English and French country pieces. At one point, Altman asked her what she enjoyed most about her job.

"Just about everything," she answered. "I am allowed to make my own decisions, and I travel a great deal, especially between London and the Continent." She looked at Altman and then at her father. "There is a real sense of adventure, a sense of excitement to the work."

Later, when Harrington excused himself for a minute during dessert, Altman asked Elizabeth, "Do you always accompany your father when he entertains foreigners?"

"No," she laughed. Her eyes shone in the candlelight. "Neither of us needs a chaperone, if that's what you're suggesting."

"Not at all." Altman smiled.

"And you?" She folded her hands on the edge of the table. "Are you here alone?"

"Yes." Altman held her gaze.

"You've left your wife at home in the States?"

"No." Altman drank from his coffee cup. "I mean, I'm not married." He shrugged. "I was, but it didn't work out."

She nodded, and then her expression became more somber. "I came with my father," she said, "because I've been worried about him." Leaning forward, she cupped her chin in her hand. "My mother died this past Easter, and my father has taken it hard."

"They were very close?"

"They were," she answered, "but more than that, because of his work, my father had to spend a lot of time away from home." She sighed and let her hand fall again to her lap. "He was due to retire this autumn, and they'd planned to finally spend time alone together at a cottage my mother's family has in the Highlands." She paused, putting her cloth napkin on the table. Her eyes were clouding. "She had lung cancer diagnosed last Christmas, and she was gone by Easter."

Not sure what to say, Altman asked, "Are you an only child?"

She smiled at him, her eyes glistening. "Does it show that obviously?" she answered.

When Harrington returned to the table, they each had a brandy. Altman asked Harrington about his experiences in the Royal Navy. Harrington lit his pipe and blew smoke over the candles. At first reluctantly and then more openly, he talked of his days aboard a destroyer escort in the Atlantic in the early fifties. When, because of his training in languages at Oxford, he had been ordered back to London to become a cryptographer, he had had mixed feelings about leaving the sea for a desk.

Altman watched Elizabeth listening to her father. The

corner of her mouth turned up slightly, and her face, somewhat flushed after the dinner and drinks, was exquisite in the candlelight.

Later, as they left the restaurant, Altman agreed to meet Elizabeth at Hyde Park Corner after his morning meetings. The Harringtons then hailed a cab, and Altman began to walk leisurely back to his hotel. As Regent Street curved down to Piccadilly Circus, he passed young couples—the boys with shaved heads and the girls with short, chopped punk hairdos. The lights of the electronic billboards flashed above the Circus. Groups of youths stood around the base of the Statue of Eros and sat on the two tiers of stone steps, talking and smoking cigarettes. Most wore T-shirts, but a few wore studded denim jackets. A boy wearing a chain belt and a derby nudged Altman as he passed him.

Along Haymarket beyond the Circus, as the crowd again thinned out, Altman began to get the feeling that he was being followed. Glancing furtively around before he crossed Orange Street, he noticed twenty-five yards behind him a man turning and gazing in Burberry's window. Altman continued on until he reached the elegant columned portico of the Royal Haymarket Theater. HIs muscles tense, he stood near the curb. Pretending to gaze across at the intricate facade of Her Majesty's Theater, he again checked the man out. The man, wearing an ill-fitting blue suit and black wing-tip shoes, passed Altman without looking at him.

Altman waited until the man turned at the next corner before continuing on himself. Reaching the corner, he looked down Suffolk Place but did not see the man. He hurried down the short block to where Suffolk Place ended at the white stone British School of Osteopathy. To his left, the cross street ended in a cul-de-sac; to his right, it led to the front corner of the National Gallery. "What the hell?" he mumbled aloud.

When he reached Pall Mall, he looked about warily and then crossed to Trafalagar Square. Pigeons waddled around his feet as he entered the square. Water cascaded from the two fountains. A few old men sat on the stone benches at the periphery of the square; a boy and girl in jeans and polo shirts stood along the edge of the closer fountain watching the cherubic figures spitting rivulets of water. Across the fountain, a powerfully built young man wearing a leather flier's jacket despite the sultry weather seemed to hesitate for a moment before meandering around the fountain toward Altman.

Starting to sweat, Altman hurried over to the Nelson Memorial and looked up the fluted granite column. From his vantage point, he could only see Nelson's head and hat, which seemed almost to hover under swirling clouds in the starless sky. Pigeons huddled at the base of the column. A boy sitting alone on the uppermost ledge of the column's foundation lit a cigarette.

Altman made his way around the base of the memorial, looking at each of the four bronze lions and simultaneously checking out every corner of the square. A man, about the height and build of the man he had seen earlier but who was wearing a raincoat, entered the square from the direction of Saint Martin of the Fields Church. The young man, his hands stuffed in the pockets of his flier's jacket, strolled toward the memorial. As Altman turned toward the second fountain, the man in the flier's jacket turned that way also. The man in the raincoat stopped walking; the boy with the cigarette climbed down from the memorial. Pigeons scattered along the flagstones as Altman hustled toward the fountain, trying to put it between himself and the men.

Fear and anger welled in Altman. He wanted to lash out at someone, but he wasn't sure what was happening. As the man in the raincoat put his hand in his pocket and moved around the fountain, Altman took off past the statue of King George and bounded up the steps. Out of the corner of his eye, he thought he glimpsed the man in the flier's jacket following him. Scurrying across the street toward Saint Martin's, he saw the stark exterior of the Charing Cross Station a block away down Duncannon Street. Three taxis were queued up in front of the train station, but there were no pedestrians on the sidewalk. Without looking back, he sprinted down the street and then, panting, slowed down.

Suddenly, as Altman reached the Strand, a burly man with a cane turned the corner in front of him. As Altman brushed by him, the man swung the cane across Altman's chest and pinned him against the side of the building. The man slid the cane up to Jones's neck and pressed hard for a second as he stared menacingly into Altman's eyes. Altman was about to knee the man when a pistol barrel was jammed against his cheek just below his right eye. He heard the pistol's hammer click back. Unable to turn toward whoever held the gun, he stared back into the dark eyes of the man with the cane.

"Stay away from that ship, Yank," the man said in a strong guttural accent. His breath was warm and fetid.

"What?" Altman gasped.

The man pressed the cane harder, cutting off Altman's air. "If you want to live, stay away from that fucking ship, Commander Altman." The man snapped the cane back, turned, and disappeared around the corner. A moment later, the gun was moved up against Altman's eye, and its hammer was let down with another click. And then the gun was gone, too.

Slumping against the wall, Altman tried to catch his breath. Sweat streamed down his chest and back. Looking back up Duncannon Street toward the National Gallery and Trafalgar Square, he saw a figure in a flier's jacket merge into the shadows near Saint Martin's. Altman slid along the wall and peered around the corner up the Strand. The man with the cane had vanished.

▽ Four ▽

As Altman ate his overdone fried eggs and undercooked bacon in the hotel's dining room the next morning, Grey approached him carrying a sleek garment bag and leather briefcase. He wore a dark suit, a starched white shirt, and a striped blue tie. He laid his bags next to the table and, as he sat down across from Altman, said, "I've been called back to Washington. I have to leave ASAP."

Altman nodded. "I've got to talk to you before you go."

"Okay, but make it quick." As Grey sat down, a waiter filled his cup with coffee. "All right, shoot."

"Last night," Altman said, "I, uh, ran into a couple of men near Trafalagar Square who warned me off the salvage."

"What?" Steam rose from Grey's coffee cup. "What happened?"

As Altman related the story, Grey twisted his university ring. When Altman finished, Grey said, "Goddamned Soviets. It's typical."

"What is?"

"This strong-arm stuff. Don't worry about it."

Altman held his gaze on Grey. "Look," he said, "the man called me by name. He knew my naval rank."

Grey looked around the room again and then waved his hand. "They won't do anything," he said flatly.

"What the hell?" Altman leaned toward Grey. "Someone threatened to kill me."

Grey glanced at his watch. "Nothing's going to happen," he said. "They're just checking you out, testing your mettle. It's standard Soviet bullshit." He stood up and took a white card from his pocket. "Don't worry."

Trying to control his anger, Altman placed both his hands flat on the table. "Grey," he asked, "what the fuck is going on here? Why the hell would they be testing me?"

Grey slipped the white card onto the table. There was nothing on the card but a handwritten phone number. "As I told you yesterday, the Soviets are up to something, but what . . ." He brushed his right eye with his hand. "Don't tell anyone about this. I don't want Jones and Harrington . . ."

"Yeah, all right," Altman answered, shaking his head, "but I don't see where telling them—"

"Goddam it," Grey interrupted, his voice low, almost hoarse, "you have no idea of the security risks." He pressed his fingers on the table for a moment and then, his tone less strident, added, "Check in with me before you board the salvage ship. Maybe I'll have some more information for you." He tapped the card. "Use a public phone."

Without looking at it, Altman put the card in his shirt pocket.

Grey picked up his garment bag and briefcase. "Oh," he said, as though he had just remembered something, "the survey ship has located another, larger wreck less than a mile from the *Hermann Schoemann* and about a hundred feet deeper."

"Well, that's good news, at least," Altman answered. "It's got to be the *Edinburgh*."

"You sail at 1600 tomorrow," Grey said. "You're on your own now. Forget about last night. Good luck." He turned and hurried toward the door.

* * *

Altman and Jones boarded the deep wooden dinghy at
Hay's Wharf near London's Tower Bridge. Altman sat on a
seat along the port gunwale. Unable to understand Grey's
glib response to what had happened, he had been on edge
all morning. But there had been no sign of anyone following
him, and he knew that the best way to rid himself of the
residual tension was to immerse himself in the work at
hand. Jones, carrying rolled charts and ship's drawings
under one arm, moved to the bow of the dinghy and stood
there staring two hundred yards up the Thames at the HMS
Belfast, the Royal Navy's floating museum and the *Edinburgh*'s
sister ship. Built from the same plans, the two ships were
alike in almost every way, the most important similarity
being their identical holds and bomb rooms.

Haze hung over the bridge, the river, and the cruiser.
High clouds ran before a damp breeze. The dinghy driver, a
grizzled, unshaven old man, settled the dinghy into the
river's current and headed for the cruiser. Squawking gulls
circled above the dinghy. The *Belfast*'s four triple turrets of
six-inch guns and dozen four-inch guns were raised to a
thirty-degree angle. She bristled with Bofors and other
smaller armaments. Gazing at the six-inch guns of her two
stern turrets, Altman imagined hearing the call to battle
stations and seeing her turrets pivot and black smoke billow
from her two smokestacks.

As the dinghy swung parallel to the *Belfast*, Jones said to
Altman, "She's big, that one. Think of my lads coming up
to her fifteen hundred feet under water." He glanced across
the Thames at the four gray Caen stone turrets of the Tower
of London jutting above the thick curtain walls. Pointing
over his shoulder with his thumb, he added, "That's more
than sixteen bloody times deeper than the Tower's 'igh,
mate."

Altman stood up next to Jones, stared at the Tower, shook

his head, turned back toward the heavy cruiser, and asked, "How thick is *Edinburgh*'s armor plating?"

"Four and a 'alf inches along 'er sides to 'er magazines and engine rooms," Jones answered. He spat into the water. "Three inches from there to 'er crowns."

"All right for a torpedo to breach," Altman said, "but a problem for divers. Any chance of entering through the blast hole?"

"I 'ad thought about that, mate, but it'd be too messy. No telling what the lads'd come up against. We'll take the straight route right into the bomb room."

"What about using an unmanned submersible?"

"Like on the *Titanic* and *Bismarck*?"

Altman nodded.

"We'll 'ave an underwater robot on a tether, but it'll be just a swimming eyeball—a video camera with a floodlight."

"Could you use something bigger with manipulator arms and a retrieval cage, that sort of thing?"

"Wish I could, it'd be easier on my divers. But there's no way to get into the bomb room except through the 'ull." Jones grinned at him. "And anyways, the *Titanic* and *Bismarck* salvages were fishing trips. They didn't 'ave a clue what they'd come up with." He rubbed his shirt sleeve across his mouth. "I know what I'm after, and what my divers 'ave to do to get it."

The dinghy's wake lapped against the side of the cruiser as they approached the section of the hull that protected the bomb room. The driver cut the engine and let the dinghy drift next to the cruiser as the two men continued to talk.

"How are you going to get through the hull?" Altman asked.

"Thermal cutting torches."

"It'll be hard work," Altman said.

"Damned 'ard work at that depth." Jones again spat into the water. "One mistake with the torch, and I'll have a diver splattered across the ocean floor."

Altman folded his arms and gazed up at the huge gray hull. "How are you going to illuminate the area?"

"We'll 'ave lights on the underwater robot and diving bell, but once the lads are inside the 'ull, they'll only 'ave electric torches, at least until we get enough space to move something bigger in. They'll be working almost blind. We'll 'ave the video cameras on the robot and bell so we'll be able to see a bit, but that won't do them any good."

"Working them in teams of two?"

Jones nodded.

"How long are the shifts?"

"Four hours," Jones answered. "Eight hours, really, four as support in the bell and four working."

"Four hours on the wreck, huh? Fatigue could become a factor." Altman was careful not to sound as though he were telling Jones his job.

"The lads are tough," Jones answered, tilting his head back. "I've got the best divers available coming in for this one."

"Where are they from?"

"All over. Two of 'em are Yanks. Five are from the North Sea oil rigs." Jones shifted the rolled charts and drawings from one arm to the other. "The Azores, the Bahamas, South Africa. I've even got one lad flying in from Australia."

They stood silently in the dinghy, dwarfed by the ten-thousand-ton cruiser. During his days as a diver Altman had done a dozen deep dives, but nothing approaching the depth of the *Edinburgh*. In that cold, dark world, under hundreds of pounds of pressure, even the act of breathing would be strenuous. He shook his head and looked beyond the ship at a red double-decker bus passing between the twin gothic towers of the bridge.

Finally, Jones broke the silence, saying, "Let's get aboard, and I'll show you the layout of the bomb room."

After the dinghy driver let them off on the wharf, Altman and Jones reached the ship by the public gangway, walked under the stern "Y" turret's six-inch guns, and ducked through a hatch. Jones flashed an identification card at a tall, bearded man in a Royal Navy uniform who escorted them through the public displays—a re-creation of the sick bay and dental surgery, a pictorial exhibit on the British navy, and the forward steering position. They then descended a bar ladder to the ship's hold and passed through a maze of watertight compartments and passageways to the bomb room. As Jones spread an intricate plan of the *Edinburgh* on a wooden table, Altman scanned the beige room, trying to picture what it might look like with crates of gold bars piled to the ceiling.

"The bulkheads on this deck are exactly the same on the two ships," Jones said, "so I've been able to get a good look at what we're up against."

Glancing at a diagram of the ship's hold, Altman pointed to a seemingly empty space between the ship's hull and the bomb room, and asked, "What's this?"

"The fuel-oil storage tank behind this bulkhead," Jones answered, tapping on the wall to his right. "The divers'll enter it after they cut through the 'ull. It may 'ave been breached when the ship went down." He shrugged. "So, like I said, there's no telling what they'll find."

Altman slid his forefinger along the diagram, pointing to the compartments in front of and behind the bomb room, and said, "You've got the small-arms magazine fore and the four-inch-gun magazine aft."

Jones scratched his scalp and said, "I know what you're thinking, mate. There's no way in 'ell the lads can tell if the 'igh explosive shells are still 'ot down there. Seawater may 'ave seeped into the casings, but we can't count on it. We'll 'ave to winch the shells to the surface and defuse 'em one by one." He rubbed his right eye. "Between the fuel oil and the shells, the whole bloody 'old's a booby trap."

Altman found an internal profile of the ship and spread the drawing on the table. Directly above the bomb room was a transmitter room and above that a seaman's mess. Just behind the transmitter room was a generator room. "Anything from the sailors' mess to heavy machinery could have fallen in there when she sank," he said.

"Exactly," Jones answered. "When the lads clear a path and reach the bulkhead, they'll cut through at about this level." He raised his hand to the height of his shoulders. "The bomb racks that stood against the bulkhead may still be there with the bombs still in 'em."

And, Altman thought, if the thermal torches touch off one of the shells, the ensuing explosion will splatter the divers as well as the gold.

Altman strolled with Elizabeth along the bridle path at the south end of Hyde Park. The sun shone through high, thin clouds. Elizabeth wore a sleeveless white dress with a blue belt tight around her thin waist. The top three buttons on the front of the dress were unfastened, and the collar fluttered in the light breeze. Altman's beat-up brown leather camera bag hung from his shoulder by a worn strap.

As they cut across the grass toward the Serpentine, the long lake that curved through the middle of the park, Elizabeth asked, "Shall we go over to Speakers Corner and catch up on what London's leading eccentrics have to say?"

Altman glanced over his shoulder, and, noticing no one behind them, relaxed a bit. "Let's not," he said. "I've heard enough speeches the last couple of days."

She smiled at him. "Yes, I suppose you have. My father has mentioned that Mr. Grey is a bit supercilious."

"That's putting it mildly," he answered. "This morning's meeting went better without him there."

"He's gone back to Washington?"

"Yes."

"Why in such a hurry?"

"I have no idea."

They sauntered toward the cement walkway along the

Serpentine, where people were sitting on wooden benches and blue-and-white-striped lawn chairs, talking and feeding the ducks.

"What else has your father had to say about the meetings?" he asked.

"Not much," she answered, but she stared at him as though he were clairvoyant.

They stopped, and Altman took pictures of a sailing dinghy, its red and yellow sail bright against the green trees in the background.

"Will," she said, "why did you ask me about my father?"

As he changed the lens on the camera, he answered, "I don't know. It seems sometimes as though he knows more than he's letting on." He shook his head. "More than I know, at any rate." He took a shot of two old men in baggy khakis who were fishing with antiquated spinning rods.

Elizabeth looked at Altman. "He's always been tight-lipped about his work. I don't think he wanted to burden my mother with . . ." She cocked her head to the left. "To bother her with all the boring details."

Strolling away from the lake past circular beds of brightly colored petunias, geraniums, and begonias, they crossed the wide rolling lawn toward a canopied bandstand surrounded by folding lawn chairs. As they climbed the bandstand's steps, Elizabeth took Altman's hand in hers. When they reached the raised platform, she let go of his hand, twirled around so that the bottom of her dress lifted, and, laughing, said, "The whole world's a stage, isn't it, Will?"

After he took three quick shots of her, she went over to one of the stand's ornate pillars, leaned against it, and gazed out into the sunshine. Her face was brushed with soft light, and her high cheekbones and thin nose seemed perfect to him. He took a picture of her like that, and then she reached out and took his arm in hers.

Turning toward him, her face almost grave, she said,

"Will, promise me you'll keep an eye on my father. I'm worried. Except for a little while when we were at dinner and you got him talking, he's been preoccupied . . . distant."

He looked down at the yellow and white daffodils planted around the base of the bandstand and then up at the light playing through the canopy's latticework. Smiling at her, he asked, "Is that why you suggested we go on this little photographic safari through the wilds of Kensington, to ask me that?"

She held his gaze for a moment, nodded, and answered, "Partly. Only partly. I had hoped to ask Jones. But being so uncouth and all, he's, well, not my father's sort of man." She brushed her fingers along his forearm. "And when I met you, I . . ." She let her voice trail off.

He smiled at her and said, "I doubt your father needs it or that I would do much good if he did, but of course I will, Elizabeth."

She turned and looked out across the park.

"And what was the other part of your reason for bringing me out here?" he asked.

She turned back toward him, smiled into his eyes, and punched him lightly in the ribs.

"I think we might find a bottle of champagne back at my hotel," he said.

She leaned into him and answered, "That sounds rather nice, but I have an appraisal at three." She laughed. "More impoverished gentry selling off centuries of priceless family heirlooms." She brushed her lips against his. "After dinner, perhaps."

▽ **Five** ▽

When Altman arrived at Sotheby's to meet Elizabeth and her father for dinner that evening, he found them standing by the entrance. It had begun to drizzle, and both of them were standing by a large flower urn under the auction house's front awning. Harrington was smoking a pipe, and Elizabeth was fidgeting with the latch of her purse.

"Good evening," Altman said as he gave Elizabeth's shoulder a squeeze.

"Will," Elizabeth said, glancing at her father before looking at Altman, "my father needs to talk with you."

Altman looked from Elizabeth to Harrington. "Of course," he said. "What's up, Trevor?"

Harrington took the pipe from his mouth, blew pale smoke skyward, and answered, "There is someone I'd like you to meet before dinner."

Altman glanced at Elizabeth, who looked down at the ground. "It concerns the *Edinburgh*," she said. "I'll meet you at the Ritz Hotel restaurant in an hour or so, if that's all right."

"Okay, sure," Altman answered. He glanced over at two men unloading a mahogany table from a lorry parked in front of the green iron doors of Sotheby's service entrance. He then nodded to Harrington and said, "Lead on, McDuff." As he left, he touched Elizabeth's arm and whispered, "We *will* see you later?"

"Definitely," she whispered back, smiling at him.

As Altman and Harrington sat in the cab a few minutes later, Harrington said, "You and Elizabeth seem to have hit it off rather nicely."

"Yes," Altman answered as he brushed the lapel of his sport coat. "Elizabeth is, as I'm sure you're aware, a very attractive woman. And she's the most pleasant and interesting person I've met in a while."

"Are you, ah, involved with someone else?" Harrington's tone was almost avuncular.

"No, actually I'm not." Altman unbuttoned the sport coat. "What's going on here, Trevor?" he asked, smiling at the older man.

"I am, ah, just inquiring about your inten..."

"Not that," Altman interrupted, shaking his head and laughing, "this meeting you're dragging me off to."

Harrington knocked the ashes from his pipe into the ashtray, cleared his throat, and said, "Oh. Well, while I was preparing the papers for the salvage—I had to explain the legality of the mission from the war-grave angle—I came across a chap who was aboard the *Edinburgh* when she was torpedoed. I thought you might like to hear what he has to say."

"Fine," Altman answered, although he could not think of what the man might say that would be as interesting as anything Elizabeth might be saying to him at that moment.

The taxi dropped them in front of the Dove and Star, an old pub with a white mortar Tudor facade. The interior of the Dove and Star provided a testament to wood. The floors were dark fir, and the tables and chairs were oak, as were the upholstered seats built into the walls. The walls were paneled with wood; thick wooden beams crossed the ceiling. Old pewter mugs lined high wooden shelves, and prints of hunting scenes hung in thick wooden frames. Harrington led Altman to a round table in the corner, where an elderly, balding man sat with his back to the wall. As Harrington reached the table, the man stood up. He was tall and thin and pallid, perhaps a decade older than Harrington.

Harrington shook the man's hand and said, "Frank, this is William Altman, the American representative on the *Edinburgh* salvage."

The man turned and cocked his head, reached across the table, clasped Altman's hand, and said, "Frank Swanson, sir. Royal Navy, retired. At your service."

Altman sat down, and Harrington got a round of ale from the bar. He then said, "Frank, I'd like you to tell Will, here, what you told me about the *Edinburgh*'s last hours."

After drinking half the glass of ale, Swanson said, "I will, that." He looked down at his glass and then up at Altman. "Have you ever been aboard a sinking ship?" he asked.

"No," Altman answered, "and I hope I never am."

"The saddest experience of my life, it was," Swanson said. "Seeing the *Edinburgh* go down with sixty of my mates aboard."

Altman sipped the ale, wishing it were colder. Harrington filled his pipe from his tobacco pouch and said, "Perhaps you should start at the beginning, Frank."

Swanson cocked his head again, saying, "Sorry, my left ear went deaf, it did."

"Perhaps you should start with Murmansk, Frank," Harrington said.

"Righto. With Murmansk. Yes, I should," Swanson answered. He emptied the glass and wiped his mouth on his shirt sleeve. "Jolly cold, it was, even though it was

May. We were sitting up outside Murmansk, Russia's god-forsaken arctic port, waiting for the convoy to form. I was in the petty officer's mess when we got the call to fall in.''

Harrington fetched Swanson another pint of ale.

"When I came on deck," Swanson continued, "it looked like some sort of military parade, it did. Electric torches were everywhere. Our contingent of Royal Marines was topside. There was this Russian gunboat with a lot of Reds on board.'' Swanson smiled to himself and sucked the ale through his teeth. "And one American who looked like he wanted to be someplace else.''

"An American?'' Altman asked, glancing at Harrington, who was lighting his pipe. "Are you sure?''

"Yes, sir, on the deck of that Red gunboat.'' Swanson sat straighter in his chair. "A young bloke. Tall and brawny, he was. Had all the papers. I ought to know, I signed 'em, I did. You see, I was the chief petty officer on duty, so I was ordered to load the cargo. Mind you, we weren't told what the cargo was. It was in wooden crates, more than a hundred of 'em, 'bout the size of ordnance boxes. Bound up with wire, they were. Markings I couldn't read on every box. But with all those Reds around, I knew it was special, I did.

"We carried the crates aboard through the bloody sleet. That's when I heard what it was—gold. All kinds of stories was in the air about where the gold was from and what it was for.'' He paused, looking into his glass. "There was a bloody lot of it, let me tell you, wherever it was from.''

"What records we have,'' Harrington said, "indicate that the gold was mined and processed in some ultrasecret Siberian slave-labor camp from which prisoners never returned.''

"As far as I know, that gold came straight from hell!'' Swanson said with a vehemence that surprised Altman. "From the time that gold came aboard,'' Swanson went on, "the *Edinburgh* was a cursed ship. As we hauled those crates, the red markings smeared in the sleet. It looked like blood, Russian blood, it did." He picked up his glass and finished his ale in one draft. "I knew it was going to be a hell of a trip." His pale cheeks were beginning to color, and beads of sweat were forming on his forehead. "I'm not a superstitious bloke, mind you, but that gold was evil." He held up his glass so that Harrington could get it refilled.

Altman, who had been sitting back in his chair, leaned forward and asked, "Did you actually see the gold?"

"Not then, not in Murmansk, but I did later. I didn't have to see it, though, to know it was evil. It's a feeling you get sometimes, you know. I went down to the bomb room later that night to double-check the inventory. I tell you the paint was smeared all over 'em like the Reds had bled to death getting 'em there." He stopped speaking for a moment, shook his head, and added, "And I knew more blokes was going to die, lots of 'em."

Altman leaned farther forward, his elbows resting on the table, and asked, "When did you actually see the gold?"

"I'm getting to that," Swanson answered. He waited for his next ale, raised the glass, and said, "Cheers." He then drank deeply and said, "We were running 'head of the convoy, forming a screen between the tubs and the Nazi destroyers. It was bitter cold, it was. The second day, early on, we got into a scrap with the Nazis." He wiped his lips with the back of his bony hand. "We put it to the bastards. Sent the flagship to the bottom, we did."

"That would be the *Hermann Schoemann*," Harrington said.

"Aye," Swanson answered, "the *Hermann Schoemann*. Blasted her right out of the water. Didn't see it myself, being down in the bomb room and all, but that we did."

"You were in the bomb room?" Altman asked.

"Yes, sir, sending munitions topside, I was." Swanson bit his lip. "That's when we were torpedoed—once amidships and once astern. Right when the *Hermann Schoemann* was going down. Nobody saw the fish coming. The second one opened her like a tin of meat, it did. Blew the decking right over the Y turret.'' He paused, staring down into his glass. ''It was bedlam below decks, I tell you. The whole ship went dark. Sounded like hell broke loose, the machinery crashing and the water flooding the gangways.'' He paused again.

Altman drank more of the warm ale, waited a moment, and asked, ''What was it like in the bomb room? I mean, what did you see?''

Swanson's hands, cupped around the glass, were shaking. Slowly, he began to speak again. ''It was hell . . . All dark and tilted and smoky. Two of the blokes in my crew was wounded. But we . . .'' He rapped on the table with his knuckles. ''The armor bulkheads was all that saved us.'' He did not look up from his ale. ''One of the bomb racks had broke. There was munitions all 'bout the place. Shells all over. The wire had held on some of the crates, but some had fell and broke open. And there was all that bloody gold. That's what did in the *Edinburgh*.'' He finished his ale but then did not continue talking.

''And?'' Harrington said.

''The gold was in long bars, gleaming between the shells like something from the devil himself. It . . .''

''It was what?'' Altman asked.

''It was evil, that's all. Evil bloody gold.''

Shortly after two in the morning, Elizabeth let Altman out the door of her flat in Blackburne's Mews just behind the American embassy. The rain had stopped, but the night was humid and overcast; a light mist hung in the air. Wearing only a silk robe and slippers, she glanced about before leading him through the courtyard toward the locked wrought-iron gate. Altman slung his sport coat over his shoulder. His shirt was unbuttoned at the collar and cuffs, and his tie was folded in his coat pocket. After dining with her father, Elizabeth and Altman had gone back to her apartment, ostensibly so that she could show him the antique furniture she had collected. They had made love first on the Oriental rug in the drawing room and then on her ornate Edwardian four-poster bed.

Elizabeth took a key from her robe pocket and paused before unlocking the gate. Looking up at Altman, she smiled and said, "I enjoyed the evening, Will."

"The pleasure was mine," he answered, returning her smile. As she turned the key in the lock, he added, "Your flat's beautiful."

"Thank you." She swung the gate open a foot. "The rent is dear, but I couldn't pass up the place when I heard about it. I've only a five-minute walk to Sotheby's."

Nodding, he asked, "How did you ever find it?"

"A friend of a friend." She shrugged. "You know." Putting her hand on his side, she said, "Will, I . . . You . . ."

He touched her cheek and said, "Take care, Elizabeth."

"You take care, too," she answered. She reached up, put her arm around his neck, and kissed him. Her nipples were hard against his chest. "Take care, Will," she repeated, "and keep watch over my father." Her eyes, reflected in the light from the embassy across the mews, were watery.

Altman walked by the embassy toward the Grosvenor Square Gardens. A sign on the fence warned that the gardens closed at dusk, but the gate had been left open. He stopped by the elliptical rose gardens and, with the fragrance of the flowers hanging in the mist around him, gazed at the statue of Franklin Delano Roosevelt. The roses' scent reminded him of Elizabeth. At least part of his attraction to her, he knew, was that she was independent—a woman who understood her own mind, traveled where and when she pleased, and had singular, if expensive, tastes.

He jumped the gate at the far end of the gardens and strolled up Grosvenor Street toward Regents Street. As he crossed New Bond Street, he saw Sotheby's white, blue, and gold awning to his right. Recalling the conversation with Swanson, he wondered why the man had been so insistent that the *Edinburgh*'s gold was evil. Did it stem from the deaths of so many of his mates? Or was it merely the rantings of an old sot?

▽ **Six** ▽

Just before noon the following morning, Altman stood in a phone booth on a steep hill overlooking the docks in Aberdeen, Scotland. As he waited for his call to Grey in Washington to go through, he scanned the area outside the phone booth. Up the street, a woman pushed a baby carriage along the sidewalk, and a mailman stopped to talk to an elderly man leaning against a gate post. A flatbed truck moved laboriously up the hill from the docks. Seagulls, gliding in the midday thermal currents, hovered in the sky and then dove to the water's surface.

The dive support ship *Seerauber*, fully provisioned, was moored along the stretch of wharf below him. Although the ship was 256 feet long, all the mechanical and electronic equipment on her deck made her appear shorter. The communications antennae stood between her forecastle and wheelhouse. Near the starboard entrance to the bridge, the enclosed lifeboat, a dark capsule with a sliding hatch cover on each side, hung from its davits. Amidships, behind her bridge, the tall steel tower housing the heave compensation gear and the suspension system for the diving bell jutted into the sky. Below the suspension system, the diving bell was set at the top of the moonpool, the circular shaft through which the bell could be lowered directly into the ocean. Aft of the moonpool there was a large yellow derrick with an operator's cab and a telescoping boom. Two smaller cranes stood along the port and starboard railings. A cubic white steel brace hung from the port crane's boom. Farther aft, the diving gas-storage pods, each consisting of nine long cylindrical canisters, lined the deck. The A-frame lifting rig rose at a sixty-degree angle from the ship's stern.

The overseas operator finished putting the call through, and Grey, sounding a little out of breath, answered on the third ring and accepted the charges.

"Good morning, Mr. Grey," Altman said, "This is your envoy in the British Isles."

"Altman?"

"Did I wake you?"

"No. I generally do my calisthenics at dawn. It gets me going for the day."

Oh, Christ, thought Altman, *I should have known*. "The *Seerauber* is ready to sail," he said, "so I'm checking in as you requested."

"Good," Grey answered. "Have you met your Soviet counterparts?"

"Haven't had the pleasure yet. I heard, though, that they went aboard yesterday."

"Keep a close eye on them. Our sources have confirmed that they are Igor Strinivitch and Vladimir Petrosky." Grey paused and then said, "I've got the info here in my briefcase. Hold on a minute."

While Grey was off the phone, Altman watched a gliding gull rise effortlessly, its wings arced and its feathers spread. Finally, the sound of paper shuffling let him know that Grey was back on the line.

"The info on Strinivitch," Grey said, "is that he is a party bureaucrat and a middle-level KGB stooge." The paper shuffled again. "Petrosky is a bit more shadowy. He has been a cultural attaché in various Western capitals—

Bonn, London. There is no clear link to the KGB, but he still bears watching.''

"Am I watching for anything in particular?" Altman asked as the gull swooped toward the docks.

"Anything suspicious. How have the final arrangements gone?"

"Smoothly enough."

"Good. What's happened since I left?"

"Not much. I spent some time aboard the *Edinburgh*'s sister ship, the *Belfast*. The salvage is going to be both tricky and dangerous, but it has a reasonable chance of success. Jones knows what he's doing."

"Yes, of course," Grey answered.

Altman asked, "Did you find out anything related to my little adventure in London?"

Grey hesitated before saying, "Oh, with the Soviets? No, nothing."

Altman was dissatisfied with Grey's answer, but, realizing that it was useless to pursue the matter, he said nothing.

After a moment, Grey asked, "What else occurred in London?"

"Nothing. I spoke with a man who had been aboard the *Edinburgh* in May of '42."

"Really?" Grey paused, as though he were writing something down. "Did he present any information that the White House should know?"

"Not really. Just that the whole experience was miserable." Two gulls soared above *Seerauber*'s steel suspension tower.

"What was his name?"

"Swanson. Frank Swanson. A bit rummy. Royal Navy, retired."

"All right. Keep the White House abreast of events. And, let me know personally the moment the divers discover anything."

"Will do." Altman was relieved that there was no last-minute bureaucratic haggling.

"Contact me the minute the gold is found." Grey's voice was almost strident. "It doesn't matter what time of day or night."

"Yeah, okay," Altman repeated as the two gulls swung around each other in the sky.

Altman climbed the stairs from his stateroom to the *Seerauber*'s wardroom. Trailed by a flurry of seagulls, the ship had left Aberdeen an hour before. Altman had organized his gear, checked his cameras, and laid out his scrimshaw on a small writing table next to his bunk. He had then shaved, something he had not done before catching the flight from London that morning.

The wardroom was empty except for two men who were playing chess at a game table built into the bulkhead. One man, in his early forties, was short, corpulent, and balding. The other, in his middle fifties, was tall and gaunt. Both wore drab shirts and dark pants, but the taller man's clothes, which were tailored, were less baggy. Engrossed in their game, neither man spoke to Altman as he entered the room. Altman fixed himself a scotch, went over to the two men, and said, "Afternoon. I'm Will Altman, the American rep on the salvage."

The tall man looked up, extended his hand, and said politely, "It is a pleasure to meet you, Mr. Altman. I am Vladimir Petrosky, the Soviet representative." His accent was pronounced, but his English was perfect. He glanced at the chessboard and then at the man seated across the table, who, arms folded over his chest, glared at the chess pieces. "You must forgive the rudeness of my comrade, Mr. Igor Strinivitch. He is about to be mated and clings to the vain hope he will escape."

Strinivitch grunted, stared at the board for another minute, reached for his king, and knocked it over. He looked up at Altman, flashed an unfriendly smile that revealed a gap between his two front teeth, and said, "You arrived at a not good moment." His accent was thick and strong. He then said something to Petrosky in Russian.

"Comrade Strinivitch," Petrosky replied in English, "you must speak in a language that Mr. Altman understands. I will get you a vodka. It will ease the pain of defeat."

As Petrosky poured the two vodkas, Altman gazed out the porthole. The North Sea was placid, the water glimmering in the afternoon sun. The ship's twin eight-hundred-horsepower diesels hummed, and the decking beneath Altman's feet vibrated slightly. Petrosky took the two vodkas over to the large rectangular wooden table that would serve as both mess and conference table for the salvage representatives. The table and six chairs dominated the center of the wardroom; around the periphery of the room were three soft reading chairs, a couch, a magazine rack, bookshelves, and a wet bar.

"Join us, Mr. Altman," Petrosky said. "We will drink to the success of the *Edinburgh* salvage."

Petrosky asked Altman about his job and about living in Washington, D.C., one Western capital in which he had not served. When Petrosky talked, he made subtle hand movements, as though he were speaking to some foreign diplomat at an embassy party who would pick up on the nuances suggested by the gestures. Strinivitch joined them at the table, drank his vodka quickly, and said little. His face was round and puffy, his eyes small.

A short time later, Harrington came into the wardroom and said, "Ah, I see that you have discovered the ship's liquor closet."

"Yes," Petrosky answered. "Mr. Altman and I have been discussing the cherry blossoms in Washington in the spring, a pleasure I have unfortunately not experienced."

"Nor I," Harrington said. He wore gray slacks, a blue

shirt, a dark tie, and a herringbone tweed blazer. "May I freshen anyone's drink?"

Strinivitch nodded and handed his glass to Harrington. As Harrington refilled the glass and then poured himself a sherry, he said over his shoulder, "Captain Jones would like to convene a general meeting here at 1800 hours. He has promised that it will be over well before dinner is served at 1900."

▽ **Seven** ▽

Jones began the meeting promptly. He sat at the head of the conference table with four fingers of dark rum over ice in front of him. Harrington and Altman sat to his right, and Petrosky and Strinivitch sat to his left. Harrington had his pipe and pouch at the ready, but he had not begun to smoke; Altman slowly nursed his second scotch. Petrosky, his hands folded on the table, looked at Jones, and Strinivitch stared at his third vodka. Jones's manner was informal, but he left no doubt as to who was running the meeting. He explained the shipboard protocol for the three days en route to the Barents Sea and the changes in procedures that would occur when they arrived at the salvage site.

When Jones finished describing the responsibilities of the crew, Petrosky said, "The crew, I have noticed, is mostly German. It is my understanding that the *Seerauber* is also owned by a German shipping firm."

"It is," Jones answered, leaning forward, his forearms resting on the table. "State of the art."

Petrosky unfolded his hands, waved them in the air, and asked, "The firm, it did not supply its own captain?"

Jones stared Petrosky in the eye. "No, it did not."

"Is this the normal arrangement?" Petrosky asked.

Altman sipped his scotch, glanced at Harrington, and shook his head almost imperceptibly.

"It's the procedure here," Jones said flatly. Then he smiled and added, "You see, Mr. Petrosky, the shipping company 'as made similar arrangements with me on other salvages, and it 'as often worked out profitably for them. I really don't know if they like it or not, but they like the six-to-one return on their investment just fine. Now that may be 'ard for a communist to understand . . ." His smiled widened.

"Does the shipping company have a senior officer aboard?" Harrington interrupted in a pleasant voice.

Petrosky nodded, rubbed his hands together, and then folded them again.

Jones sat back in his chair. "Yes, Gunter Schmidt, who you'll sometimes see on the bridge with me. Big bloke, must be close to sixteen stone, with a mustache. When we reach the salvage site and I take over as dive supervisor, Gunter'll run the ship."

"What are the captain's responsibilities at that time?" Harrington asked.

"Not a lot—keep tabs on the weather and make sure the thrusters that keep the ship stable over the diving bell are functioning." Jones pushed up the sleeves of his knit fisherman's sweater so that the wide scar on his forearm showed white. "As dive supervisor, I'll 'ave complete responsibility for the salvage. Trevor will advise me about the war-grave angle."

Harrington nodded and picked up his pipe and tobacco pouch.

"Anyone else," Jones continued, "is welcome to say what they want. But I will make the final decisions about the gold."

"The *Russian* gold," Strinivitch said. He raised his glass, finished the vodka, and put the glass down hard on the table. His neck and face were ruddy.

Jones stared at Strinivitch and said, "The gold belongs to whoever salvages it."

"The gold, it is Russian," Strinivitch repeated.

"The gold is on a British ship sunk in international waters." Jones scooped an ice cube out of his drink and cracked it with his teeth.

"Gentlemen," Harrington broke in. He put down the pouch that he had just opened. "This has all been gone over before in London." He shook his head. "It would be most pleasant if we didn't have to go through it again. A legal agreement has been signed by the three nations and by the consortium, represented by Mr. Jones."

"Mr. Harrington is right, Igor," Petrosky said. "An agreement has been reached, and as the representatives of the Soviet people, we must see that the agreement is honored..." He glanced at Altman. "... By everyone."

Strinivitch frowned and looked down at his empty glass.

Just before midnight, Altman, who was at the writing table in his stateroom hunched over the ivory, inscribing the design for his scrimshaw, stood, stretched, and opened the table's upper drawer. He took out a beige envelope containing the photographs of Elizabeth that he had developed in the ship's darkroom after dinner. The shot of her he had taken on the bandstand had turned out even better than he had hoped. He gazed at the photograph for a time and then, after placing it next to his scrimshaw, headed out of the cabin and up to the *Seerauber*'s foredeck.

The temperature had dropped to the high forties. The sky was indigo, and pale stars flickered in the twilight. The odors of diesel fuel and pipe smoke mixed in the salt sea air. Harrington stood by the port railing gazing out to sea. Altman came up to him, clapped him on the shoulder, and said, "Evening, Trevor. How's it going?"

"Not bad, Will," the older man answered. Although he

still wore a tie, he had changed from the blazer into a thick wool cardigan sweater.

They stood silently at the rail for a minute, the splashing of the ship's wake echoing past them. Altman noticed, far to the north, the running lights of a large ship.

"I had forgotten how much I liked to be at sea," Harrington said. "I haven't been aboard ship in open waters for years." He put his pipe in his mouth and took a long drag from it. "I used to especially like the slow, quiet hours of the late watch."

"There's a different time to life at sea all right," Altman answered.

"Yes, there is," Harrington agreed, the pipe still clenched in his teeth. "You know, I spent my summers as a boy near Bournemouth with my cousins who had a house there." He took the pipe from his mouth, cupped it in his hand, and leaned against the railing. "A different time, that was. Were you lucky enough to spend any of your boyhood by the sea?"

Altman smiled. "No, I'm from Colorado—America's Wild West to most of the rest of the world."

"Really? I got the impression at dinner the other evening that you had been brought up around boats. At the very least, on one of America's inland seas."

"The Great Lakes? No." Altman rubbed his hand along the railing. "I grew up only dreaming of boats. My father was an amateur geologist, and I spent a lot of time roaming the Rocky Mountains with him. There were long distances between places and people. And that lonesome wandering with my father gave me a lot of time to dream."

"An amateur geologist? What did your father do to provide the family's daily bread?"

"He was the principal—it's similar to a headmaster—of a small rural high school. He had been a science teacher. My mother was an English teacher. They met at the school, married, and never left it." Altman turned and, leaning with his back to the railing, looked up at the light on the ship's masthead.

"And you joined the navy to see the world."

Altman laughed. "No, nothing so romantic as all that. I joined the navy because it paid for me to go to college back East. It was only when I went on my first training cruise that I realized I had struck the right bargain."

"Yes, we do make bargains in life," Harrington said wistfully. "Did you learn to dive in the navy?"

"Yeah. I eventually commanded diving teams in Norfolk."

Wisps of smoke twisted above Harrington's pipe and then vanished in the breeze. "But you didn't become a career man?" he asked.

"No. After Vietnam, it became clear to me that I had gone about as far as I could in the navy. When I got wind of a job in the Office of Undersea Research, I took it."

They were quiet for a minute. Altman turned so that he faced the ocean again. The smell of the salt water and of Harrington's pipe washed over him. The breeze ruffled his hair. He saw himself as a nineteen-year-old standing at the railing of the square-rigged training ship *Constitution* as it left Newport with its sails billowing in the wind. The young man had seen the world, all right, even if he had not consciously set out to do so.

"What do you think of our Soviet colleagues?" Harrington asked.

"That Igor Strinivitch is a piece of work."

Harrington smiled. "Yes, a pugnacious chap, that one."

"Petrosky doesn't seem too bad," Altman said. "At least he's civilized—the new Soviet of *glasnost* and *perestroika*. I get the feeling, though, that Strinivitch would be happier as a pillaging cossack." He paused and then added, "I hope you don't mind acting as a mediator. It looks like you're going to have your hands full."

"That is what I was thinking about when you came on deck—how dear a price I am going to pay for this return to my youth at sea." Harrington nodded toward the distant ship's lights.

Altman looked again at the lights he had noticed earlier.

"Soviet," Harrington said. "Light destroyer. It picked us up an hour out of Aberdeen."

"What?"

Harrington knocked his pipe against the railing, and the ashes fell toward the dark water. "I'm sure if we were to query our Russian friends, we would discover that it is merely a protective escort. A goodwill gesture from the Kremlin."

In the distance, the pricks of light wavered in the darkness.

▽ Eight ▽

Altman stood by the moonpool examining the orange and blue diving bell. Like the other diving bells he had seen, this one looked more like a customized space capsule than a bell. Steel cables and tightly wrapped umbilical hoses ran from the top of the bell. Thick steel bars held gas cannisters to the bell's exterior shell; floodlights were clamped above the bell's viewing ports.

He took a wide-angle lens and a strobe from the leather camera bag slung over his shoulder and put them on his 35-millimeter camera. The first eight divers were to begin compressing down in the deck decompression chamber the next day, and he wanted to get some photographs before there was a lot of activity in the area. He took one shot down along the bell's base at the swirling water of the moonpool and another shot upward at the bell's curved dome, the cables and umbilicals, and the dark steel suspension tower rising into the cobalt sky.

He unscrewed the lens from the camera and replaced it with a fish-eye lens from the bag. As he straddled a cable in order to get a clear shot through one of the bell's portholes into its interior, a wiry, bearded diver sidled over to him. The diver wore only a nylon swimsuit, a T-shirt, and deck shoes despite the cool temperature. He smoked a Camel, which hung at an angle from his mouth.

"Getting a good look before the work begins?" the diver said with a Southern accent.

"Trying to," Altman answered. "You're American?"

"A cracker from Georgia," the diver answered. "Name's Jeremiah Percy. Friends call me Jem."

Altman leaned over and shook Percy's hand. "Will Altman," he said. "I'm the American rep."

Percy blew smoke through his nose and then took the cigarette from his mouth. "Glad to meet ya," he said. His smile was open and friendly.

"You one of the first in the deck decompression chamber?" Altman asked

"Yep. Already stowed most of my gear in the DDC." Percy flipped the cigarette down into the moonpool, where it disappeared in the foaming water beneath the diving bell.

"Navy?"

"Nah. Learned to dive at home, outside of Savannah. Done most of my work in the Gulf on the oil rigs. The other American is navy, though, just mustered out a month or so ago."

Altman made a mental note to look up the other American. "Have you done a lot of deep dives?" he asked.

"Quite a few. I've been in saturation a dozen times. Nothing nearly as deep as the *Edinburgh*, though." He tapped the diving bell's steel brace. "And never with this new gas mix. Oxygen and helium, sure, but not hydrogen, too."

Altman nodded. "I haven't either, but on experimental dives almost as deep as the *Edinburgh*, the mix has worked much better than straight oxygen and helium."

Percy scratched behind his ear and smiled. "I hear it's slightly narcotic."

Altman laughed. "Can be," he said as he slipped his

camera back into the leather bag. "Want to show me around the chamber?"

"Sure." Kicking a closed hatch on the deck and pointing to the bag, he added, "We could get to the DDC through the diving entry port, but you might hang yourself."

Percy led Altman down a flight of stairs, past the door to the dive control room, and over to the three interconnected orange modules of the deck decompression chamber. All three modules, shaped like huge metallic sausages, were nine feet high. The modules at either end were fourteen feet long, but the one in the center, which had an extra hatch on top mated to the deck above, was only ten feet. Percy opened a thirty-inch circular hatch, grabbed the top rim, lifted his legs, and swung himself into the chamber. He then took the camera bag so that Altman could follow him. As Altman clutched the hatch's rim, he gazed up at the sky through the wide opening in the deck above the diving entry port. He then pulled himself into the chamber.

"Welcome to my home for the next month or so," Percy said.

The quarters, much like those on a submarine, were close but not as cramped and cluttered as some of the older habitats that Altman had been in. Because the seven-foot ceiling and the white interior walls gleamed in the light, Altman took the strobe off the camera and changed film before taking any photographs. Percy showed Altman the living quarters, which had a small galley, a mess table, and chairs. He then waved his arm expansively at the stereo, compact disk player, television, VCR, and bookshelves filled with an assortment of paperbacks and videotapes.

"All the comforts of home," Percy said, "except that you can't smoke or drink." He laughed. "And you can't exactly bring any of the local belles back for a nightcap." Pointing to the communications console, he added, "Actually, this'll provide our only real link with the world."

Taking a photograph of the console, Altman asked, "Is it hooked into the diving bell as well as the control room?"

"Sure is," Percy answered, "the control room, the bell, and even the bridge. We can keep tabs on pretty much any of the ship's internal communications."

After Percy pointed out the emergency escape port, Altman checked the air lock through which food and supplies would be passed.

"It may not exactly be fresh," Percy said, his tone ironic, "but we'll be enjoying the same fine cuisine you'll be eating."

The two men entered the dive locker/wet room through another circular hatch. A steel ladder led up to the hatch in the ceiling through which the divers would enter the diving bell. Wet suits hung on a rack near the shower stall, and tool belts and umbilical harnesses hung above the equipment bins along the far wall. Percy showed Altman the new gas-recovery unit the divers would use to recycle the mixed gases they would be breathing while working from the bell.

As Altman took a series of photos of the unit, which looked like a thick red and black rubber collar with gauges attached, Percy said, "It's supposed to save almost thirty percent of the gas mixture, but nobody's ever used it at a depth anywhere near the *Edinburgh*'s." He shook his head and smiled at Altman. "We're guinea pigs on this one in a lot of ways, but that's what makes the whole thing exciting."

They pulled themselves through a third circular hatch into the sleeping quarters and stood by a table between cushioned seats built into the bulkhead. The toilet faced the dehumidifier and the environmental control system, both of which hummed loudly. At the far end of the chamber, four piggybacked bunks were set above storage cabinets.

Altman shook his head and said, "You've got every bell and whistle imaginable in here."

"Yeah," Percy answered, patting the back of one of the seats. "The table can be stowed, and these fold down into more bunks—just like on a yacht." He rubbed his hand along the top of the seat. "And if there's a problem, each of the chambers can be sealed off from the others." He pointed over his shoulder with his thumb. "The aft chamber even doubles as a life raft. It can be jettisoned from the ship and operated from the enclosed lifeboat amidships."

Putting a fish-eye lens back on the camera, Altman said, "I've read about emergency chambers like that, but I've never actually seen one operate."

As Altman took a photograph through one of the decompression chamber's observation ports, Percy laughed and said, "Well, I hope to hell ya don't see it here."

Later that afternoon, Altman climbed the stairs to *Seerauber*'s bridge, which contained an odd mixture of old equipment and new electronic gadgetry. A wooden and brass wheel stood before a one hundred eighty degree expanse of windows. To the left of the wheel were radar and sonar monitors; to the right, a ship's compass, a depth finder, and an assortment of gauges. Along the rear bulkhead, to the right of the passageway to the captain's cabin, were a loran and a chart table. On the wall above the chart table hung an old three-foot gaff. The gaff's handle was wooden with leather bindings, its shaft burnished steel, and the point of its hook extremely sharp.

Jones was alone at the wheel. "Aye, mate," he said as Altman came through the door.

"Thought I'd come up and catch the view from the bridge, if you don't mind," Altman said.

"Don't mind at all. I could use the company, as a matter of fact."

Altman glanced around the bridge and then went over to look at the charts on the table. "When do you reckon we'll reach the *Edinburgh*?" he asked.

"If the weather 'olds, sometime after sunrise the day after tomorrow. We're about thirty-eight hours away."

As Altman flipped through the charts, Jones locked the wheel off and turned toward him.

Altman replaced the charts and glanced up at the wall. "Did that come with the ship?" he asked, pointing to the gaff.

Jones's eyes flashed. "No," he said, "I took it off a bloke in Algiers a few years back." He rubbed his left forearm with his right hand. "I keep it as a . . . memento."

Altman looked at the gaff, and then at Jones again. "You took it off a guy, huh?" Altman said.

"Yeah. Some frog in a waterfront pub thought I was coming on to 'is Moorish mistress," Jones said, turning back to the wheel. "The bloke came at me with that gaff." He turned the wheel one point to starboard and looked over his shoulder at Altman. "If I 'adn't got my arm up, he would 'ave yanked my throat out." He grinned at Altman. "When I finished with 'im, I 'ad to get out of Algiers fast. I mean, fast."

Altman went over to the windows. Light, fluffy clouds encircled the horizon of an otherwise clear sky. To the east and south, the horizon was a clear, undulating line that met the clouds. Off to the north, the horizon was broken by the silhouette of a ship on the same tack as *Seerauber*.

"I see that our shadow is still with us," Altman said.

Jones glanced to the north. "The *Zorky*. I raised 'em on the radio last night. They're supposedly on a routine North Atlantic training run." He shrugged. "As long as the bastards give me enough leeway, they can play all the games they want."

"Can I borrow some binoculars?" Altman asked.

"Sure, 'elp yourself," Jones answered, pointing to a dark leather case on the ledge in front of the wheel.

Rather than binoculars, Altman found a heavy antique spyglass in the case. He lifted the spyglass out, felt its cold, polished brass, pulled it so that it telescoped to its full length, and said, "Nice. Another memento?"

Jones shrugged again. "Just something I picked up."

Shutting his left eye, Altman looked through the spyglass with his right eye, focused, and found the destroyer. He scanned it once quickly and then, starting with the bow, gave it a closer look. "Hundred and fifty meters?" he asked.

"Closer to one-forty," Jones said. "But big enough to blow us the 'ell out of the water if they 'ave a mind to."

Altman sharpened the focus. The *Zorky* had two forward turrets with 57-millimeter guns. The bridge was large, and the two funnels belched light smoke. Twin 30-millimeter guns were visible near the after funnel; five torpedo tubes angled from the starboard decking. A twin SAM launcher stood aft, just ahead of a large helicopter pad at the stern. "Armed to the gills," he said. "She certainly looks battle ready."

"She does, at that," Jones answered. He gave a short, almost contemptuous, laugh. "If she comes anywhere near us, I'm going to 'aul Igor's ass up the bloody masthead."

As Altman was leaving the bridge a few minutes later, a sailor came in, handed Jones a yellow sheet of paper, and said with a German accent, "From Kirkenes, this just arrived."

Altman paused in the doorway as Jones read the paper. Jones's neck and face reddened, and he crumpled the paper in one hand. "God*damn* it," he hissed. He then turned to the sailor and said, "I want 'arrington and that Russian Mutt and Jeff in the wardroom in fifteen minutes." He uncrumpled the paper, grabbed a pencil from the chart table, scribbled a note on the paper, and handed it to the sailor, saying, "And send this to our fishermen friends in Kirkenes right away. Tell 'em I need an immediate reply." He looked over at Altman, who still stood in the doorway. "You, too. All the reps," he said in a harsh voice.

▽ **Nine** ▽

"We 'ave a problem," Jones announced, tapping his fore-finger on the yellow sheet of paper folded in front of him on the wardroom table. Altman and Harrington again sat to his right, and Strinivitch and Petrosky to his left. Jones lifted his wide glass and swirled the rum in it. "The signal buoy marking the *Edinburgh* has been cut loose from its cable."

Altman, who had wondered what had caused Jones to become so angry, exhaled. He had expected worse. Strinivitch sipped a vodka; none of the other representatives had a drink. Petrosky glanced at Strinivitch. Harrington slowly spun a box of stick matches on the table. He then raised his right hand to the knot of his tie and asked, "Might the buoy have broken loose?"

Jones's eyes met Harrington's. "It could 'ave," he said, his voice low with anger, "but it didn't." He rubbed his hands across his mouth. "I . . . the consortium 'ired some Norwegian fisherman to check it every day. While they were checking it today, they realized it was drifting."

"But it could still have broken loose?"

"No. Goddamn it." Jones raised the folded yellow paper and waved it in the air. The scar on his arm was clear white. "I wired 'em. The buoy's cable was cut clean."

66

"Why would anyone want to cut the cable?" Altman asked.

"To keep me from the gold," Jones answered. "To cost the salvage time we 'aven't got. There's only three or four weeks before the 'eavy weather sets in again. As is, we've barely got the time to make the salvage work. It's common bloody knowledge that if we don't find the gold in a 'urry, we'll 'ave to wait almost a year before we get another shot at it."

"But why stall the salvage?" Harrington asked.

"To keep the Soviet peoples from having what is theirs," Strinivitch said.

Oh, Christ, Altman thought, *I'm not going to listen to this again.* "Or," he snapped, "they want to take all the gold when the salvage fails."

"It is the Americans," Strinivitch said.

"That's bullshit," Altman said.

Strinivitch muttered in Russian.

"Igor," Petrosky said, reaching out and placing his hand on the table in front of Strinivitch. "May I ask," he said to Jones, in a voice overly polite, "what you are trying to do, summoning us here and making accusations?"

Jones bit his lip. "Somebody," he said, "is trying to sabotage the salvage. It's going to stop." He pointed his index finger at Strinivitch. "I want you all on notice about that."

Strinivitch's hand was clasped so tightly around the vodka glass that his knuckles were white. "Speak to Mr. Altman about sabotaging," he said.

"What the hell does that mean?" Altman asked, his voice icy.

"You know," Strinivitch said.

Jones stared at Altman. Petrosky's hand moved in front of Strinivitch again.

"Like hell I do," Altman said, although he knew, or thought he knew. He pushed his chair back from the table,

stood up, and walked over to the liquor cabinet. He dumped
ice in a glass and poured four ounces of scotch. He took a
long drink and then slid the glass onto the bar.

Harrington cleared his throat and said, "The salient
point, gentlemen, is that someone has sabotaged the buoy.
We don't know who . . ." He looked around the wardroom
at each of the others. "Or we don't appear to know who."

Leaving the scotch on the bar, Altman walked back to his
chair, but he did not sit down.

"The important question, it seems to me," Harrington
continued, "is, what effect does it have on the salvage?"

Jones's anger had abated somewhat. The yellow sheet lay
partially crumpled on the table in front of him. He said, "If
I 'adn't 'ired the goddamned fishermen . . ."

"But what tangible damage has been done?" Harrington
interrupted, irritation slipping into his voice for the first
time.

Jones shook his head. "The survey ship got an exact
fix—three lines of position down to the exact second. If the
ship is still in the Arctic Ocean, she could relocate the
Edinburgh quick enough." He looked at Harrington and
added, "But if we 'ave to locate the wreck, we'll lose at
least two days. I've got divers ready to compress down."

In the silence that followed Jones's statement, Strinivitch
picked at the skin around his thumbnail. Petrosky leaned
slowly forward, toward Jones, and said, "It is possible, is it
not, that this sabotage was done by some private group and
not by one of the countries involved." He waved his hand
around the room. "A group that wanted the gold to further
its own ends."

"Doubtful," Jones answered. "No private group could
muster the men and technology to make the dive without
drawing a lot of attention."

"But possible?" Petrosky repeated.

"Yes."

Altman, standing with his hands on the back of his chair,

thought about what Petrosky was saying. "But sure as hell not likely enough," Altman said, "that we would need the protection of a destroyer."

Jones's head jerked up as Altman mentioned the destroyer. "No," Jones said. "We'll need no 'elp from anybody." He turned to the two Russians. "The *Zorky*, Mr. Petrosky, is to keep its bloody distance."

That evening, when Altman entered the wardroom, Petrosky and Strinivitch were playing chess. Petrosky leaned forward over the table, his arms resting at the edge of the board. Strinivitch sat straight, his arms folded across his chest. No one else was in the room. Altman took a chair from the conference table, turned it around so that its back faced the two Russians, sat down, and leaned forward, his arms on the back of the chair. He did not say anything.

Petrosky glanced at him and said, "Igor believes that this is the night that he will mate my king."

Altman said nothing. He watched as Petrosky moved his knight. Strinivitch unfolded his arms and lowered his head closer to the board. It took Strinivitch almost three minutes to decide to take Petrosky's rook. With a flourish, Petrosky moved his queen and said, "Check." Strinivitch glared across the board.

"Vlad," Altman said. His voice was amiable, his use of the Russian's first name conscious. "I'd like to know what Igor was referring to when he suggested I had been involved in sabotage."

Petrosky waved his hand and said, "It was nothing. A reference to your military record."

Remembering the man with the cane in London, Altman made an effort to keep his voice low. "Which you have access to?"

Strinivitch looked angrily at Altman and then went back to glaring at the chess pieces.

"Like you," Petrosky said to Altman, "we have been fully briefed about the other salvage representatives."

"I was not briefed about you."

Smiling, Petrosky said in a suave diplomatic voice, "Of course, you Americans are not like us—what would the word be—*clandestine* Soviets."

Altman lowered his left arm and tapped on the slats of the chair's back. "I received no information about you other than your names and recent positions," he said. "But that's not the point. I want to know what Igor was talking about."

Strinivitch knocked over his king. "I can not think," he muttered, "with noise around."

"Igor," Petrosky said, "you will perhaps have better luck tomorrow. Mr. Altman would like to know what you meant this afternoon."

Strinivitch's gap-toothed smile was antagonistic. He looked at Petrosky rather than at Altman. "The Americans send underwater demolitions expert on this ship. A veteran of their imperialistic war in Vietnam. And he wants to know why I accuse him of sabotaging?" He snorted and then began to clear the chess pieces from the board.

"It does seem quite clandestine," Petrosky said.

Altman wrapped his fingers around one of the slats. "If you have a goddamned file on me," he said, "then you know I was involved in removing mines from Haiphong Harbor."

"Publicly, you said that there were mines left at the entrance to the harbor," Strinivitch answered. "Mines that could blow up unarmed Soviet merchant ships bringing food and medical supplies to the peoples of Hanoi."

"That's because we were unable to—I don't have to answer to goons like you," Altman said to Strinivitch.

"It does seem strange, Mr. Altman, that your government would choose a man with your background for this mission," Petrosky said in a calm, even voice.

Altman slapped the palm of his left hand against the back

of the chair. "Goddamn it," he said, "you've got to understand that my job here is to represent the American government and to keep a record of the salvage, nothing else."

"And you understand something, Mr. Altman." Although Petrosky's voice remained calm, his eyes gleamed darkly. "My job is to protect Soviet interests—and I am fully prepared to take whatever measures are necessary to do just that."

▽ **Ten** ▽

Altman awoke to rain beating against the hull outside his stateroom. Faint light passing through the porthole cast the room in dark gray shadows. The rain seemed to encompass the ship, to shroud it from the rest of the ocean. He shut his eyes and listened to the rain and the ship's engines. He had always liked the tapping of rain on a ship's hull, even when he had known it meant he had to get up, pull on foul-weather gear, and head out on watch with a mug of steaming coffee. He had especially liked the pattering of rain on the wooden deck of the *Halcyon*, anchored in some isolated inlet in Chesapeake Bay.

As he lay in his berth with his eyes closed, he wondered if it was raining in England and if Elizabeth was awake listening to it, too. He remembered her standing at her apartment gate when he was leaving that night in London. Her robe had been tied loosely, and the smell of her body had lingered with him in the rose garden in Grosvenor Square. He missed her, although he had not really expected to. Going to sea had always been a release, even in the years that he had loved his wife deeply and had known he would not see her for months. He wondered if he was changing.

He wanted to talk with Elizabeth now, to explain to her that he had blown up North Vietnamese gunboats and Vietcong barges and even civilian fishing boats suspected of running supplies to the Vietcong. He had not considered then whether what he was doing was right, and he had only later understood that it had not been right. It had been his job, and he had done it well, and a lot of people, some of them civilians, had died. He had only stopped when a charge he had set had gone off prematurely, injuring his right eardrum, almost drowning him, and preventing him from making any more dives. He had been decorated, promoted, and transferred.

He wanted to tell Elizabeth what he had been unable to tell his wife on his return to the States—that, ironically, he had gotten into trouble only after the war was over, at least for the Americans. Having commanded one of the "Endsweep" teams removing the mines from Haiphong Harbor, he had admitted to a wire-service newsman that there was no way that all of the mines could be found, much less detonated. His statement had made headlines the next day and effectively ended his naval career, even though no mention of it was ever made again after a severe dressing down in an admiral's office.

He wasn't sure why he wanted to tell Elizabeth all of this, but he knew he did, just as he knew he would get no more sleep that night. He flipped the switch on the lamp next to his berth. As the room lit up, the beating of the rain seemed to fade. He stood up, ran his hand through his hair, stretched, and went over to the small writing table. He glanced at the photograph of Elizabeth that lay next to the polished whale-tooth ivory, the cheesecloth, and the Eskimo styles. He then took stationery from the upper drawer and began to write Elizabeth a long, rambling letter. As he finished the first page, he paused, wondering what it was about her that made him want to confide in her.

* * *

When Altman entered the bridge, a stout man dressed in white stood at the wheel. Jones was seated at the chart table, calipers in hand, hunched over the charts. Although it had stopped raining about an hour before, at six-thirty, the sun had still not broken through the towering clouds. Jones glanced at Altman and then back at the charts. "Gunter," he said without looking up, "this is the American I told you about, Will Altman."

The man twisted his thick mustache with his stubby fingers, said "*Guten Morgen*," and turned back to the wheel.

"Mr. Altman, this is Gunter Schmidt," Jones continued, "the crew chief and my second in command for ship's operations."

Altman nodded to Schmidt and then said to Jones, "I'd like to speak to you for a minute."

"Go ahead." Calipers still in hand, Jones swiveled on the chair. His expression was blank.

"I'd prefer to speak to you alone."

Jones waved the calipers in the air. "Whatever you 'ave to say, you can say in front of Gunter." The corner of Jones's mouth curled. "Anyways, last night, 'arrington filled me in on your background."

"Trevor?"

"Yeah. He 'as a full file on you and on that Soviet Laurel and Hardy."

Altman's head ached with the thought that the other salvage representatives seemed to know everything about him, while he was in the dark about them.

"It's all there." Jones shook his head slowly. "U.S. Naval Operations for two years, assigned to 'Special Ops,' —whatever the 'ell that means. Sabotage, if I am to believe Igor. Followed by the minesweeping operation in North Vietnam."

Altman leaned against the bulkhead and said, "But none of that has anything to do with the *Edinburgh* salvage."

Jones snorted, "Damned right. It bloody well doesn't." He nodded toward Schmidt. "The crew is going to be keeping an eye on you." He stood, reached up, and rubbed his hand along the gaff's steel shaft. He then turned back to Altman and said, "I don't know what your bloody orders are, but if you do anything to jeopardize this salvage, you'll regret it, mate, believe me."

Altman felt himself flush. He took a step toward Jones and said, "Look, I came up here to tell you my only role here is as a photojournalist. That's it." He cocked his head. "And I don't need you or Strinivitch or anyone else threatening me."

Schmidt, his back to the two men, continued to stare out over the bow of the ship.

"Now, you look." Jones came up face to face with Altman. "If the Americans want to send a demolitions man as their rep, that's their bloody business." He tapped Altman on the chest with his forefinger. "My business is to bring up the *Edinburgh*'s gold, and nobody's going to get in my way."

Altman brushed Jones's hand away. "Don't..." he started to say, but did not go on. He stared into Jones's eyes, turned, and stormed out of the bridge.

The first eight divers due to go into saturation bantered on the deck near the decompression chamber. Jones had been able to contact the *Twain*, which had been working along the Norwegian coast, and the American captain had agreed to attempt to relocate the *Edinburgh* before *Seerauber* arrived in the Barents Sea. The storm had finally passed, and the sun shone like a hollow white circle behind a sheet of high, translucent clouds.

Altman had gathered the divers together for a couple of group photographs. In addition to Altman, Petrosky and two of the crew members were taking pictures. Strinivitch, his arms folded across his chest, stood behind Petrosky. Jones

strutted among the divers. Harrington leaned against a stack
of helium containers, gazing with a bemused expression at
all of the activity.

After the photo session, Altman walked over toward a
stocky diver who wore a sleeveless blue T-shirt. The diver
was clean shaven, and his black hair was cut short. There
were tattoos on each of his arms above the elbow. On his
left arm was an anchor, on his right a devil's head. As
Altman approached him, the diver nodded.

"Are you the other American diver?" Altman asked.

Through a crooked smile, the diver said, "Jem Percy is
the other American. I'm Sam Mathewson, *the* American
diver."

"I'm Will Altman, the American rep."

"I know," Mathewson said, "and I hear that you and the
Soviet reps went at it pretty good yesterday."

"Is that right?" Altman opened his camera and removed
the roll of film he had just shot. The fact that almost
everyone aboard *Seerauber* seemed to know his business
rankled him.

"That's what I hear," Mathewson answered, with a low,
guttural laugh.

"It's not true." Altman snapped the camera shut and
slipped it into the leather bag. "You're navy?" he asked.

"That's right. Twelve years."

"Ever stationed in Norfolk?"

Mathewson shook his head. "Not recently." He set his
feet farther apart and rolled his neck. "I was a SEAL for
seven years, till last summer. Spent the ten months before
my discharge in Florida training divers at the Ocean Simula-
tion Facility."

Altman nodded. "I've been there. It's good duty." He
took a marking pen from his pocket and scribbled the date
and a note on the roll of film he had taken from the camera.

"Yeah, I guess," Mathewson said. He looked beyond

Altman at the divers who were loading last-minute supplies into the decompression chamber.

"A lot of divers would give their left nut to be stationed there," Altman said.

"Not me. Not enough action."

"Is this your first civilian job?"

"You got it."

"Not a bad first job."

"No, not bad." Mathewson's laugh was indifferent. "With all that gold for the taking, I expect there'll be some action."

▽ **Eleven** ▽

The night before *Seerauber* arrived at the salvage site, the Barents Sea was calm and the wind light. Faint stars appeared in the dark blue sky; the northern lights flickered on the horizon. The *Zorky*, having headed southeast in the late afternoon, was no longer in sight.

Altman paced the foredeck. He had spent a lot of time the previous thirty-six hours alone in his stateroom, incising the whale's tooth. The solitude and the slack time during which the divers were compressing down and the other dive preparations had slowed had done him good, he thought. His anger had abated, and he had begun again to become excited about the impending salvage.

As Altman turned by the forecastle, Harrington emerged from the main cabin's hatchway. "I thought I might find you up here taking your constitutional," Harrington said.

Without answering, Altman stopped at the port railing.

"I was just talking with Elizabeth on the wireless," Harrington said. "She sends her best to you." He put both his hands on the railing.

"That's nice," Altman answered. "How's she doing?"

"Fine. Just fine. She said she'd written you, although I'm sure what mail delivery we receive will be sporadic."

Harrington turned so that he faced Altman. "She would like you to write her when you have the chance."

"I already have," Altman answered. He looked out at the shimmering northern lights. Occasionally, a shaft of light shot skyward, like distant fire from a large cannon.

Harrington patted his pockets in search of his pipe but did not find it. He then cleared his throat and said, "I'm sorry that my showing your file to Jones caused such a row."

Altman shrugged but didn't say anything.

"After Strinivitch's statements," Harrington went on, "I assumed that the truth would be less damaging than whatever Jones imagined."

"You did, huh?" The muscles in Altman's neck tightened. "And you figured *you* were the one to tell him?"

Harrington gripped the railing. "Well, yes, at the time, I did."

Altman turned so that he faced the older man and said, "That's pretty fucking patronizing."

Harrington looked out to sea. "I hadn't thought that it was, really."

"Look, Trevor, I went up to talk to Mick early the next morning. By that time, thanks to you, he was almost out of his goddamned skull."

"I thought I was helping you out, helping to alleviate the problem."

"Well, you weren't. You worry about yourself, Trevor. I'll take care of my end just fine."

Harrington didn't answer. Still gazing out to sea, he scratched his head above his ear. He then folded his arms and rocked back and forth on his feet. "You know," he said finally, "Elizabeth is rather taken by you."

Not sure what to make of the change in the conversation, Altman said nothing.

"She does not," Harrington continued, "give freely of her emotions. She never married, I think, because she grew up with the loneliness my wife felt when I was so often away. I think she resented my not being there for her."

"I very much doubt that is the case," Altman answered, his voice softer than it had been. "She has nothing but fondness for you, nothing but pleasant memories of her childhood. At least, that's the impression I got."

"She is my only child," Harrington said, as much to the night as to Altman. "And really all that I care about in this world."

Altman again did not say anything.

Harrington put his hands in the pockets of his wool pants. "A parent cannot really..." He began to turn away from Altman. "Whatever happens, be good to her, Will," he murmured as he walked along the deck.

Harrington's final words had been said so softly that Altman, left standing alone by the railing, could not be sure he had heard them. In the distance, the northern lights licked the sky.

When *Seerauber* arrived at the salvage site, the Barents Sea was still placid and the sky clear. The captain of the *Twain*, which remained at the site, motored over in a launch to *Seerauber* to report that his crew had had little difficulty relocating the *Edinburgh* and that electronic homing devices had been placed on the wreck as well as on the surface buoy. He also confirmed that the original buoy's cable had been cleanly severed.

Preparations for the first bell run began even before the *Twain* was out of sight. Jones had the salvage ship's diesel engines shut down. The delicate wind-velocity indicator was hoisted to the masthead, and the current and position measurement devices were connected to the computer on the bridge. The powerful thrusters were switched on, and the ship's dynamic positioning equipment was activated. The derrick's main winch was rechecked, and then cables for the bell were sunk to the ocean floor.

Each element of the divers' umbilical was also double-checked. Every inch of the gas hoses for the mixture of hydrogen, helium, and oxygen that the divers breathed was examined for kinks and tears. Because a diver without hot water circulating through his wet suit would lose conscious-ness in less than five minutes at the depth the *Edinburgh* lay, the water heater, pump, and hoses were inspected again. The communications system that linked the divers with the supervisors in the dive control room was given one last test. Finally, all of the hoses were wrapped tightly together with silver duct tape at one-foot intervals, starting with the end of the umbilical that attached to the diver's harness.

As the time for the first of the round-the-clock bell runs approached, Jones and the technicians in the dive control room moved carefully through a sequence of procedural tasks. In the deck decompression chamber's dive locker, Percy and the Australian, the divers scheduled to make the first run, went over their checklists. They then slipped into their wet suits and taped the seams between their suits and diving boots with two-inch silver duct tape like the tape that had been used on the umbilical system. Another diver in the DDC helped them put on the gas-recovery collars and the diving helmets.

Altman and Harrington waited by the moonpool for the start of the first bell run. Harrington, who had just lit his pipe, leaned against the guardrail and smoked. Altman finished attaching the auto-advance mechanism to his cam-era so that he could get a series of quick shots of the diving bell's initial descent. Technicians in dark blue overalls scurried around them checking the bell's umbilical connec-tions, auxiliary gas cannisters, and deep-sea lights one final time. As the bell was raised and set into its white steel brace, Altman took half a dozen photographs. The suspen-sion system's engines whirred, and the bell, locked snugly into the brace, began to shift along the steel tracks on the deck.

"When the bell's air lock is mated with the decompression chamber's diving entry port," Altman said, pointing to the round air lock on the deck that Percy had shown him earlier, "the divers'll be able to enter the bell without any loss of pressure.

Harrington inhaled and then cupped the pipe in his hand. Smoke swirled in the cool air as he said, "My God, the whole process looks as complicated as a space launch."

Altman nodded. "Almost," he said, "and the divers are probably even more dependent on the technology than astronauts are. If anything goes wrong here, there's no way to save them fast."

Altman couldn't see the divers enter the bell, but he noticed shadowy movement inside the bell's portholes. He changed rolls of film and then, as the sound of the engines reverberated around them again, took four photographs of the bell shifting back along its track to the moonpool. When the bell was directly over the moonpool, two sailors, shouting to each other in German, unclamped and slid back the heavy steel brace. The technicians made last-second adjustments, and then the bell dipped toward the water and vanished in roiling foam. The slow unwinding of the main cable and the umbilical marked the bell's descent.

"Come on," Altman said to Harrington, "I want you to meet Newt."

Harrington followed Altman over to the port railing, where three technicians and a barrel-chested German crane operator stood near the six-foot crane. A pale blue underwater robot, just over three feet long and shaped like a turtle, hung in a white steel housing attached by a cable to the crane's boom.

"That's Newt?" Harrington asked, his tone a little baffled.

Laughing, Altman took a photograph of the technicians fussing with the video camera's protective lens cover protruding between two lights at the front of the robot. "Yeah," he answered, "Newt is science's latest aquatic marvel. And, as you can see, his tenders have developed a doting affection for him."

Harrington took an old leather tobacco pouch from his tweed sport coat's pocket. Refilling his pipe, he asked, "And what exactly does he . . . it . . . do?"

"Newt's sort of a diver's buddy, although the divers aren't nearly as fond of him as the technicians are," Altman answered.

Harrington tamped the tobacco in the pipe's bowl and, turning his back to the wind, gave Altman a quizzical look.

Pointing to the flexible cable coiled in the wooden bin next to the railing, Altman said, "The tether's connected to a console in the dive control room, and Newt's operated from there. The divers'll never admit, though, that having an aquatic friend that lights their work and sends a video picture up to the ship is necessary."

Harrington relit his pipe. The technicians stepped back from the robot, and one of them nodded to the crane operator. The German swung the boom around and over the water. The robot's steel housing rocked on the cable before becoming still.

As Altman continued to take photographs, he said, "There's a compass, depth finder, and propulsion plant under Newt's cover. The four cylinders sticking out are directional thrusters that enable him to maneuver almost anywhere, and the lights and video camera provide such a clear image that most of the time the staff in the dive control room'll have a better view of what's going on than the divers on the wreck do."

"It is rather a technical marvel, isn't it," Harrington said.

The crane operator pressed the winch's switch, and, as the robot descended and sank into the sea, Altman said, "What's most amazing is that Newt's weightless under water. The shell's made entirely of syntactic foam and epoxy. Though he weighs two hundred and fifty pounds aboard ship, the billions of air-filled glass bubbles in the foam make him float like a phantom in water.''

For a moment, the two men continued to watch the spot where the robot's tether slipped into the water, and then they hurried down a flight of stairs to the dive control room just forward of the DDC. Two crewmen were monitoring the life-support system, communication lines, and video camera. Jones was seated at the dive console, an entire wall of toggle switches, gauges, digital meters, and video screens. He had on headphones even though the divers' voices were amplified and broadcast over a speaker on the wall above the console. During the bell's descent, which took almost thirty-five minutes, the video image from the camera attached to the bell showed only a small, hazily lit world of bright motes and darting fish. Percy, who was to do the first stint on the wreck while the Australian provided support, reported gauge and meter readings from the bell. As always, it took Altman a while to get used to the divers' squeaky voices, caused by the gas mixture.

As the bell neared the ocean floor 1486 feet below *Seerauber*, conversation in the bell and control room ceased. The only sounds were the divers' breathing amplified through the speaker, the incessant humming of machinery, and the intermittent clicking of the control-room monitors.

When the bell reached its bottom platform, Jones switched off the hydraulic winch and said, ''Bell run number one is a go. Let's 'ave a look, lad.''

''I'm leaving the bell,'' Percy said, his voice like that of a Southern Donald Duck.

''Roger,'' Jones said into the microphone as he raised his left hand, thumb up, to the others in the room. He turned to the technician to his left and said, ''Get Newt out there with 'im, mate.''

The floodlights on the bell illuminated an immense gray wall in the surrounding darkness. When the underwater robot's lights were also switched on, a cloud of silver-white bubbles appeared on the monitors in the control room for a moment before dissipating to reveal the figure of the diver. With the small emergency tank on his back and the umbilical trailing after him, he looked tiny, almost fragile, against the *Edinburgh*'s vast gray hull. As he headed upward and the technician at the robot's controls followed him with Newt's lights and deep-sea camera, the *Edinburgh* loomed on the monitor like a ghost ship in a curling fog. Although the ship listed to port, the hull had not broken apart. "Jesus," Percy said, "it's huge." He sounded almost breathless. "I can't tell you how . . . how big . . ." His voice trailed off.

The men in the control room watched mesmerized as Percy and the robot, like some pudgy aquatic pet, glided along the deck. The railing was encrusted and bent but only broken in spots. The six-inch guns of the "A" and "B" turrets jutted above the forecastle into the darkness. Smaller antiaircraft guns came into view on either side of the bridge and flag deck. Harrington glanced over at Altman and nodded. Altman's skin tingled. Forgetting that he had planned to take photographs of the procedures in the control room, he was taken by the fact that the wreck looked remarkably like the ship on the Thames. For the first time on the mission, he wished that he were one of the divers in saturation in the DDC, waiting his turn to descend to the wreck.

When the robot's light reached the four-inch guns amidships, Jones shouted into the microphone, "Move down, Jem. Down more, lad." His voice only a little less excited, he then told the technician to tilt the robot's camera, too. Jones leaned forward, both hands planted firmly on the console table.

As the camera tilted down, a gaping blast hole came into view on the monitors. Jones stroked his chin, and Altman let out a low whistle. "Shit," Percy said, his Southern accent giving the word three syllables.

"That's what did her," Jones remarked to Altman. "Okay," he said into the microphone, "Let's see the rest of her."

Petrosky came into the control room as the monitor showed the twisted wreck of the *Edinburgh*'s "Y" turret and stern. Harrington shook his head and stepped closer to the monitor. "The remains of sixty British sailors are still aboard that ship," he said.

Petrosky, who had stayed back from the others, said, "More Russians gave their lives for the motherland at the battle of Stalingrad alone than British died in the entire war."

Harrington glanced over his shoulder at Petrosky but did not answer. Jones looked over at Altman and raised one eyebrow. Jones then said into the microphone, "That should do it, Jem. Start the survey."

"Roger," came the squeaky reply over the speaker.

"And get on it, lad," Jones said, grinning at the others. "There's gold to be found."

▽ Twelve ▽

As the arctic night passed from dull gray to the light gray of dawn, two seventy-five-foot patrol boats flying the red Soviet flag appeared on the horizon. One stayed a half mile to the southeast of *Seerauber*; the other cut across the ship's bow and took up a position three-fourths of a mile to the northwest. Sophisticated antennae rose above the gray cabin of each boat, and each had twin 14.5-millimeter guns forward and a 12.7-millimeter gun aft. Both boats began to tack back and forth, but neither strayed far from its position.

The arrival of the two patrol boats put Jones, who had been cheerful the night before, in a foul mood at breakfast. Before Strinivitch and Petrosky were even seated at the wardroom table, Jones said, "I've got to 'and it to your comrades, Igor. It's bloody clever of the bastards to send out *two* shadows—one in the direction of the nearest port and the other right in our path back to the UK."

"Russian boats fish in these waters often," Strinivitch grunted as he sat down. "Their labors support their families and the Republic."

Jones laughed spitefully and said, "Apparently you 'aven't been topside to see 'em."

Strinivitch, who had already begun to shovel food onto his plate, shook his head.

"No, I haven't either," Petrosky answered as he sat down and picked up his napkin.

Jones looked over at Harrington, who was sipping a cup of Cambridge tea, laughed again, and said, "No wonder the Russian economy is such a bloody mess."

Relieved that Jones's volatile temper was again directed at the Russians and not at him, Altman sat silently eating his scrambled eggs and sausage.

"What do you mean?" Strinivitch asked as he chewed a biscuit smeared with butter. Crumbs dropped on his plate and the table.

"I mean, Igor, that they aren't fishing boats. They're bloody patrol boats a long goddamned way from the coast." Jones picked up a piece of sausage, bit it in half, and pointed the section still in his hand at the Russians. "And, besides being armed to the teeth, they 'ave enough electronic equipment aboard to broadcast to Mars." He paused, looking around the table first at Harrington and Altman and then back at the Russians. "Now, should we all take a guess at what they're doing here?"

"These are international waters," Petrosky said, enunciating the words slowly. "Those boats have every right to be here."

"That's true," Harrington said, just as slowly and carefully. "But they have no right to interfere with an internationally sanctioned salvage operation. No right whatever."

"You have my guarantee," Petrosky answered, "that the Soviet government has no intention of interfering with the salvage. Those boats are here strictly to observe the progress of the salvage and to ensure that there is no outside interference."

Jones stuffed the other half of the sausage in his mouth and scoffed at the Russian. Strinivitch, who had stopped eating, stared at Petrosky.

Harrington nodded and asked softly, "What exactly does 'no intention of intervening' mean?"

"It means," Petrosky said, turning toward Altman and leaning forward, his forearms on the edge of the table, "that the Soviet government will not intervene unless some other government interferes first."

A vein pulsing in his neck, Jones looked from Petrosky to Altman and back to Petrosky.

Altman did not say anything at first. When the silence had lasted almost a minute, he said, "The Russians have gunboats on either side of us. There are no American ships in the area." He pushed his chair back and stood up. "I'm tired of this Soviet bullshit blaming their belligerence on some phantom American threat. There was a Russian destroyer out there, and now there are a couple of gunboats. You want a threat, there's your goddamned threat." He tossed his napkin on his plate and stared down at Jones. "Get it through your fucking skull that there is no American threat." He walked out of the wardroom, leaving each of the others glancing around the table.

During the first six bell runs, each eight hours long, the divers measured the ship, located the exact spot in the hull nearest the bomb room, and began the arduous and dangerous task of cutting the entrance hole. The going was slow because of problems with both the underwater robot and the thermal cutting torches. During bell run three the robot's glass and epoxy hull leaked, causing the motors to short out; on the fifth bell run the robot circled out of control, almost tangling its tether with the divers' umbilical. The technicians worked constantly to rid their pet of its glitches, and by the end of the sixth run they pronounced the robot entirely fit. Whenever the divers got the thermal torches working, the oxygen blew silt around, sometimes reducing the divers' visibility to less than a yard. Ironically, the video cameras on the robot and bell, when they were operational, provided a better view for those in the control room than the divers had on the wreck itself.

Late in the afternoon of the third day of diving, Altman came into the control room just in time to view the divers' changeover midway through bell run number seven. The first diver had finished cutting the third edge of the entrance, and Sam Mathewson was just leaving the bell to begin the fourth and final cut. One of the English divers, a lanky man who had not yet compressed down, was seated at the control console acting as dive supervisor in Jones's absence. None of the other salvage representatives was in the control room, so Altman merely nodded to the supervisor and pulled up a chair.

As he was sitting down, Altman heard Mathewson say over the speaker, "I'm ready to fire the torch."

"Roger," the supervisor answered.

Altman watched the video monitor as Mathewson flipped down the special welding visor that fit over his dive helmet. Newt hovered nearby, its reflective disks a bright curved line in the bell's floodlights. A moment later, when the flame from the torch touched the hull, orange liquid sparks formed a halo around Mathewson's head. The halo soon shrank, but bubbles bursting with light continued to drift across the screen as Mathewson worked. Over the speaker, Mathewson's breathing, a hoarse sucking followed by gurgling, gradually became shorter and more labored as the fatigue of working at depth inevitably set in.

"He's fast, the fastest we've got," the supervisor said to Altman after about twenty minutes.

Altman nodded.

"And a tough SOB," the supervisor added. He then said into the microphone, "Going good, Sam. Keep at it, mate."

Altman stood, stretched, and meandered around the control room, checking the instruments. He liked watching the divers at work, especially when Jones and the others were not in the control room. Despite the various equipment failures, the work had developed a rhythm to which he had become attuned. He went back toward the control console, put his hands on the back of the chair he had been sitting in, and said, "Who's doing the next run?"

As the supervisor was about to answer, the monitor flashed bright orange. A split second later, a loud pop came from the speaker.

"What the hell?" the supervisor yelled.

Altman clenched the back of the chair.

Mathewson's image disappeared from the monitor, which suddenly showed only the faint outline of the ship's hull. His low moaning and erratic breathing were the only sounds coming from the speaker.

"Oxygen blowback," Altman shouted at the supervisor. "Get Jones down here fast." Altman took the microphone from the supervisor, who hustled over to the ship's public address system. "Sam, can you hear me?" Altman yelled into the microphone.

The only response was the continued moaning over the speaker.

The supervisor flicked the switch and shouted over the PA, "Captain Jones. Captain Jones, you're needed in the dive control room immediately."

Altman put his hand over the microphone and asked the supervisor, "What's the name of the diver in the bell?"

"Tierney. John Tierney."

Altman sat down in the supervisor's chair and said into the microphone, "John, do you read me?"

"Roger," came the reply. "What's happening? I can't see anything out the viewing port."

"Mathewson's been hit by a blowback. He's out. Get to him as fast as you can. Use your emergency tank if you have to."

"Roger."

"He's got to be below the entrance hole. Somewhere close. Follow his umbilical. Get going."

The moaning ceased; the erratic breathing became more shallow.

Jones burst into the control room as Altman shouted to the supervisor, "Tilt Newt down. Pan the area below the entrance."

Jones leaned across Altman to get a better look at the monitor and asked, "What 'appened?"

"Oxygen blowback."

"Shit. Who's the diver?"

"Mathewson."

"Bad?"

"Don't know. He's out, but he's still breathing."

Jones leaned back and began to say, "I'll take . . ."

"That's it," Altman shouted to the supervisor. "Hold Newt right there."

A limp figure, barely discernible in the silt, lay on the ocean floor.

Jones leaned against the console table and glanced over at the dive supervisor at Newt's controls.

Altman yelled into the microphone, "He's ten to twelve meters to the stern of the hole."

"Roger, I've got his umbilical," the diver answered.

Altman turned to Jones and said, "You want to take it from here? I'll get the emergency medical team organized in the DDC."

Taking the earphones from Altman, Jones said, "Thanks." He paused and then added, "Good work, mate."

Altman nodded. "Who's the medical officer?" he asked.

"Percy."

"Jem Percy?"

"Aye. The bloke's an MD. Why don't you go over to the DDC instead of using the PA? We don't need the whole crew getting wind of this till we know how bad the diver's banged up."

Altman nodded and headed out of the control room. As

he was crossing the deck toward the decompression chamber, he saw Harrington, who asked, "What's going on?"

Altman did not stop walking. "Accident down on the wreck," he answered. "Excess oxygen from a thermal cutting torch blew back in the diver's face. Jones may need another hand in the control room."

At the hatch to the decompression chamber, Altman pushed the intercom button and said, "Jem Percy—emergency." His mouth was dry, and he was sweating despite the cool sea breeze. He could see his reflection in the hatch porthole.

Percy came to the hatchway and said through the intercom, "What's the matter? What happened?" A modulator on the decompression chamber intercom made the diver's voice less squeaky.

"A blowback. Mathewson's hurt. We don't know how badly."

"Jesus," Percy said. "I'll get the med kit out, and I'll have a med station set up in plenty of time before the bell surfaces."

"If he's critical, it'll take . . ."

". . . Almost seven days to decompress him," Percy finished Altman's thought. "But I can handle in here almost anything a blowback could've done to him."

"Just a Georgia cracker, huh?" Altman smiled. "We'll bring him up as fast as we can."

Percy said, "Roger," and turned away from the hatch.

By the time Altman reached the dive control room again, Mathewson had been brought aboard the bell. The report from the other diver was that Mathewson's helmet was dented but had not leaked. Mathewson, who was only semiconscious, did not know where he was; his nose and one ear were bleeding, but there did not appear to be any deep cuts or gashes.

During the interminable thirty-five minutes it took to haul the bell up to the moonpool, Jones paced back and forth in front of the console. Harrington stood off toward one corner chewing on the stem of his unlit pipe; Altman stared at the monitor as though that action might somehow speed the bell's ascent. When the bell reached sixty feet below the surface, he headed over to the moonpool.

Altman arrived at the moonpool just as the bell emerged from the foaming water. Although he could see the yellow of the divers' wet suits through the bell's porthole, he could not tell what was happening. Once the bell was locked to the decompression chamber, he hurried over to one of the dive locker's portholes. For more than five minutes he could see nothing except the shadows of figures, playing on the stark white walls. Finally, he glimpsed Percy and two other divers carrying a stretcher into another section of the chamber. Mathewson, wearing only a nylon swimsuit, lay immobile on the stretcher, the blue anchor tattoo visible below his left shoulder, which was cocked at an awkward angle.

▽ **Thirteen** ▽

Altman lay in his bunk in the half-light, staring at the ceiling. Unable to sleep, he tried to stave off a flow of jumbled images in his mind: the orange flash on the monitor, the limp figure on the ocean floor, Mathewson lying on the stretcher. When Altman had taken over from the dive supervisor, he had felt for a moment the excitement he had known during combat missions in Vietnam—and he had liked the feeling again. He had felt alive, clearheaded, vibrant. Now, the feeling was gone, and all that remained were a headache, sleeplessness, and the images.

He got out of bed, put on corduroys, sat at the writing table, and wrote another letter to Elizabeth. In the letter, he described what had happened to Mathewson and how the accident had affected each of the salvage representatives. He told her more about his experiences in Vietnam, and how Mathewson's accident had dredged up old feelings from that time. When he finished, he slipped on a heavy sweater and headed out of his stateroom.

On deck, his breath clouding in the cold wind, he walked to the ship's stern. There was no one else on deck, but a light was on in the bridge, and the derrick's floodlights shone above the moonpool. The stars were faint in the sky above the ship's A-frame lifting rig, and the northern lights shimmered behind the Russian patrol boat to the northeast. Although a light chop ran before a brisk wind that made him shiver, *Seerauber* remained stable.

He cut back across the afterdeck, climbed down the ship's ladder to the decompression chamber, and pushed the intercom button next to the main entry lock. Percy peered around a bulkhead, saw that it was Altman, and came over to the viewing port.

"You're putting in long hours today," Altman said.

Percy shrugged. "I've got a patient who still needs some tending," he answered.

"How's he doing?" Altman shifted his weight from foot to foot to keep warm.

Percy took a can of tobacco from his pocket, twisted the top off, and pinched a wad of tobacco. "He's still out of it. Delirious. Believes he's in combat, I think." He stuffed the tobacco into the side of his mouth. "I've got him sedated. I had to increase the dosage. He keeps mumbling something about a mission."

"Any further report on his injuries?"

"No." Percy shook his head again. "His blood pressure— all his vital signs are good. He was damned lucky. And the fact that he's in incredible shape helps a lot."

Altman nodded.

"Just a second." Percy went over to the galley's cabinet and returned with a Styrofoam cup. Smiling and holding the cup up in front of the porthole, he said, "Can't smoke in here for fear of blowing the place up." He spat into the cup. "Don't get me wrong. The man's got a concussion and a separated shoulder. He's finished on this dive, but he'll be able to dive again in a month or so. As I say, he's been damned lucky."

"You do good work," Altman said.

"Thanks," Percy answered.

Altman tugged at his ear and said, "Do you practice medicine in the States, in Georgia?"

"Nah," Percy answered, "I liked diving more than I liked the office, the water more than the telephone. And I found I could make a decent wage as a dive doctor." He smiled to himself. "Not what a surgeon makes, but . . ."

"Where did you get your MD?"

"Columbia." Percy spat into the cup. "I hated the New York winters. Hated New Yorkers, for that matter. They were always in a hurry to go nowhere."

Altman looked at his reflection in the porthole. He realized that at some point Percy had clearly chosen a life at sea rather than in an office. Altman himself had tried to have it both ways—an office that provided him with the chance to return occasionally to the sea. And he wondered now if one really could have it both ways. "Well," he said, "I'll let you get back to your patient. And get some sleep, Jem. You'll be down on the wreck yourself soon enough."

On the second bell run after Mathewson's injury, the diver reported that he was within a few inches of completing the final cut through the *Edinburgh*'s hull. A steel shackle and cable were lowered to the wreck, and the salvage representatives and *Seerauber*'s crew began to gather by the small crane at the starboard railing between the moonpool and the ship's stern. The crew milled about, bantering with each other. The two Soviets stood off to one side, Strinivitch doing most of the talking and Petrosky occasionally waving his hand while making a point. Harrington stood at the rail with Altman, who had his camera bag over his shoulder and his auto-advance Nikon around his neck.

Jones, who had been down in the dive control room supervising the final cut, strutted through the crowd and clapped the winch operator on the shoulder. "Bring 'er up, lad," Jones said. Turning to the others, he shouted, "We've breached the bloody 'ull."

The men on deck grew silent as they watched the cable
winding around the winch. Altman took a photograph of the
winch operator and then leaned against the railing and
focused his camera on the spot where the cable disappeared
into the sea. Drops of water fell from the cable as it rose
until suddenly the jagged gray steel plate, five feet long and
four feet wide, broke the surface.

The men cheered as the plate rose into the bright, clear
sky. The cable ran through two fist-sized holes that had been
cut near the center of the plate, and, as the winch operator
turned the boom, the sun reflected off the oil splattered on
the steel. Altman took photographs until the plate, twisting
on the cable, had been swung above the railing and lowered
to the deck.

Jones stood beside the plate, one hand on it and the other
raised in the air, and said, "For those of you that 'ave been
wondering if there really is a ship down there, 'ere's the
proof." He closed his fist and hammered the plate. "The
first 'ard proof."

The crew shouted encouragement, and even Harrington,
Petrosky, and Strinivitch clapped heartily. As dull and ordi-
nary as it might seem in any other setting, the steel plate,
the first palpable evidence that the *Edinburgh* lay 1486 feet
below, rested, dripping oil and seawater, on the deck—and
Altman's neck tingled with excitement. He took one final
photograph of two crew members unshackling the plate,
nodded to Harrington, and headed up to the bridge, where a
bottle of champagne was being uncorked.

The rancor of some of the earlier meetings was forgotten,
at least for a time, and the celebratory atmosphere continued
through dinner and into the evening. After eating, the
salvage representatives remained seated around the wardroom table drinking and talking. Jones, who was more
affable than he had been at any time during the voyage, tried
to get a card game started, but there was no game that all
five of them played. Jones drank dark rum over ice with a

lime and told stories of his earlier salvage missions. Petrosky asked Altman more about life in Washington, D.C.—the art museums, the restaurants, and the theaters. Harrington smoked his pipe and drank little; he listened to the others but did not say much. The conversation continued to meander until Strinivitch, who had been drinking vodka straight up, asked Jones about the scar.

Jones rubbed his arm, leaned forward, and said in a mock theatrical tone, ''You want to know about this scar, do you, Igor?'' He rolled up his shirt, revealing the full eleven-inch jagged white line. ''This scar saved my life.'' He glanced around the table. ''You ever been in Algiers?''

''No,'' Strinivitch answered. Both Petrosky and Harrington shook their heads.

''No, I wouldn't expect it. It's much too 'ot a town for the likes of you.'' Jones grinned. ''There's a woman to blame, a Moorish woman with a mouth to drive a man wild,'' he said, shaking his head. ''There's always a woman to blame, right, mates?''

Strinivitch laughed loudly; Petrosky stirred the ice in his drink. Harrington gazed up at the swirling pipe smoke he had just blown into the air.

''The long and the short of it is, a bloke made the mistake . . .'' Jones paused for a moment, looking at each of the others in turn. ''. . . The fatal mistake of attacking me with the gaff I 'ave 'anging in the bridge. Maybe you've seen the gaff. A sharp bloody mother, that.''

Petrosky bit the corner of his lip and squinted at Jones.

''I have seen it,'' Strinivitch said.

Jones drank his run, glanced at Altman, and said, ''Well, Igor, I disemboweled the bastard. Ripped the gaff, which was still stuck in my arm, out of the bastard's 'and. And I got 'im good. I left 'im 'olding 'is guts, watching 'is intestines slipping through 'is fingers, spilling all over the floor.''

Strinivitch exhaled loudly; Petrosky still squinted at Jones.

Harrington, who had stopped gazing at the smoke, stared at Jones. Altman wondered if Jones had included the gore to impress the Russians.

"No one attacks me, Igor," Jones said, grinning again, "unless he wants to die."

Harrington went to his stateroom soon after the story, and the two Russians, Strinivitch weaving as he walked, left a short time later. When Altman stood up to go also, Jones said, "Aye, mate, 'ave another drink. The night's still young."

The genuinely amiable tone of Jones's voice surprised Altman. He poured a short shot of scotch over ice and sat back down at the table.

Jones asked Altman about his childhood in the American West. Altman described how, each summer, he and his father had headed out away from the school and town with a pack horse and enough gear to sustain them for a couple of weeks. Occasionally they went for five days or more without seeing any other people. His father searched outcroppings for minerals, and Altman tagged along, learning from his father, breathing the thin, clean air, gazing at the mountain peaks and valleys, and daydreaming. In the afternoons, storms sometimes came up fast, and they had to stand under their ponchos and wait out the lightning, blustering wind, and driving rain before they could return under a clearing sky to their camp. Jones reveled in Altman's memories of that open, unrestrained, almost wild life.

Jones talked of wandering the Cornish seacoast as a boy, in search of flotsam washed ashore from the ships that were periodically wrecked there. In heavy weather, ship's captains, both British and foreign, sometimes mistook the Bristol Channel for the English Channel and struck the reefs along the coast. Jones, occasionally with other boys but more often by himself, scavenged the beaches and cliffs.

The two men fell silent for a moment, and then Jones took a long swig of his rum, wiped his mouth, cocked his head to the right, and said, "You did a damned good job yesterday during the blowback. A 'ell of a job."

"Thanks," Altman answered. He waved his hand as if to dismiss the subject.

"My dive supervisor said you reacted fast—much faster than 'im. You acting like that may 'ave saved the diver's life. It sure as 'ell saved us some downtime on the bell runs."

Altman nodded.

Jones rubbed the back of his hand across his nose. "What I'm saying is, when you're in the dive control room, you're welcome to say whatever you think." He picked up his glass and gazed at the dark rum. "A man around with your skill won't 'urt the salvage any."

"Okay," Altman said, "I'm willing to help in whatever way you need."

"When I 'eard you were a demolitions expert, I . . . well . . ."

Realizing that what he was hearing was Jones's clumsy attempt to apologize, Altman answered, "I've already forgotten what was said before."

Jones finished his rum. "The thing you 'ave to know," he said, "is that the Americans I had to deal with in London were all pricks. Grey and the others acted like I was some bloody communist conspirator or something." His speech was becoming slurred. "It was like they didn't want the salvage to come off. They just wanted to cover their asses."

"I don't know much about that," Altman answered, as he thought about how Harrington had said almost the same thing in different words.

▽ **Fourteen** ▽

For the next few days, the divers worked around the clock to clear a path through the oil tank to the bulkhead and the bomb room beyond. Although the underwater robot was small enough to fit through the hole cut in the hull, the oil tank was far too cluttered for Newt to maneuver inside the ship. Because the sediment and oil in the tank also reduced the divers' visibility to a few inches, they worked more by feel than by sight. Machinery, pipe work, and debris that had fallen through from the upper decks slowed the divers' progress even more. At the great depth of the *Edinburgh*, the divers felt that every movement they made was like pushing against a wall. They quickly became short of breath, and, even if they stopped to rest for a while, they never really got their wind back for the rest of the dive.

Steel shards were winched from the wreck during each bell run. The larger pieces had to be slung individually and moved laboriously through the hole in the hull. During bell run eleven, the divers sent a metal trolley to the surface; a Royal Navy teapot came up in the basket two runs later. All of bell run fifteen was spent winching a large engine through the hole. It loomed there for a moment, a bright metallic beast in the floodlights, before slipping its cable and crashing to the ocean floor. The divers lost a full day trying to move a heavy compressor out of the way, before giving up and changing by five feet the spot for the final cut through the bulkhead to the bomb room.

During that period, Percy had Mathewson in the DDC's forward chamber decompressing so that after seven days Mathewson could be moved to the ship's sick bay. While the replacement diver was compressing down, the divers doing the bell runs worked doubly hard to keep on schedule. Once the divers reached the bomb room, they found a jumbled mess of silt, smashed piping, and munitions. Whenever a diver touched anything, he stirred up the silt and, losing all visibility in the area, had to pause to let the muck settle again. Each of the unexploded shells that the divers discovered had to be brought to the surface and defused. Four 250-pound bombs had to be moved safely out of the way. During bell run twenty-one, a diver sent an entire wooden crate of shells to the surface. On deck, the oily blue and brass shells, still neatly arranged in the open crate, glistened in the sunlight.

With each bell run, the anticipation in the control room heightened, and the number of salvage representatives and crew members gathered in front of the video monitor increased. Altman began to bring his camera with him each time he came to the control room. During bell run twenty-three, the diver working with Jem Percy found a strip of copper wire that matched the description of the wire used to bind the wooden crates that had been brought aboard the *Edinburgh* that night in Murmansk fifty years before. Two bell runs after the wire was discovered, a diver sent to the surface a piece of wood, like a slat from a crate, with indecipherable red stenciling still faintly visible along its grain. Although Petrosky tried to match the stenciling with numbers from the original invoice, no one could be sure the board came from one of the Russian crates.

Wearing the communications headset, Jones sat at the dive

console for the start of bell run twenty-six. Altman also sat at the console, monitoring the mixed-gas and hot-water gauges. Four technicians were working at various tasks in the room. Percy and Tierney were the two divers making the run, with Percy having the first stint on the wreck. For more than an hour, nothing happened that those in the control room could see. Newt's video camera remained focused on the shadowy hole cut in the *Edinburgh*'s hull. Altman cleaned a set of filters he had in his camera bag; Jones stood and stretched.

"I found the gold! I found the gold!" The high-pitched voice squealed from the speaker.

Instinctively, Altman squinted up at the video monitor, but there was nothing to see.

"I found it. I found the gold!"

"Jem," Jones yelled into the microphone, "you're shouting like 'ell. Where is it?" He sat down, stood up again, and leaned over the console.

"I found the gold!" Percy repeated, his voice cracking with excitement.

"Roger, roger," Jones shouted. "Well bring it out, lad. Send it up in the bloody basket." He then turned to Altman and added, "My 'ands are shaking, they are."

A few seconds later, the figure of a diver emerged from the hole in the hull and hovered there holding an object to his chest. He then did a slow-motion jig as though he were doing some arcane aquatic dance.

Jones laughed into the microphone. "Look at 'im, will you!" he yelled.

The news spread quickly; by the time Altman reached the winch along the starboard rail aft of the moonpool, Petrosky and Strinivitch and eight of the crew members were already there. Harrington, pulling on a tweed sport coat, hurried along the deck. Jones, who had stayed at the dive console until a dive supervisor arrived to take over for him, reached the deck just as the heavy canvas and steel-mesh bag was hoisted over the railing. The winch operator squatted, pulled the bag open, and lifted out a glittering, oily bar. When he saw Jones, he reached over and handed the dripping bar to the captain.

Jones's shoulders slumped for a moment under the weight of the bar. He then raised it over his head and turned a full circle while those around him cheered. Water and oil dripped down over the scar on his arm. "The *Edinburgh*'s treasure," he shouted. "And there's 'undreds more of these beauties just waiting to be plucked."

The crew cheered again, and the winch operator tossed Jones a white towel. As Jones wiped the bar clean, it glinted in the sunlight. Like the others around him, Altman stared at the shining bar. It was long and thin and rectangular—longer and thinner than he had expected.

Jones motioned to Petrosky and Strinivitch. As Petrosky smiled wryly, Strinivitch stepped forward and took the bar. He grunted, laughed, and said, "Heavy." While Strinivitch held the bar, Jones rubbed his fingers over its smooth surface and read the serial number aloud—KT 328. There were no other markings on the bar.

Jones nodded toward Altman, and Strinivitch passed the bar to the American. It was heavy, almost twenty-five pounds. He held the bar at chest level and balanced it so that the setting sun caught the bar and made it gleam brilliantly.

"Careful with that, mate," Jones shouted to him over the hubbub. "It's worth more than a 'undred thousand quid."

More than a hundred and sixty thousand dollars . . . as much as I make in three years, Altman thought. He shook his head slowly and glanced at Jones, who was grinning at him.

When Altman offered the bar to Harrington, the older man waved him off. Harrington smiled, but his expression seemed almost befuddled. Pale smoke swirled above his pipe.

△ **Fifteen** △

Throughout the evening, those aboard *Seerauber* could talk of nothing but the gold. Percy found five more bars, and Tierney, during his four hours in the bomb room, discovered nine bars, bringing the total for bell run twenty-six to $1.5 million. Jones radioed the news of the discovery to London in code so that anyone monitoring the radio would not know that the *Edinburgh*'s cargo had been located. Petrosky sent a cryptic message to Moscow, and Altman cabled Grey, using the code words agreed upon earlier. Champagne was uncorked for the crew as well as the salvage representatives. Only the divers in the deck decompression chamber and those crew members supervising bell run twenty-seven were excluded from the festivities.

At ten that evening, Altman carried the first bar—KT 328—over to the decompression chamber to show the divers. He pushed the intercom switch and held the bar in front of the porthole. A motley, bearded group after two weeks in the DDC, the divers gathered around the viewing port chattering and laughing and gesturing like children. Then they cleared a path for Percy to have a closer look at the bar. When he saw the glistening bar, he whistled, the sound shrill through the chamber's intercom.

Altman lowered the bar, leaned against the exterior of the chamber, and said, "You looked pretty damned happy when you came through the cut in the hull."

"I was," Percy answered. He had a pinch of tobacco in his mouth. "I mean, that's why we're here. I'd been busting my butt down there, and suddenly I'm feeling around in the muck . . . I couldn't see a thing . . . and I feel this object. I knew it couldn't be a shell. It wasn't round and it was too heavy for its size. Even as I was lifting it, I couldn't believe it. I was surprised as hell."

The other divers continued to mill around behind Percy for a moment before dispersing.

"You about popped our eardrums with your yelling over the squawk box."

"I did, huh?" Percy laughed. "I remember shouting, but I didn't know it was that loud. I just . . . Well . . ." He scratched his beard. "It's hard to explain. The fact that it's valuable, worth a lot of money, wasn't important. It's finding it that sends you. You're at that incredible depth in almost total darkness in that steel tomb, and suddenly . . ." Percy shook his head.

"I think I understand," Altman said. He then raised the bar again and added, "I better get this back to the strong room. The Russians didn't want me taking it out in the first place." He laughed. "They're goddamned possessive about it." He started to go, stopped, and turned back. "Oh, I almost forgot. How's Mathewson doing?"

"Great." Percy smiled. "By the time he's decompressed, he should be fit enough for light duty. He can't use the shoulder any, but the ear is healing nicely. And so is the concussion."

When Altman returned the bar to the ship's strong room, Strinivitch was there waiting for him. Strinivitch had placed the other fourteen bars on the table next to the log in which Petrosky had registered their serial numbers. He took the bar from Altman and carefully lined it up with the others.

Altman didn't say much because he didn't want to hear any more about the "Russian" gold. Instead, he went back over to the wardroom, where Jones, Petrosky, and Harrington were sitting. Three bottles of champagne stood empty on the table. Petrosky was flushed, and Harrington appeared somewhat dazed. Red-faced, Jones was saying, "They're sending up more than a million quid on this run alone."

Altman clapped Jones on the back and said, "Congratulations, Mick. You've done what you said you were going to do."

"That I did," Jones answered. "Did you show that bar to the divers?"

"Yeah," Altman answered as he sat down. "Being able to actually see the gold made their day. And Jem Percy's still walking on air."

"I'll bet," Jones said. He reached down into a bucket of ice on the floor, pulled out a chilled bottle of champagne, and filled the glass in front of Altman. He then refilled Petrosky's glass and his own.

Harrington covered his glass with his hand.

Jones shrugged and said, "Just leaves more for the rest of us."

Petrosky raised his glass and gave the tenth toast of the night, "To the discovery of the Russian gold."

"To the gold," Jones said. "I'll drink to that."

Harrington, who had raised his empty glass, asked Jones, "When you saw that gold bar on deck today, was that the high point of your salvage career?"

Jones swirled the champagne in his glass and gazed at the bubbling liquid. He then looked over at Harrington and said, "It was a damned fine moment, mate. Damned fine." He gazed down again at the champagne. "But not the best, no."

"What was the best?" Petrosky asked, slurring the last word so that it sounded like "besht."

"The best moment," Jones answered, "came almost

twenty years ago. I was only a few months out of the Royal
Navy. I 'ad learned to dive in the navy, and that's all I
wanted to do. I was working different jobs in Falmouth—
bank teller, bartender—and was out on the water any chance
I got. Me and my mates rented a fishing boat from a bloke
who was done with it by midafternoon every day. Thought
'e 'ad a good deal, that bloke, but 'e should 'ave gotten a
salvage contract instead of taking the quid a day off me. The
boat was named *Vagabond*, which suited me fine. She was
forty-two feet.'' He looked over at Petrosky. ''About 'alf the
size of those Russian gunboats 'anging like vultures out
there.''

Jones cleared his throat. ''Me and three mates were
working the Cornish coast. When we could get *Vagabond*
for a couple of days, we'd 'ead over to the reefs off the
Scilly Isles. A graveyard for ships, those reefs are. We'd
sell anything we found—trinkets, bottles, iron works, anything that the antique dealers could sell up in London. We
didn't make much but it paid for our supplies.'' He waved
his hand. ''And anyway, it was the diving itself that mattered
then.''

As he spoke, his voice softened with the memory. He
seemed to be speaking as much to himself as to the others.
''One summer day, a peaceful day with the surf barely
breaking on shore, we were following a reef north. We
dragged a diver.'' He glanced at Harrington. ''You motor at
slow speeds, towing a diver on a line. The diver checks the
bottom for any sign of a wreck—ballast stones, discolored
straight lines cut in the sand. You get 'ypnotized sometimes
watching the bottom as you move above it. Some people
think dragging is dangerous, but we 'ad already found
scores of wrecks that day.

''The diver was off the drag line. I took *Vagabond* about
and headed back. 'Ballast stones,' 'e shouted, and I anchored.
We set our marker buoy on the reef, and me and another
man dove. One of my mates stayed on board to keep watch.

We began to circle around the ballast stones, searching, the same way we always did. We found nothing at first except for some iron spikes and whatnot.''

No one else said anything as Jones refilled each of the champagne glasses except Harrington's. ''It was getting late. My mates were ready to give up, but I 'ad been on too many wrecks. I wasn't about to leave. The others went to the surface, while I circled the ballast stones one last time. With the large, round chunks of granite all around me, I fanned the sand with my 'ands, knowing all the time that my mates were 'aving a bloody laugh at my stubbornness. Then I dug a couple of little craters in the sand. I was about to pack it in myself. I was fanning the sand, watching it swirl, then a gold coin slid below my hand. Then another coin and another.''

Jones looked around the table at each of the others. ''My breath was caught in my throat. I'm not sure I breathed at all. Then I was shouting like Percy was down there today, but there was nobody to hear me. I fanned some more and saw something that looked like a chain. But it shined. I mean, it shined like no chain I ever saw. I pulled on it, and it eased out of the sand—grudgingly.

''It was a chain, all right, a gold-link chain eight feet long. I felt like the world above me disappeared. It was like the water was magic. As if every fish, every creature in the water 'ad stopped. As if time 'ad stopped. As if the universe 'ad froze for that moment I pulled the chain out of the sand.''

He stopped talking, sipped his champagne, looked up at the ceiling, and exhaled. ''Today, 'olding that bar was great, but nothing will ever compare with that moment on that reef.'' He was silent again.

''What did you do?'' Petrosky asked.

''What the 'ell do you think I did?'' Jones answered, grinning, his voice once again harsh. ''I swam to the surface. I could barely get the chain up. I still 'ad those gold coins clutched in my hand. You should have seen my mates' faces when they pulled the chain aboard. I watched, 'anging onto *Vagabond*'s gunwale. Then I tossed the coins onto the deck. My mates scrambled into their gear. We were all down at the ballast stones, fanning the sand like mad crabs.

"By the time our tanks ran out, we 'ad the deck of the *Vagabond* covered with gold. Gold everywhere. Gold nuggets . . ." He pointed to the salt and pepper shakers that had been left on the table after dinner. "Some as big as that. Gold rings. Gold coins—dated from 1626 to 1665. Gold bracelets and necklaces. Gold bars with markings we couldn't understand. And silver and pearls. All of it shining there on the deck." He shook his head, finished his champagne, and said, "It was something."

"What happened to it?" Harrington asked. He had been staring at Jones through the second half of the captain's story.

"The bloody government took most of it in taxes. But I've been able to call my shots ever since."

▽ **Sixteen** ▽

Unable to sleep at three that night, Altman sat at the writing table in his stateroom. He had begun to incise the whale's tooth, working on the masts and spars, but the champagne made his hand unsteady. His mind was not clear enough for him to write Elizabeth. Hoping that fresh air would calm his hand and slow his mind, he headed up to the deck.

He could just discern the horizon in the gathering light. The air was crisp and the breeze brisk. Wanting to be buffeted by the gusts, he climbed the steel ship's ladder to the flying bridge above the wheelhouse. Although he wore a heavy sweater, he shivered. The lights near the top of the communications antenna on *Seerauber*'s forecastle seemed to twinkle. The dark enclosed lifeboat hung from its davits along the starboard railing a deck below him. Behind him, the diving suspension tower's cables whined in the wind, but the heave compensation gear kept the tower absolutely stationary over the dive bell that at that moment hovered fifteen hundred feet below as the divers searched the *Edinburgh*'s bomb room for more bars.

His head began to clear, but he could not help thinking about the gold. Just before he had gone to his stateroom two hours earlier, the basket, swung onto the deck, had con-

tained six bars—almost a million dollars worth of gold. . . .
Smudged with silt and oil. . . . Piled haphazardly in a steel
mesh basket. . . . Worth as much money, perhaps, as he
would make the rest of his life . . .

Hearing footsteps on the ladder behind him, he turned as
Harrington reached the flying bridge's deck and, panting a
bit, pulled at the sleeves of his thick turtleneck sweater.

"Good morning," the older man said. "I see you're
keeping baker's hours."

Altman shrugged and answered, "Couldn't sleep."

"Neither could I," Harrington said. "I heard you in the
passageway." He glanced over at the suspension tower. "I
couldn't at first figure out where you'd gone."

"I needed the wind to sober me." Altman shook his head
slowly. "I can't get my mind off all that gold."

"Yes, a lot of bars have been raised already."

Altman stuffed his hands in his pockets, laughed, and
said, "It certainly doesn't look cursed."

At first, Harrington did not answer. He gazed up at the
burgeoning light on the horizon. "No," he said, "it doesn't
appear cursed. Still, it . . ." His voice trailed off. He put his
hands together and, fingers locked, stretched his arms forward.

Altman nudged him. "Are you still bothered by that tale
of doom that old sot told us?"

"Swanson? Yes, I guess that's it. Or part of it, anyway."
Lowering his arms, Harrington looked closely at Altman for
a moment. "You know, Will, the fact that the cargo is being
brought aboard doesn't mean that the salvage is complete."
He grabbed the railing. "See that patrol boat out there?"

As Altman looked out to sea, the cold wind blew through
his sweater. He could barely detect the low, gray silhouette
of the boat in the half-light.

"It's a *Zhuk*-class craft," Harrington went on. "For what
it's worth, the *Zhuks* are supposedly manned by the KGB."

"KGB?" Altman asked, taken aback for a moment. "But

there's no reason . . . They're not stupid enough to . . . They're not going to hijack the gold . . ."

"I agree," Harrington answered, "but still one has to ask why . . ."

"Trevor," Altman interrupted, "we're part of the most remarkable salvage operation in history. You've got to drop that crusty British reserve of yours and get into the spirit of it."

Harrington turned away from Altman, looked out to sea, cleared his throat, and said to the wind, "The spirit of the thing. Yes, that's it."

The next afternoon Altman crossed the deck to the decompression chamber to meet Mathewson, who was due to come out. Altman had slept for a few hours, updated his log, and marked the rolls of film he had shot of the celebration when the first gold bar reached the deck. Now, his head ached and the camera slung around his neck felt heavier than the entire camera bag had felt the day before. One of the ship's radio operators handed him a cable, said, "It's just come in, sir," and scurried away.

Altman stood near the moonpool, unfolded the cable, and read it: "Altman. Thank you for the good news. Everything goes well, I trust. Grey." Folding the sheet of paper again, he wondered about the message. Grey had insisted that Altman contact him the moment the gold was discovered. And now, almost a full day had passed before Grey had responded, and the response was so nondescript. Figuring there was no point in trying to fathom, especially with a hangover, the mind of a bureaucrat, Altman put the cable in the pocket of his wool shirt and looked out at the white crests beginning to form on the waves. The wind had picked up to fifteen knots, but *Seerauber* still barely moved.

When Altman approached the decompression chamber, Mathewson, assisted by a burly crew member, was pulling himself awkwardly through the entry lock. The crew mem-

ber pulled the DDC's hatch shut and spun the wheel on the
lock. Mathewson wore a dark shirt and jeans but no shoes.
His beard was scraggly, his skin pale. His left arm was in a
blue cloth sling, and bandages covered burns on parts of his
feet where he had been scalded by the hot water trapped at
the base of his wet suit when he had tumbled to the ocean
floor. He lifted his duffel bag from the deck and carried it in
his right hand. When he saw Altman fumbling with the
camera to take pictures, he frowned, walked over, and said,
"What the hell are you doing?"

"Recording this for posterity—and Uncle Sam," Altman
joked. "An American diver injured during the quest for the
gold. I can see the caption already."

"Cut the crap," Mathewson said. He dropped the duffel
bag and put his hand in front of the camera. "And stop the
fuckin' pictures. I feel rotten enough about this without 'em."

Altman picked up the duffel bag, and the two men
climbed the ship's ladder and began to walk toward the
ship's bow. The wind blew Mathewson's sling, causing the
material to flutter like a luffing sail. Mathewson took a deep
breath of the cool sea air.

"It's too bad, a big dive like this, and you have to sit it
out," Altman said.

Mathewson snorted, "It's damned bad luck. I've worked
with thermal cutters a hundred times and never had an
accident." He turned and spat over the railing.

"At least you came out of it in one piece," Altman said
as they ducked through a hatchway into the ship.

"Shit, I've been hurt worse and been back on the job
faster."

"Not a deep dive, though. You can't chance it," Altman
said.

"Well, I got a private berth out of it," Mathewson said
sarcastically. Despite Mathewson's protests that he was fine,
Jones has assigned him for forty-eight hours to sick bay. For

Mathewson, Altman realized, the order had heaped insult on injury.

When dinner was finished that evening, Altman stayed on in the wardroom after the others had left. Jones had gone back to the dive control room, and Petrosky had headed to the radio room to make his evening report to Moscow. Harrington and Strinivitch had returned to the ship's strong room. Fifty-nine gold bars had been discovered in the twenty-four hours since Percy had found the first bar. During dinner, Petrosky had suggested that Harrington, as nominal head of the salvage, should take responsibility for the key to the strong room. Agreeing reluctantly, Harrington had accompanied Strinivitch to count the newly discovered bars, clean them, log their serial numbers, and line them in neat rows on the steel shelves.

Altman spread his cheesecloth on the wardroom table, took out the whale's tooth and scrimshaw tools, and began to incise the square-rigger's spars where he had left off the night before. His hand was steady and his head clear; alone in the wardroom, he soon lost himself in his work. His mind wandered from the *Edinburgh*'s gold to his own experiences as a diver. He thought about how different it must be to find gold than it had been to plant explosives or to survey the ocean floor. Although he had never lost his awe of the sea and he had often felt satisfaction after completing a job, he had never experienced anything approaching the ecstasy that both Jones and Percy had spoken of the night before.

Gunter Schmidt, dressed as always in his white uniform, hurried into the wardroom. Red-faced and panting, Schmidt said, "Herr Altman, you must come to the dive control center. Captain Jones needs you immediately."

When Altman entered the control room, Jones was standing between two technicians seated in front of the dive console. Jones, who had the headset on, motioned to Altman and then shouted into the microphone, "Goddamm it. Get out of the bomb room—NOW."

Altman said, "What the . . ."

He was interrupted by a high-pitched voice screaming over the speaker, "Gold. Gold. Everywhere there's gold. Gold here. Gold there. Gold everywhere."

Jones yelled, "Glenn, get out of the bloody bomb room." He ran his hand along the back of his neck. "John, are you there?"

"I'm here, capt'n," a second, slightly less shrill voice came over the speaker. "What can I do for ya?"

"Get off your ass and 'elp me talk Glenn out of the bomb room."

"No can do, capt'n," the voice answered. "He's just dancin' with the gold, that's all."

"Oh, my God," Altman murmured. He moved closer to the console and gazed up at the monitor, which showed only a diver's umbilical trailing into the dark hole in the hull. "How long has this been going on?" he asked Jones.

"Ten minutes," Jones answered. "Since just after the bell reached the ocean floor."

"Gold, beautiful gold," a voice squeaked over the speaker. The diver's breathing was hurried.

"They're pissed out of their skulls," one of the technicians said.

Jones glanced at Altman and said, "It can't be nitrogen narcosis." It was both a statement and a question.

"The symptoms are right, but, with the mixture we're using, it can't be," Altman agreed. "What's the mixed-gas reading?"

"Looks okay," the technician sitting in front of the gauges answered. "Pressure's been a little low, but well within a safe range."

Altman leaned over and looked at the gauges himself. They were nowhere near a dangerous level.

"I keep dropping the gorgeous gold bars," the squeaky voice announced over the speaker.

"We can't get 'im out of the bomb room," Jones said, his forehead perspiring. "If we raise the bell, we'll 'ang him by 'is umbilical."

"Don't lose those bars, buddy," the other shrill voice laughed. "I want to get my mitts on some of that beautiful bullion, too."

Altman checked off the symptoms in his mind: intoxication, clumsiness, euphoria, bizarre behavior. "How fast do they respond to questions?" he asked.

"Slow," Jones answered.

Altman glanced again at the mixed-gas gauge. "Who's in the bomb room?" he asked.

"Glenn Hall."

"In the bell?"

"John Tierney."

"Can I try talking to Hall?"

Handing the headset to Altman, Jones said, "They 'ave no idea they're barmy."

Altman sat against the edge of the console. The rate of his breathing was increasing, as though he were subconsciously trying to synchronize it with the hyperventilating divers. He composed his voice and said, "Glenn, do you read me?"

"Roger, dodger. Dodger, roger, dodger," the high-pitched voice answered after a couple of seconds.

Tierney howled with laughter. Altman grimaced. Jones slammed his fist on the console table and said, "Shit."

Trying to keep his voice calm, Altman asked, "How's it going in the bomb room?"

"Great," came the answer. "I keep finding gold bars." He laughed shrilly. "But I lose 'em before I can get 'em into the basket."

Altman rubbed his hand across his forehead. "Glenn," he said, "we've got a problem with the robot's video camera. Can you give us a hand?"

"Little Newt's got something in his eye?" Hall laughed.

His breathing was coming in long, deep drafts. "Hang on a minute. I'll go fetch him."

Jones raised his hand, thumb up, and nodded to Altman.

"What's the problem?" Tierney asked from the bell. "I can scoot to Newt faster than Glenn can."

"That's okay, John," Altman said, keeping his voice conversational. "We need you in the bell. You're doing great."

"Dodger, roger," Tierney laughed.

Altman exhaled and sat down in the chair. He figured that the only chance of getting the divers up from that depth was to coax Hall out of the wreck and into the bell. If Tierney left the bell, they'd never get the divers back alive. His mind checking the symptoms against the possible causes, he looked at the clock above the console and then at the mixed-gas gauges. "Hypoxia," he said suddenly. "That's got to be it." He turned to the technician and shouted, "Raise the oxygen level."

"The mix is all right," the technician protested.

"Just do it," Altman yelled.

"Wait!" Jones shouted. He cocked his head, listening intently.

"We've got to raise the oxygen level. It's . . ." Altman said to Jones. Then he realized what Jones was listening to: silence. The high-pitched hyperventilating of one of the divers had ceased.

"Raise the bell! Raise the fucking bell!" Jones yelled at the technician seated in front of the control switch.

"But, sir, the diver in the bomb room . . ." the technician answered.

Jones pushed the technician from the chair and punched the hydraulic switch. Wide-eyed, the technician sprawled across the floor.

"Maybe we can yank 'im out, like on a leash," Jones said to Altman.

"Glenn," Altman shouted into the microphone. "Do you read me, Glenn?"

"Hey, what's going on?" Tierney yelled through the speaker.

"Keep adding oxygen," Altman shouted to the technician monitoring the mixed-gas gauges. "More, dammit!"

The technician Jones had pushed stood up, brushed his pants off, and stood next to the console.

Altman stared at the monitor. As the bell rose, the slack went out of the umbilical leading into the cut in the *Edinburgh*'s hull. The umbilical first became horizontal, and then its angle increased until it was almost vertical. The tubing seemed almost to stretch, but no diver appeared against the dark hole in the hull.

"That's it," Jones said. "If I raise the bell anymore, it'll rip 'is 'elmet off." He hit the hydraulic switch, pushed back his chair, and stood up.

"Glenn," Altman yelled, "if you read me, respond."

The speaker was silent for a moment, and then Tierney, his voice cracking, said, "What's happened to him? Where is he? You can't leave him."

Altman stood up, put his hand over the microphone, and said to the technician, "Hold that oxygen level. Tierney seems to be coming out of it."

"It's too bloody late," Jones said, anger in his voice. His shoulders were slumped as he leaned, fists on the console, toward the monitor. He stood up straight, kicked the steel leg of the console, and turned away.

Altman glanced at the clock and then squeezed his temples with his thumb and middle finger. "Come in, John," he said, his voice lower than it had been.

"Where the hell is Glenn?" Tierney asked.

"How do you feel, John?" Altman asked. He sat down slowly, his head throbbing.

"I'm all right," Tierney answered. "But would someone tell me what the hell is going on?"

"We need you to go after Glenn in the bomb room," Altman said, his neck and back drenched with sweat.

▽ **Seventeen** ▽

By the time Tierney reached Hall, the men in the dive control room had given up hope. They went through the emergency procedures mechanically—contacting Percy so that he could set up the medical kit in the deck decompression chamber, having Tierney administer artificial respiration, and raising the bell. Altman, who had seen death often, was subdued. Livid, Jones stomped around the control room yelling that the gas mixture couldn't have been wrong, that it was the same mixture used on every other bell run, and that he was going to find out what went wrong even if he had to tear apart every piece of equipment in the umbilical system.

When the diving bell neared the surface, Altman went over to the moonpool to organize the removal of Hall's body from the bell. Outside, the wind blew even more briskly; white caps foamed atop five-foot waves. Clouds rolled through a darkening sky. He was only at the moonpool a short time when, as news of the accident spread around the ship, the crew began to gather near the base of the bell's suspension-system tower. Harrington arrived soon after four of the German sailors had set the steel brace over the dripping bell. At first, he stood off to one side, out of the glare of the ship's lights above the moonpool, and said nothing.

Strinivitch ambled across the deck toward Altman and asked, "There has been an accident? Another diver is injured?"

"A diver is dead," Altman answered.

The raw wind blowing his thinning hair, Harrington approached the two men and asked, "How did it happen?"

"Hypoxia," Altman answered. "The oxygen level in the gas mixture was too low." He shrugged. "Hall hyperventilated— basically used up his oxygen and lost it."

"That is too bad," Strinivitch said. He buttoned his dark coat. "Will it stop the search for the gold?"

Harrington scratched the side of his nose, turned away, and looked out at the lights of the Russian patrol boat on the horizon.

Altman glared at Strinivitch. "No, it won't," he said icily. "But it'll slow it down."

Looking stricken, Harrington turned back toward Altman. "Damn," he said. "What caused it?"

Zipping up his windbreaker, Altman answered, "Equipment failure, somewhere in the umbilical system."

"That damned cargo." Harrington brushed his hand through his hair. "Something must be done."

Mathewson, who stood at the top of the ladder down to the deck decompression chamber, called to Altman and waved him over. The diver had shaved, but his skin was still wan and his left arm was still in a sling under his wool naval watch coat.

Before Altman moved to follow Mathewson, Strinivitch asked, "The delays in the search, how long will they take?"

"I have no fucking idea," Altman answered. "You may have to go a day or two without fondling any new gold."

"What does that mean?" Strinivitch demanded. His upper lip was curled, revealing the gap between his front teeth.

Altman shook his head and said nothing.

Grabbing Altman's sleeve, Strinivitch said, "What do you mean?"

Altman stood face to face with the Russian, staring down into his small eyes, and said, "There's a dead diver I have to get out of the bell." He pulled himself from Strinivitch's grasp and, without looking back, went over to the ladder.

As Altman followed Mathewson down the ladder, Mathewson said, "Jem Percy wants to talk to you. What the hell happened?"

"Hypoxia," Altman answered. "The gas mixture was off."

"Shit," Mathewson said. He rubbed his left shoulder with his right hand. "What the hell? There was no problem before."

"There's one now," Altman said. "Somewhere in the umbilical system."

Percy was waiting by the DDC's viewing port to talk to Altman over the intercom. Before Altman could speak, Percy said, "I've already been in the bell. There's no hope of reviving Hall. Tierney's pretty shook up, but he'll be all right."

Altman leaned toward the intercom in order to make the conversation as private as possible. "We assumed as much," he said.

Apologetically, Percy went on, "Even if I could've gotten his heart going, he'd have been a total vegetable." He wiped his face and then smacked the palm of his hand against the hatch. "Jesus, shit, I was supposed to make that run."

"What?" Altman asked.

"It could have been me down there. I was scheduled for the run. But one of the divers came down with an ear problem during the last run. I had to treat him immediately, so I scratched at the last minute."

Altman exhaled slowly. "Makes you stop and think, huh," he said.

"Damned straight," Percy answered.

Ten minutes later, two crew members passed the stretcher bearing Hall's body through the air lock at the bottom of the diving bell. Altman and Harrington accompanied two other crew members carrying the stretcher by the moonpool and along the port deck. The corpse was covered with a sheet, but as they turned by the bridge a gust of wind blew the sheet off. Harrington, who was walking behind the stretcher, grabbed the sheet, catching it just before it blew over the railing. Hall's body was naked except for a nylon swimsuit. His skin was a moribund bluish color and his face was gray-blue. His fingers and toes were darker. Harrington bit his lip as he and Altman covered the corpse again, carefully tucking in the corners of the sheet.

Jones was not at breakfast with the four salvage representatives the next morning. Altman, who had slept little, did not eat anything. Writing to Elizabeth had provided his only solace during the slow, murky hours before the arctic morning. Now, his mind foggy, he drank his second cup of coffee and wondered if Jones, who had been inspecting the wiring connecting the gauges to the oxygen, hydrogen, and helium tanks when Altman had left the control room the night before, had slept at all.

Harrington hunched over his tea and said nothing. He looked bleary eyed, older, almost decrepit. He had developed a dry, hacking cough during the night. Strinivitch was dour, Jones having announced that there would be no more bell runs until the cause of the accident was discovered. Occasionally, Strinivitch took another biscuit from the table, dunked it in his coffee, shoved it in his mouth, and chewed it with his mouth half open. Petrosky paged through a copy of *Punch* while he ate his eggs. When he finished his tea, he asked Altman, "Is there any more information about the accident or when the divers will begin work again?"

Altman shook his head and picked up his coffee mug. He felt as though he were under water, weighed down by ten atmospheres of pressure.

The four men sat around the table in silence for a few more minutes. Then, as Harrington sighed and stood up to leave, Jones burst through the doorway. He had on the same dark corduroys and turtleneck sweater he had been wearing the night before. There were dark circles under his eyes; the stubble growing on his chin was mostly gray. "All of you on deck," he said, his voice acid.

Petrosky slowly wiped his mouth with his napkin and then said, "Good morning, Mr. Jones." He smiled sardonically. "That sounds suspiciously like an order, which would be inappropriate here." He waved his hand languidly around the room.

"That is right," Strinivitch said. "We are representatives of the Soviet peoples, not members of a crew to be ordered around."

Jones leaned forward, letting his shoulders drop a little, and cocked his head slightly—the pose a street fighter assumes just before tearing someone apart. "Just the same," he said, "you're coming on deck—now."

The wind had subsided some, but white caps still swirled atop the four-foot waves. Cumulus clouds slid through the overcast sky. Jones led the men over to the moonpool, where the bell had been positioned so that its top was level with the deck. Gunter Schmidt, his arms folded across his chest, stood at the derrick's controls, but none of the ship's crew was around.

Jones ran his hand along the top of his turtleneck as though he were trying to loosen the sweater's grip on him. "I spent all night looking for the bloody problem," he said. "I checked the wiring—every goddamned gauge. Worked my way through the control console and the bell. Found nothing.''

Altman scanned the sky for a spot where the sun might break through, warm him, and clear his head.

Jones stepped across the moonpool's railing and onto the top of the bell. ''Things go wrong. It's the nature of ships. The nature of diving. I checked the connections between the tanks and the tubing, between the tubing and the bell, between the bell and the divers' umbilical.'' Squatting, he rubbed his fingers on each one of the bolts and washers where the umbilical tubes entered the bell.

Harrington coughed into a monogrammed handkerchief.

''I inspected every millimeter of feed tubing coming from the tanks,'' Jones continued. ''You can't always see or 'ear leaks, so Gunter pumped oxygen while I sprayed the tubes with water. If there's a leak, the water bubbles up. There were no bloody bubbles.''

Schmidt stood impassively, his arms still folded. Strinivitch, his hands deep in his coat pockets, rocked back and forth on the balls of his feet. Petrosky leaned against the moonpool railing and asked, ''Is this lecture necessary, Mr. Jones?'' His voice was coldly polite.

Jones raised his arm, pointed at Petrosky, and said, ''You better...'' Dropping his hand, he paused. ''It's goddamed necessary, Mr. Petrosky,'' he said. ''And you'll listen... Unless you're too busy filing reports to Moscow Central.''

Strinivitch glanced at Petrosky.

''Or is this something they already know about?'' Jones asked.

Petrosky moved away from the rail, stood up straight, pulled the cuffs of his shirt down from under his sweater, and, his voice steady, said, ''Do proceed, Mr. Jones.'' He waved his hand toward the bell.

Jones stared at Petrosky for another moment and then said, ''I expected to find the problem fairly easy. You don't always, but I thought I would.'' He nodded to Schmidt.

"This morning, I lowered the bell. Then, as Gunter raised it, I checked every meter of the tubing as it fed back into the 'olding tank. It took three bloody hours. I almost gave up." He raised his arm and grabbed the umbilical tubes above his head. "Almost," he repeated. He then pointed at the different-colored tubes. "The oxygen is the orange one." He stretched so that he could cup the tube with his hand. The base of the scar on his arm showed above his sleeve. Torn silver duct tape hung near his elbow. "Above the bell, 'ere . . . above a man's line of sight, but not above 'is reach." He twisted the orange tube a little. "There." He looked at each of the salvage representatives. "There," he repeated, anger in his voice. "See anything there, Trevor?"

Harrington coughed and shook his head.

"Will?"

"No," Altman answered.

"Igor? Vlad?"

Strinivitch shook his head and glanced at Petrosky.

"No, I do not," Petrosky said.

"No, you wouldn't, would you?" Jones muttered. He gave the tube a violent twist so that a razor-thin gash, almost eight inches long, appeared. He held the tube like that, the veins in his wrist bulging from the exertion and suppressed rage.

Harrington gasped and coughed. The others looked at each other.

"The cut is very thin and very neat," Jones said, still twisting the tube.

"Mick," Harrington said, clearing his throat. "Is it possible that the hose caught on something sharp?" He looked around. "On some metal apparatus or something?"

Jones's smile was ominous. "Is it possible it wasn't sabotage, you mean? Is it possible someone didn't murder one of my divers? Is that what you're asking me?" he scoffed. "It's possible, but only if you believe in mermaids and the bloody tooth fairy." He stared for a moment at each of the salvage representatives and then held Altman's gaze. "You see, Trevor, whoever cut the tube . . ." He let go of the tube quickly, as if he were trying to fling it away. ". . . Knew that at depth, the pressure would make the tube contract. Almost no oxygen would escape at the surface, but down at the *Edinburgh*, the tube would buckle." He stepped off the bell and over the railing and stood facing the others. "Whoever cut the tube knew that the divers wouldn't lose oxygen until they were already down on the wreck—until it'd be too late for anybody to save 'em."

▽ **Eighteen** ▽

"No, definitely not," Harrington said. He tapped the bowl of his pipe on the ashtray in front of him. "First, you tell us there is a murderer aboard this ship. Then you say you are continuing the bell runs. You're asking for trouble."

"Aye," Jones answered slowly. "Maybe I am." He sat at the head of the table, leaning forward, his dirty hands in front of him. When he and the four salvage representatives had returned to the wardroom, Jones had immediately announced that he intended to begin the bell runs again that evening.

"You can't risk the lives of the divers," Harrington protested. "You must stop the salvage." He turned the pipe over in his hand.

Jones sat back and stared at Harrington. "Trevor, do you know who the killer is?" he asked.

Harrington waved his pipe. "Of course not. Don't be ridiculous."

"Neither do I," Jones answered. "There's no witnesses. No bloody evidence. But I'm gonna find 'im. And the only way to flush 'im out is to keep the bell runs going."

"Have you any suspicions?" Petrosky asked as he nonchalantly leaned back in his chair.

"I suspect everybody," Jones said. "Even you blokes." He glanced at Altman. "The killer is either a diver . . ." He turned toward Strinivitch. ". . . Or knows enough about diving to sabotage the operation."

Strinivitch, who had been slouching in his chair, sat up straight and glared at Jones.

"This is absurd," Harrington cut in. "You are electing yourself prosecutor and judge. I can't allow this." Red blotches were appearing high on his cheeks.

Jones laughed spitefully. "Don't be so bloody dramatic," he said. "Somebody's murdered one of my divers. I've reported the death to London and the consortium. If I wait for a goddamned inquiry when we return to port, we'll never nail the bastard. And 'e will 'ave got what 'e wants."

"What does he want?" Altman asked. While the others had been talking, he had been trying to figure out a motive for the killing. Someone might have done it simply to stop the bell runs, but the killer should have known that Jones would react the way that he had—that nothing would stop the bell runs. "Why was Hall killed?" he repeated.

"To sabotage the salvage," Jones answered.

"But why?" Altman asked again. His head ached worse than it had earlier.

"Why did some bastard cut the buoy?" Jones asked. He looked at Petrosky, who had taken a stick match from a box on the table and was cleaning his fingernails. "Why? Because some government wants all the gold."

Petrosky did not look up, but Strinivitch again glowered at Jones.

"Or because some government wants to make damned sure that nobody gets the gold," Jones continued, glancing first at Altman and then at Harrington.

"Whatever the motive," Harrington said, "you must curtail the bell runs and call in the proper authorities for an investigation."

"Proper authorities?" Jones's condescension flashed to

anger. "We're in international waters. This is my ship, and I'm the goddamned proper authorities."

"But . . ." Harrington began coughing, put his pipe down, took his handkerchief out of his pocket, and held it in front of his mouth. He then cleared his throat and said, "But you can't further jeopardize the lives of your divers."

Jones slammed both his hands on the table and shouted, "Wake up, goddammit, Trevor. My divers' lives are already in jeopardy. Your life's in jeopardy. My life's in bloody jeopardy." He clenched his fists. "There's a killer aboard. He could be one of the divers. Or one of the crew. Or even someone in this room."

"Excuse me," Petrosky said, "but are you suggesting a diver could have left the chamber"—he waved his hand in the air—"to cut that tube?"

Altman glanced at Harrington and shook his head.

"No, of course not," Jones answered. "I'm just saying we 'ave no bloody idea who the killer is."

"Then anyone on the ship is suspect?" Petrosky said.

"Damned straight," Jones answered. He stood up, kicked his chair back, brushed his hand through his hair, and turned around. He then turned back and, fists on the table, said, "I'm going to nail the bastard. And until I do, nobody except us and the killer is going to know that the diver's death was no accident."

Harrington looked up at Jones. "As the head of the salvage operation," he said, "I feel it necessary to reiterate that continuing the bell runs at this time is inadvisable." As he reached for his pipe, his hand trembled.

"Excuse me," Petrosky said again, his voice almost saccharine. "It appears to me that there are two issues here. The first is whether—how do you say it?—outside authorities should be brought aboard. I would like to suggest that it is possible to have Soviet investigators from Murmansk arrive here today."

Jones, who was still standing, grumbled, "Not a goddamned bloody chance, Vlad.'' He pulled his chair back over to the table, sat down heavily, and continued, ''I already thought this could be some Russian trick to get aboard. It would be just like your goddamned government to murder a diver so that you'd have an excuse to take over the ship.''

Strinivitch leaned across the table, but Petrosky held his arm and said, ''I did not believe that you and Mr. Altman would agree to such an eventuality.'' His voice remained calm. ''So, we are in agreement that no one should come aboard.'' He looked triumphantly at the others. ''Mr. Harrington?''

Harrington had slumped back in his chair, staring at his unlit pipe. ''Agreed,'' he answered without looking up.

''Mr. Altman?'' Petrosky asked. He was leaning forward now.

Altman nodded. He felt that any outside investigators would only muddy the waters. Still, he resented the fact that Petrosky was making the decision seem like some sort of Soviet victory.

''Okay,'' Jones said, ''I . . .''

''Mr. Jones,'' Petrosky interrupted, ''I mentioned that there were two issues.''

Jones rubbed his right eye. He appeared to have grown suddenly weary, as if the energy that had sustained him through the inspection of the umbilical system had finally drained away. ''Go ahead, Vlad,'' he said.

''The second issue,'' Petrosky said, ''that of whether to again begin the bell runs for the gold, is something that, given Mr. Harrington's attitude, we may never agree upon.'' He smiled. ''I suggest we put the matter to a vote—something that surely my colleagues from the West could not object to.'' He nodded at Harrington and then, smiling coldly, turned to Altman and added, ''I am even willing to concede that there should be only one Soviet vote shared by Igor and myself.''

Strinivitch stared incredulously at Petrosky. Harrington still did not look up from his examination of the stem of his pipe.

Altman rubbed the back of his neck and tried to think. His would be the deciding vote. If he voted against continuing the bell runs, there would be a hopeless stalemate; if he voted for them, he would cut Harrington off from the others. Agreeing with Jones that the only way to catch the killer was to give the appearance of carrying on business as usual, he had no choice but to vote for the bell runs.

Looking up from his pipe, Harrington first glanced at Altman and then looked Petrosky in the eye. "Very astute, Vlad," he said softly. He slid back his chair and stood up.

Jones leaned back and folded his arms. Strinivitch, seemingly confused by what was occurring, gaped at the others. Altman avoided Harrington's gaze.

Harrington coughed, cleared his throat, and said, "Whatever happens is on your heads. On your head, Mick. And on the heads of the rest of you." He turned and left the room.

▽ **Nineteen** ▽

As Altman approached the DDC late that afternoon, a crew member in blue overalls was placing a large foil-covered pan into the air lock. Smelling the fried chicken, Altman pressed the intercom button. He then cupped his hands around his eyes to cut the glare and looked through the viewing port. One diver, wearing a headset, sat at the communications console; a second diver was tying off the top of a white plastic garbage bag so it could be passed out through the air lock.

Both divers glanced over at the porthole as Altman asked, "Can I talk to Jem Percy?"

The diver put down the garbage bag, pushed the intercom button, and said, "Aye, I'll get him." He went over to the far hatch and called into the next chamber.

Altman watched the crew member place two stainless-steel coffee pots into the air lock, close and lock the hatch, spin the wheel, and turn the gas gauge's handle.

Percy pulled himself through the chamber's far hatch, clapped the diver at the communications console on the shoulder, and came over to the intercom. He scratched his beard and said, "Hey, Will, I was hoping you'd check in."

The diver behind him flipped open the air lock's interior

hatch, pulled out the foil-covered pan, and set it on the table.

"Dinner smells pretty good," Altman said.

Percy glanced over his shoulder, took a deep breath, smiled, and said, "It's not exactly Southern fried, but I won't complain."

"How are you . . . all of the divers doing?"

"Not bad." Percy shook his head. "Accidents happen. We all know that going into any dive."

Altman nodded.

"Risk's the nature of the business . . . especially at these depths. Lost another buddy of mine in an explosion on a Gulf rig two years ago." He waved his hand. "Having the bell runs going again helps, keeps everybody busy." He laughed ironically. "When there was nothing to do for sixteen hours after Hall's accident, it started getting a little close in here."

The diver behind Percy stuffed the white plastic bag into the air lock and shut the hatch.

"What about Tierney?" Altman asked.

"He's okay. Normally I'd have him skip a turn in the bell, but with Hall gone and Sayers down with an ear infection, we've only got six divers active . . . It's a good team, though. If anything, it'll make the stints in the bomb room count even more. Fitzsimons has already found . . ." He turned to the diver at the communications console and asked, "What's Fitz got coming up this run?"

Altman couldn't quite make out the answer.

"Thirty-eight bars," Percy said, turning back to the porthole. "In just four hours."

"Great," Altman said. "Well, I just wanted to check in and see how things were going."

Percy glanced over his shoulder and then leaned closer to the intercom. Behind him, one of the divers was taking plates out of the galley's cabinet, and the other was speaking into the headset's microphone. "Any more info on the cause of the accident?" Percy asked.

Altman looked closely through the porthole at Percy. "A cut in the oxygen hose in the umbilical above the bell. Almost impossible to detect, but easy enough to fix once it was discovered."

"Yeah, that's what Jones told us." Percy stared back at Altman. "But I'm also hearing Jones had you and the other salvage reps in some closed meetings later."

Not wanting to lie to Percy, Altman hesitated for a moment. "There was some discussion about whether the bell runs should continue, that's all. Why do you ask?"

"Not sure." Percy scratched his beard again. "Jones was sort of curt, which isn't like him at all, when he talked to us over the squawk box. Seemed like we weren't getting the full poop."

Altman looked over at the crew member carrying away the white garbage bag and then said, "Jones had been up all night checking the umbilical system. One of his divers was dead. He wasn't exactly talkative with the reps either."

"Yeah, okay," Percy answered, but he continued to stare through the porthole at Altman.

After Altman left Percy at the DDC, he climbed to the deck and headed toward the winch aft of the moonpool, along the starboard railing. The sun, breaking between dark clouds, fired the wave crests around *Seerauber*. He stopped, lifted his face to the light, and felt the warmth for a moment. The gusting wind made his eyes water.

Strinivitch stood near the winch operator, a burly man who was lowering a dripping canvas and steel-mesh bag to the deck. At their feet, a low steel trolley held almost three dozen gleaming bars. Four other canvas and mesh bags lay crumpled on the deck against the bulkhead. A thin, pimple-faced sailor stooped, unshackled the dripping bag, opened it, lifted out an oily, silt-covered bar, and handed it to Strinivitch. Using a dark rag, the Russian scrubbed the bar until it glittered. He then jotted the serial number in a small red notebook.

Saying, "*Das ist alles,*" the crane operator began to shackle off the winch's cable.

Strinivitch glanced up from his notebook, pointed with his pen at the trolley, and said, "Mr. Altman, the decision to continue the search was good, very good." He smiled broadly as he began to rub the second bar with the rag. His hands were dirty; his fingernails were black from the oil and silt.

"I see," Altman answered, "that you are working hard, as always, for the Soviet people."

Trying to determine if he was being ridiculed, Strinivitch stared at Altman for a second before registering the bar's serial number.

"Have you seen Trevor?" Altman asked.

"No," Strinivitch answered, "I have not." He tapped the pen on the notebook. "But he will go to the strong room soon. He must mark in each bar with me." He looked down at the bars stacked on the trolley. "And the Russian gold is coming up very fast."

Just after eleven o'clock that night, Altman sat on his bunk paging through a diving manual he had picked up in the wardroom. His lack of sleep the previous two nights was catching up with him, and he intermittently dozed off as he read. There was a knock on the door, and Harrington entered the stateroom. He had dark circles under his eyes, and the skin on his cheeks was still blotchy. "Hello, Will," he said. "Do you have a minute?"

"Sure," Altman answered, pointing to the chair by the writing table. He squeezed his eyes tightly shut for a moment and then shook his head to wake himself. "Missed you at dinner."

Harrington sat down, crossed his legs, and leaned his elbow on the table. "I had things to catch up on, odds and

ends, correspondence." Altman expected him to make some
comment about the continuation of the bell runs, but instead
Harrington asked, "Have you heard from Elizabeth?"

"Yes," Altman answered, "in the last mail drop, a
couple of days ago." He tossed the diving manual to the
foot of the bunk. Elizabeth's last letter had been particularly
warm, telling him that she felt closer to him than she had to
any man in years.

"Good," Harrington said. He began to pick at the flap of
the cheesecloth that lay next to the camera bag on the table.

Altman waited a moment, and then when Harrington
didn't go on, asked, "Is she okay? Is everything all right?"

Harrington looked up. "Yes. Yes, I guess so." He coughed
into his hand and then unfolded the cheesecloth and picked
up the wooden-hafted sculptor's knife.

Altman had no idea why Harrington was asking about
Elizabeth. "Have you heard from her?" he asked.

"Yes. Yes I have," Harrington answered. "Like you, in
the last post." He leaned back in the chair and gazed at the
knife's small, curved blade. "She's a good girl, Elizabeth
is," he said. "And she is fond of you. I want you to
understand that because . . . Have I told you this before?"

"Yes, Trevor, you have," Altman said. Swinging his legs
over onto the floor, he added, "Did you come in here just to
indulge in some sort of paternal interrogation?"

"What? Oh, no," Harrington answered. He pointed to
the manual on the bunk. "I'm not interrupting anything?"

Altman turned, glanced at the manual, and then looked
back at the older man. "No, not at all," he said. "I was
just passing time."

Harrington folded the cheesecloth and, starting to cough
again, pulled his handkerchief from his pants pocket.

"Is something the matter?" Altman asked.

Harrington shook his head, stood up, looked around the
stateroom, and then seemed to focus on Altman for the first
time. "Will, I . . . There was another matter I wanted to

discuss, but . . ." Coughing again, he continued to shake his head. "I won't trouble you with it." He raised his hand in an awkward salute. "Keep in touch with Elizabeth, Will," he said as he turned to leave the room.

Altman stared at the door for a few seconds after Harrington had shut it. Wondering what had been on the older man's mind, he undressed and lay on the bunk in the semidarkness. For a while he was unable to clear his thoughts, but the hum of *Seerauber*'s stabilizing motors keeping the ship directly over the *Edinburgh* eventually lulled him to sleep.

Sometime later, he was awakened by the sound of shuffling in the passageway. He listened for a time, thinking that Harrington had probably been unable to sleep and was heading up to the main deck for some air. In the half-light of the polar night, he could just distinguish the lumps on the writing table as his camera bag and scrimshaw kit. When the noise in the passageway subsided, he closed his eyes and drifted back to sleep.

Loud banging on his door woke him from a dream in which he was caught in a maze of passageways aboard an ancient wreck. He was swimming free, without tanks and mask. Gold glittered everywhere about him—gold jewelry and coins and bars. He kept swimming, afraid that his air was running out. The banging reverberated in his ears. The gold glimmered around him as he swam faster and faster. On the verge of panic, he searched for an open hatchway. There was none.

His neck and chest were drenched with sweat. "Yeah, come in," he yelled as he pulled himself up on his elbows. Schmidt loomed in the doorway, his white uniform almost luminescent in the twilight. "Herr Altman, you must come to the bridge," Schmidt said. "It is Herr Harrington."

▽ **Twenty** ▽

Wondering what Schmidt had meant, Altman pulled on his corduroys and buttoned his shirt. The German had vanished from the doorway as soon as he had spoken, and his English was bad enough that his statement might have meant almost anything. When Altman reached the bridge, Jones was standing alone by the wheel, staring out the window. Clouds scudded through the sky, periodically covering the sun. Although the wind had slackened, three- and four-foot waves still rolled around *Seerauber*. Jones had shaved and changed into clean clothes, but his bloodshot eyes suggested he had still not slept much. He held the mahogany and brass spyglass in his right hand.

"What's happened?" Altman asked.

Jones extended the spyglass to its full length. "Trevor's gone," he said.

"What do you mean?" Altman licked his dry lips. He had expected to find Jones irate, but the captain's voice was almost calm.

"Disappeared. Not on board. Gone, goddamnit." Jones tapped the spyglass against the palm of his left hand. "And a gold bar's gone with 'im."

"What?" Altman could not believe what he was hearing.

140

"Gunter discovered the strong room wide open around 0500 this morning," Jones said. "When 'e couldn't find Trevor in the wardroom or 'is cabin,' 'e woke me up." Jones shrugged. "I figured Trevor was wandering around the decks somewhere like 'e does, so I didn't hurry. By the time I got to the strong room, Igor, the SOB, was ranting about a missing gold bar. Neither Trevor or the gold bar 'ave showed up. I 'ave the crew searching the ship, but I don't expect 'em to find anything." Jones looked through the spyglass at the Soviet patrol boat to the northeast. He then swung around so that he faced the patrol boat to the southwest. As the sun broke between the clouds, light reflected from the polished brass of the spyglass. "I got the killer's attention, all right," he added, his voice low, almost unnaturally calm.

Altman pulled out the chair by the chart table and sat down. He set his elbows on the arms of the chair and tried to piece together what had occurred. "What do you mean by 'got the killer's attention'?" he asked Jones.

"Trevor's disappearance 'as to be related to the diver's death," Jones answered as he compressed the spyglass. "I don't know the connection yet, but I'm . . ."

Petrosky swung the door open and stepped into the bridge. "Mr. Jones, I must protest the loss of Russian gold," he said.

Jones twisted the focus ring of the spyglass. "There's a lot of activity on our Soviet shadows this morning, Vlad," he said, laying the spyglass carefully onto the sheep's wool that lined the teak case.

Ignoring the statement, Petrosky repeated, "Mr. Jones, I must . . ."

Altman stood up and faced the Russian. "Shut up, Vlad," he said. "Harrington is missing, and all you give a shit about is the goddamned gold."

"Missing? Harrington?" Petrosky glanced from Altman to Jones and back to Altman.

Anger over Harrington's disappearance and his own ina-
bility to do anything about it began to boil up in Altman.
From the start of the salvage venture, he had been caught up
in something he didn't understand, and now, he realized, his
ignorance might have cost Harrington's life.

"Come on," Jones said to Petrosky. "Do you expect us
to believe Igor didn't tell you that Trevor was gone?"

Shaking his head, Petrosky answered, "Igor told me only
that a gold bar had been taken from the storage room." He
gestured as he spoke. "Igor was quite angry and stated that
you would not listen to him. I offered to take the matter up
with you."

"Just the helpful mediator, as always," Altman said. His
mouth was dry, and his neck and shoulders were stiff with
tension.

"Mr. Altman," Petrosky said, his tone condescending,
"your sarcasm will do little to . . ."

Altman took a quick step toward Petrosky.

Jones clamped his hand on Altman's shoulder and hissed
in his ear, "Are you bloody daft, mate?"

Petrosky glared at Altman for a moment and then, regaining
his composure, brushed off the sleeves of his sweater as
though nothing had happened.

"All right. Okay," Altman muttered to Jones.

Just as Jones took his hand from Altman's shoulder,
Schmidt came through the door carrying a small object in a
white handkerchief. When he saw the three men, he tugged
at the end of his mustache and said, "Excuse me, Captain
Jones. I will come back."

"No," Jones answered. He pulled up his shirt collar.
"Come in, Gunter. What is it?"

Altman sat down again in the chair by the chart table.
Petrosky folded his arms and looked over at Schmidt.

Schmidt glanced at each of the men. "We have not found
Herr Harrington. He cannot still be on board the ship." He
unfolded the handkerchief. "First mate Mitzenmacher found

this knife near the port anchor housing." He handed the handkerchief and its contents to Jones.

At the mention of the word "knife," Altman lifted his head.

Jones took the handkerchief and knife, stared at the knife for a moment, and then carried it, still in the handkerchief, over to the chart table and held it in front of Altman.

"Isn't that the knife I have seen Will using on the whale-tooth cutting?" Petrosky asked, his voice cold.

"Stay out of this," Jones said to Petrosky.

Altman glanced at the knife, its blade clean and shining on the handkerchief, and looked back up at Jones. "It's my knife, all right," he said. "But I didn't..." His mind raced.

"Didn't what?" Jones asked.

Schmidt clasped his hands behind his back and stood stiffly near the door.

"Trevor was looking at it in my cabin last night," Altman answered. A little bewildered, he added, "That's the last I saw of it."

"It is just the sort of knife that could be used to cut the divers' tubing also," Petrosky said.

"I said stay out of this, Vlad." Jones scowled at the Russian and then turned back toward Altman. "Are you saying 'arrington stole your knife?" he asked incredulously. "What the 'ell for?"

Altman stood up. "No. I mean, I don't know."

"But you 'aven't been out of your cabin since you saw 'im with it?" Jones asked.

"No, not at all." Altman shook his head. "Trevor must have taken the knife, but I have no idea why."

Jones cleared his throat and said, "That's one shaky bloody story, mate." While wrapping the knife in the handkerchief, he added as much to himself as the others, "You can bet it's been wiped of any fingerprints."

As Jones placed the wrapped knife on the chart table,

Schmidt unclasped his hands, stepped forward, and said, "There is one other thing, Captain Jones." Again he glanced at Altman and Petrosky.

"Yes. What?"

"Wilhelm Kupferberg, the duty watch, heard Herr Harrington and the Russian arguing in the strong room."

Altman, who had still been trying to figure out why Harrington had taken his knife, looked over at the German.

"He is mistaken," Petrosky said abruptly.

"Not you," Schmidt said to Petrosky. "The other Russian. Strinivitch. *'Der fette Russe,'* Kupferberg called him."

"What time was that?" Jones asked Schmidt.

"He is unsure of the proper, the exact, time. Between 0400 and 0430."

"Where is Igor now?" Jones asked Petrosky.

When the four men sat down at the wardroom table, Harrington's seat was conspicuously empty. Strinivitch gripped his coffee mug and glared at Jones while Petrosky fastidiously removed the tea-strainer from the teapot. Altman turned his chair so that he was facing Jones rather than the Soviets.

"I tell you," Strinivitch said to Jones, "I was angry only because Mr. Harrington said he was taking the gold bar from the storage room. I was walking around. I saw the door open." He gulped the steaming coffee. He was unshaven, and his eyes were bloodshot. His thick hand shook as he held the mug. "I go in and see Harrington holding a gold bar. When I ask him what for, he says none of my business. He is taking out the gold bar." He glanced at Petrosky. "I get angry. It is not his gold."

"What time was this?" Jones asked. He poured himself coffee from the heavy stainless-steel pot set on the table.

Strinivitch shrugged. "I do not know. Around four."

"And you were just walking around?"

"Yes," Strinivitch answered. "I could not sleep good."

Jones leaned back in his chair, looking at the ceiling

instead of at Strinivitch. "You were probably there," he said, "so you could rub your bloody 'ands all over the gold, even in the middle of the night." He leaned forward, stared at Strinivitch for a moment, and added, his tone almost taunting, "The divers found forty-seven more gold bars on the last bell run, Igor. Forty-seven."

Altman, who had been watching the steam from his coffee swirl above the mug, slammed his hand on the table, causing the crockery to jiggle, and said, "*Fuck* the gold bars. What the hell's happened to Trevor?"

"I tell you I do not know," Strinivitch shouted back, saliva spraying from the gap in his teeth. He glanced again at Petrosky. "I have not seen him after that."

"Trevor's drowned or aboard one of those gunboats. There's no other possibility," Jones said, staring at Strinivitch.

"Gentlemen," Petrosky said, "this rancor will not solve the problem here. In order to decide how to proceed, it is necessary to establish the known facts." As usual, his words were carefully chosen, his voice moderate.

As Altman picked up his coffee mug, he thought, *the bastard is going to take over the goddamned meeting—and Harrington will never be found.*

"And just what are the bloody facts?" Jones asked.

Petrosky folded his hands on the table. "First," he said, "it is known that Trevor and the gold bar are missing."

"No shit, Sherlock," Altman said.

Petrosky, his tone condescending, said, "It is a crucial fact, Mr. Altman. For, although we know that Harrington is missing, there is no evidence that harm has come to him."

Jones cocked his head and stared at Petrosky.

Altman laid down his mug; his breathing was becoming short. "He just went for a fucking swim, is that it?" he said. "A dip in the goddamned ocean, but he'll be back in time for tea."

Petrosky sighed, as though bored with having to explain things to the dull-witted. "The fact, Mr. Altman," he answered, "is only that Trevor and the gold bar are gone. One could conclude that he has stolen it."

Altman grabbed the edge of the table and began to slide his chair back. "And where the hell would he have gone with it?"

Petrosky, his voice still calm, said, "Like you, I also assume that something has happened to Trevor. It is just not a verifiable fact."

Altman let his hands fall from the edge of the table.

Petrosky gazed at each of the others. "The question," he went on, "is, What has occurred? The only other facts are that Igor was heard arguing with Trevor at four, which establishes Harrington's place at that time . . ."

Strinivitch, his knuckles white, clutched the coffee mug.

"And," Petrosky continued, "that Mr. Altman's knife was found under the anchor chain at the ship's bow. The knife is a very important piece of evidence."

Altman clenched his fists. "You forget one other *fact*." He spat the last word at Petrosky.

"What is that?" Petrosky asked, as though genuinely surprised.

"Schmidt and Jones saw Igor in the strong room at 0500," Altman retorted.

"You will have to speak to Comrade Strinivitch about that," Petrosky said. He then took a slow sip of his tea.

Jones turned to Strinivitch and, his voice controlled, asked, "What 'appened after the argument, Igor?"

Strinivitch glanced at Petrosky and then glared at Jones. "I returned to my cabin. I was tired."

"But you already told us," Jones said, "that you couldn't sleep. You expect me to believe that you had an argument with Trevor, went to bed, and less than an hour later were back in the strong room?" His face beginning to redden, Jones asked, "What the 'ell really 'appened in that hour, Igor?"

Strinivitch's eyes grew wider. "Nothing, I tell you. I did

not see Harrington after he left with the gold. Nothing happened.''

''I'll tell you.'' Jones was standing now, leaning across the table toward Strinivitch. ''You murdered Trevor, threw his body overboard, and took the gold. Or dumped it with 'is body. You murdered 'im just like you killed the diver—so you Russian bastards would 'ave a chance to take all of the bloody gold.''

''I did not,'' Strinivitch yelled. He leaped to his feet, kicking over his chair and knocking over his mug. He pressed his hands on the table and leaned toward Jones. ''I have done nothing.''

Jones and Strinivitch glowered at one another across the table.

The hot coffee ran along the fingers of Strinivitch's left hand, but he paid no attention to it. ''I tell you, nothing,'' he said. His voice, though lower, was still venomous. ''I did not kill Harrington. I am a Soviet citizen. I do not have to answer to you, Mr. Jones.''

Jones straightened up and began to rock on the balls of his feet. He folded his muscular arms, the white scar bulging, and said in the same unnaturally calm voice Altman had heard him use earlier, ''We'll see about that, Igor. We'll sure as 'ell see about that.''

▽ **Twenty-one** ▽

During the bell run following the confrontation in the wardroom, the divers discovered sixty-two bars—worth, according to shipboard estimates, almost $10 million. Jones returned to the bridge and, when Altman asked him to stop the bell runs, refused to do so. Strinivitch went back to the strong room and the minor bureaucracy that he had established to keep track of all the bars being brought to the surface.

Altman spent much of the day pacing *Seerauber*'s windswept deck, mulling over what had happened. For a long time, he watched as the crew used the ship's main derrick, a two-story marine crane with a telescoping boom, to move the pods of empty compressed-gas cylinders aft from the moonpool and replace them with the full pods stored by the A-frame lifting rig. The wind was turning and building, and the empty pods twisted so much on the cables that the crew had to run guy lines from the pods to the deck. But nothing, not the freshening wind or the coiling cables or his own whirling thoughts, offered Altman a clue to Hall's death and Harrington's disappearance.

Shortly after four that afternoon, Altman climbed the stairs to the bridge to try again to persuade Jones to end the bell runs. No evidence related to Harrington's disappearance had turned up, and Altman knew he should contact Elizabeth.

When Altman entered the bridge, Jones was looking through the spyglass in a northwesterly direction.

"Gotten any sleep?" Altman asked.

"None today," Jones answered. He drummed his fingers on the spyglass.

Altman looked out the expanse of windows. The sky had darkened under towering cumulonimbus clouds, and long, foaming waves were starting to form again. "It's getting pretty raw out there," he said.

Jones squinted again through the spyglass. "A force-six storm is supposed to blow through here by morning." Shaking his head as though trying to clear it, he turned to Altman. "It'll be rough, but not too rough to run the bell, if that's what you're thinking."

Altman went over and sat in the chair by the chart table. "The bell runs have got to stop," he said, his tone more conversational than argumentative. "You're acting like some gambler with a weak hand who's bluffing and keeps trying to up the ante, hoping your opponent will fold."

"I am a gambler," Jones answered.

"Nobody's going to fold for you."

"Maybe not." Jones held the spyglass out to Altman. "Take a look through this," he said, "ten points west of north."

Altman stood and took the spyglass, its brass cool in his hand. At first he saw nothing but murky clouds meeting dark water. Then he made out the silhouette of a warship, barely visible on the horizon. He could just discern the twin towers of its superstructure and, at that distance, could only estimate its length at about 550 feet.

"We've 'ad radar contact for a couple of hours," Jones said. "We raised 'em on the wireless 'alf an hour ago." He paused. "It's American. The *Thorn*. A destroyer."

Altman looked through the spyglass again. The *Thorn*

had five-inch guns and missile launchers fore and aft; a
helicopter stood on a launch pad aft of the ship's superstructure. He guessed that the *Thorn* was one of the navy's newer
destroyers, probably designed primarily for antisubmarine
duty. "I don't know anything about this," he said.

"Right," Jones said sarcastically.

"I don't," Altman repeated. He handed the spyglass to
Jones. "I've been in the dark about the crap going down
here as much—more than—you have."

Jones compressed the spyglass. Without looking at Altman,
he said, "You've got your orders, whatever the 'ell they
are. But I believe you. I don't think you 'ave anything to do
with the diver's death or Trevor's disappearance." He rubbed
the spyglass with a piece of velvet and laid it in its case.
"You wouldn't 'ave left a trail, the knife and all, that led
back to you." He faced Altman. "You're not involved in
this shit. At least not yet. But whatever you're up to,
whatever Uncle Sam 'as planned, know two things." The
bravado was gone from his voice. "I'm bringing up the
Edinburgh's gold like I set out to do. And I'm going to
get the bastard who's fucking the salvage."

Altman nodded. "I don't give a damn about the gold,"
he said, "but if I find who killed Harrington, there won't be
much left for you."

As Altman entered the forward passageway on his way
back from the bridge, he saw Mathewson coming out of
Harrington's stateroom. His left arm was no longer in a
sling. "I was just looking for you," he said to Altman.

"In Harrington's cabin?"

"Nah." Mathewson shut the stateroom door. "I wasn't
sure which was your cabin." He pointed to the other door.
"This must be it."

"How are you doing?" Altman asked as he ushered the
diver into the stateroom.

Mathewson knocked on the wooden writing table. "My

wing's still shot, but I feel good otherwise," he said. "The headaches are gone." He sat down in the chair. "I was looking for you because of the Englishman."

"What?" Altman stood up, walked the few feet to the door, and closed it.

Mathewson unfolded and refolded the cheesecloth in which Altman kept the whale's tooth. "Harrington's gone, isn't he?"

"Yeah."

"Have any idea what happened?"

Preoccupied with what he would have to say to Elizabeth when he spoke to her, Altman walked back over toward the bunk. "No. Hell, I wish I did."

Mathewson began to pick at a scab on his forearm. Not looking up from what he was doing, he said, "I've been hearing that Hall's accident fits into this somehow."

"Is that right?" Altman asked, wondering what Mathewson really wanted from him. "Where'd you hear that?"

Mathewson tilted the chair back against the table. "The divers . . . Jem Percy and the others. They're locked in the DDC with nothing much to do but listen to the squawk box. Things are getting pretty weird in there."

"Well, don't believe what you're hearing," Altman answered, his voice almost curt.

Mathewson let the chair fall forward again on all four legs. He leaned forward, turned so that he was looking squarely at Altman, and said, "I heard the Soviets had Hall killed so that they had an excuse to take over the ship."

Altman wondered about the source of that particular rumor. "Hall's death will be investigated fully when we return to port," he said tersely. "For now, it's officially an accident." He knew he was beginning to sound like the bureaucrats he disliked, but he didn't want to tell Mathewson anything more.

Mathewson sat up and hung his good arm over the back of the chair. "I saw you and that fat-assed Soviet having words yesterday by the moonpool when Hall's body was being brought up," he said.

"Strinivitch? What about it?" Altman went over to the sink in the corner, ran cold water over his hands, and splashed the water on his face. Picking up a towel, he turned back toward the diver.

"He wants to kick your ass." Mathewson laughed.

Altman didn't answer.

Mathewson stood up and hooked the thumb of his right hand in the belt loop of his jeans. Grinning, he said, "If you need any help with the Soviets, remember I'm around." He laughed again. "I could use the exercise."

After Mathewson left, Altman sat at the writing table. He estimated that he still had three or four hours before Elizabeth returned to her apartment. Apprehensive about what he had to tell her, he worked for a while on the scrimshaw, trying to lose himself in the incising of the sails. The curved lines of the billowing sailcloth allowed him to drift for a time to memories of *Halcyon*'s running before a fresh breeze. Inevitably, though, his mind returned to Harrington and the salvage mission, which had become anything but the pleasant summer cruise he had hoped for. He again mulled over why Harrington might have borrowed the knife, and then wondered where the trail of violence would end.

When he went to dinner in the wardroom, no one else was there. The steward told him that Jones had stayed in the bridge and that the two Russians were taking their meal in Petrosky's stateroom. Although it seemed strange to be alone in the wardroom, Altman welcomed the solitude. After eating, he paged through a couple of the magazines on the table near the bulkhead. Unable to concentrate, he marked the time until he would call Elizabeth. Finally, he headed up to the radio room, which was just aft of and a deck below the bridge.

When Altman entered the radio room, the radio operator on duty sat in a padded steel chair in front of the transmitter and receiver. A photocopier stood below the room's one porthole, and a large red fire extinguisher hung near the clock. Along the opposite wall, log books and manuals lined the shelf above a row of cabinets. Altman explained that he needed a London telephone operator, and then he sat down on a straight-backed wooden chair to wait.

He imagined Elizabeth arriving home, a briefcase in one hand and a bag of groceries in the other. In the vestibule, she placed the briefcase on the library table and glanced in the mirror. Her thin gold necklace accentuated her white blouse. Her face was tan and her hair a little lighter from her buying trip in southern France the previous week. She ran her hand through her hair and carried the groceries into the kitchen. She began to unpack the bag—first the fresh lettuce and tomatoes and then . . .

"I've got London," the radio operator said, startling Altman.

Having expected it to take much longer to get the call through, Altman hadn't yet decided what to say. He took the headphones and told the London operator the telephone number. He listened to the ringing and then heard Elizabeth's voice. The London operator told him to go ahead.

"Elizabeth," he said.

"Yes," she answered tentatively, not recognizing his voice.

"It's Will . . . Altman."

"Oh. Will!" At first her voice was warm and animated. Then, suddenly, as though she already knew what he was going to tell her, fear took her voice. "What is it, Will?" she asked. "What the matter?"

"We don't know for sure."

"What's happened to my father?" Her voice was low, almost a whisper.

The radio operator wheeled his chair over to the other side of the room and took a manual from the shelf. Altman leaned against the transmitter table. "He's disappeared," Altman said. "We don't know what's happened to him."

Elizabeth made no reply.

"We . . . I . . ." Altman raised his hand to his forehead. "He's dead, isn't he?"

"No . . . I mean, we don't know."

"Will!" She began to sob.

"He was last seen early this morning . . ." Altman paused and licked his lips. ". . . Arguing with one of the Soviets. He's gone without a trace—no sign of violence, of a struggle. He just disappeared."

Elizabeth was silent for a time, and then, her voice low and distant, she said, "He somehow knew he would never return, but I hoped you'd be able to help him." There was no hint in her voice that she was trying to make Altman feel guilty.

He wanted to ask her why Harrington thought he would not return, but he couldn't bring himself to intrude anymore on her grief. He promised to contact her the moment there was news, and he jotted her phone number at Sotheby's on the notepad in front of him. When they hung up, he stood still for a moment, his chest and back damp with sweat. He then took off the headphone and laid it by the receiver. The radio operator, who had been pretending to study the manual, closed it and put it back on the shelf.

When Altman left the radio room, he felt lonely in a way he had never experienced before while aboard a ship or even while single-handing *Halcyon* along the East Coast. He went out on deck. The world had turned gray-black under a thick layer of storm clouds. Streaks of foam ran along the crests of the waves. The westerly wind, blowing at twenty-five knots, chilled him as he walked toward *Seerauber*'s bow. The sea and wind were cacophonous. He stood at the railing for almost fifteen minutes, shivering and staring into the northwest, where he could make out the lights of the Russian patrol boat but no sign of the *Thorn*.

Finally, the salty spray beating against his face, he turned away. Unable to make any sense out of what had happened, he headed toward the stern. As he passed the moonpool with its cable running into the depths, he wondered how many bars the divers had discovered that day—and if the salvage was worth the life of even one man. He saw no one else on deck. Silver light diffused from the floodlights on the suspension tower. The underwater robot's steel housing stood on the deck and its tether lay coiled in its bin, but the technicians had taken the robot below for more repairs.

As he turned by the base of the A-frame lifting rig, he stopped abruptly. Ahead of him, between two of the gas-storage pods that had been moved there that afternoon, a bulky body lay facedown on the deck. Approaching the body, he saw that it was Strinivitch. The steel shaft and wooden handle of Jones's gaff protruded at an angle from under Strinivitch's head. Blood darkened the deck.

Altman peered in all directions but saw no one. His heart pounding and adrenaline rushing to his head, he stooped and touched the blood, which was cool, beginning to congeal. He then turned the body on its side. The gaff's point was buried deep in Strinivitch's neck. The Russian's throat was splayed and his carotid artery torn. His face was frozen in a scowl of unendurable agony.

▽ **Twenty-two** ▽

"I demand that *Seerauber* sail for Murmansk immediately," Petrosky said, his voice cold with anger.

"No chance," Jones answered.

Petrosky, Jones, and Altman stood near the stern crane, while Schmidt directed three of the crew members in the removal of Strinivitch's body. Altman, who had taken photographs of the corpse, rewound and removed the roll of film from his camera. After discovering Strinivitch's body, he had gone to find the captain, who had been alone in the wardroom finishing a late dinner of cold ham and potatoes. A bottle of rum stood on the table next to a tumbler half-filled with melting ice and dark rum. When Altman had told Jones that Strinivitch lay dead on the deck, the gaff having ripped out his throat, Jones had barked orders to Schmidt over the intercom and rushed out to the stern of the ship.

"A Soviet citizen has been brutally murdered—with your weapon," Petrosky snarled at Jones. "A Soviet citizen you threatened this morning."

"You bloody bastard," Jones bellowed over the noise of the waves and wind. He pointed a finger in Petrosky's face. "There's two Brits dead, and I'm going . . ."

Schmidt and the three sailors stopped their work and stared at Jones and Petrosky.

Jones scuffed the deck with his shoe. "We'll finish this . . . in the wardroom," he said. The veins in his neck were bulging as he turned and stomped past the moonpool toward the hatch amidships. As Altman followed, the wind whipped at his camera bag. It had not yet begun to rain, but spindrift from the lashing waves had drenched the deck.

When the three men reached the wardroom, no one sat down. Petrosky faced Jones across the table, the captain's half-eaten dinner lying between them. Altman stood off to one side near the liquor closet.

Petrosky repeated, "The *Seerauber* must sail for Murmansk—or Kirkenes—immediate . . ."

"Shut up!" Jones cut him off. The captain's eyes were cloudy, not quite focused.

"I will not. A Soviet citizen has . . ."

"I said shut up!" Jones's words echoed around the wardroom. He raised his hand to his forehead and, less vehemently, said, "I 'ave got to think. Give me time to think." He picked up the tumbler and finished the rum.

"There is no time," Petrosky insisted.

"Shut up, dammit."

Altman stepped forward and put his camera bag on the table. "You've got to give him time," he said to Petrosky. He wound the camera strap tightly around his hand.

Jones sat down in the chair and poured another shot of rum into the tumbler.

"There is a Russian dead on the deck of this ship," Petrosky said, his voice almost shrill.

"If you don't shut up"—Jones's voice had become abnormally calm; his words were almost slurred—"there are going to be two dead Russians."

The shift in Jones's speech made Petrosky hesitate. Sweat dripped down the Russian's temples. Finally he said, "You threaten me, Mr. Jones, and you ask for trouble." His finger shaking, he pointed at Jones. "I am going to report this at once. You will regret it." He stormed out of the wardroom, slamming the door.

"The bloody bastard," Jones muttered. He stood up, raised the tumbler, and drained the rum in one long draft.

Altman wondered how much Jones had already been drinking.

"The bloody bastard," Jones repeated as he sat down again, poured more rum, slid the bottle back onto the table, and said, "I didn't kill Strinivitch. Why the 'ell would I kill 'im with all this treasure aboard? I 'ave more to lose than anybody." The last word of the sentence was so slurred that it was almost indistinguishable. He shook his head. "Jesus, my own gaff."

"We'll probably have a Soviet warship bearing down on us tomorrow," Altman said.

"To 'ell with 'em." Jones drank half of the rum.

"You could order the radio operator not to send any messages."

"No. Let 'im file whatever goddamned reports . . ."

Altman leaned forward and asked, "Will you at least stop the bell runs?"

"No."

"The weather is getting too messy anyway."

"No. Keeping the bell runs going is the only chance I 'ave."

"What?"

Jones sat up straighter, his eyes momentarily focused, and said, "If the bell runs stop, there's no reason for the bloody Russians not to take over my ship."

Altman realized that Jones had a point—shutting the bell down was like closing the betting window. "Then what the hell can you do?" he asked.

"I can flush out the goddamned murderer." Jones finished the rum and shook his head. "What the 'ell, I figured it was Strinivitch." He reached over, stuck a fork into what was left of his ham, looked at the meat, and dropped the fork on the plate. "My own goddamned gaff," he added, standing up slowly. "It's a bloody mess, it is."

When Altman left the wardroom, he knew he should sit down somewhere and think, but he was at once too tired and too keyed up. He walked along the passageway to his stateroom doorway and then, on an impulse, turned and entered Harrington's cabin. After switching on the light, he stood in the middle of the room. There was no sign of a disturbance, no evidence of violence. The bunk was neatly made, the corners of the blanket tucked in military fashion. Harrington's suitcase lay closed on the floor. Two pipes rested in an ashtray on top of the writing table. Altman pulled out the chair by the writing table and sat down. He then ran his fingers along the edge of the table and opened the top, right-hand drawer, where he found only beige stationery, envelopes, and a ballpoint pen. The drawer below was empty.

He opened the wide, flat drawer in front of him only to discover that it too was empty. He then picked up one of the pipes, the stale odor of burnt tobacco catching in his nostrils. When he turned the pipe over, bits of charred tobacco fell from the bowl into the half-open drawer. He held the pipe up and leaned back.

Glancing down at the burnt tobacco, he noticed a sliver protruding from the small crevice where the front of the drawer had been glued to the bottom of the drawer. He pressed his forefinger against the sliver and raised it in front of his face. He then rolled the sliver between his thumb and forefinger and looked at it again. It was gold, a minute shaving that gleamed as he raised it toward the light.

His heart racing, he pushed back the chair and dropped to his hands and knees. His breathing became short, and the palms of his hands perspired. Rubbing his hand along the floor, he at first found nothing. He moved his hand in an arc under the table but came away with only dust. He then hooked two fingers behind the leg of the table. When he again raised his hand, a gold shaving, three-eighths of an inch long and shaped like a capital J, clung to the tip of his index finger.

Sliding both shavings into an envelope he took from the drawer, he remembered the noise that he had heard in the passageway shortly before Harrington's disappearance. What had Harrington known that made him cut into the bar? Why had he needed a knife as sharp as the sculptor's knife? Were the bars really gold-plated lead that the Russians had loaded aboard the *Edinburgh*? Had the Russians leaked information about the convoy just so that the *Edinburgh* would be sunk? What exactly had Harrington discovered—and who had he told of his discovery? Where had Harrington been going? Or was it even Harrington who had been in the passageway? Altman recalled that he had heard no coughing that night.

Altman rushed out of Harrington's stateroom and into his own cabin. He rooted through his scrimshaw materials until he found his sharpest style. After putting the style in his pocket, he took his wool watchman's coat from its hook and hurried out of the room. He tried the strong room first, but it was locked. Putting his coat on, he headed out on deck and toward the starboard crane that lifted the bars from the *Edinburgh*. *Seerauber*'s cables whined in the gusting wind. The sea was beginning to heap, and white foam blew in streaks along the crests of the waves. Jones would be forced to stop the bell runs soon, Altman realized, because not even *Seerauber*'s electronic gadgetry could keep her stable in a near gale.

As Altman approached the crane, a young sailor, his pimply face purple from the cold wind, stood by the controls. Altman nodded to him and said, "How's it going?"

A befuddled look on his face, the sailor answered, "*Ich spreche kein Englisch.*"

Altman exhaled, turned up his collar, and stuck his hands

in his coat pockets. "The gold," he said. "When is the next load of gold coming up?" He made a circular motion with his hand in an attempt to imitate the winch.

"*Ja.*" The sailor smiled and nodded. "*Das geld.*"

Realizing he was getting nowhere with the sailor, Altman nodded, crossed the deck to the moonpool, climbed down the ladder, and went over to the deck decompression chamber. When he pushed the intercom button, the diver monitoring the communications console put down his headphones and came over to the porthole.

"Is Jem Percy around?" Altman asked.

"Aye," the diver answered curtly.

"I need to talk to him," Altman said.

Without replying, the diver stared at Altman.

"Get him," Altman said.

The diver turned and disappeared behind the bulkhead.

Altman did a little jig to keep warm, the damp sea air blowing under his coat.

Percy, wearing an Emory University sweatshirt, sidled up to the hatch, shook his head, and said, "It's getting bad in here, Will."

"What do you mean?" Altman asked.

"The bell started to yaw near the surface the last run— almost tore apart the umbilical. When the supervisor told Jones half an hour ago, he yelled at him to shut up and keep the runs going. He apparently sounded drunk." Percy tugged at his beard. "The divers have a lot of respect for Jones, but with what's going on out there . . . If he's blitzed, and another diver is hurt or . . . Man, that's it."

"I've already asked him to stop the runs," Altman answered. "He's got his reasons for keeping them going, but I'll talk to him again as soon as I can."

"I'll tell the men," Percy answered. He paused, cleared his throat, and said, "We're hearing that Jones killed one of the Russians tonight."

Altman leaned closer to the intercom and said, "Strinivitch, the younger Soviet, was killed . . . with Jones's gaff. But that doesn't mean that Jones murdered him.''

Percy whistled. "With the gaff, huh?''

"Yeah." Altman pointed over his shoulder toward the stern. "Back by the gas pods."

"You found the body?''

"Yes." Altman did not want to talk about it.

"And the Englishman's disappeared from the ship?''

"Yes."

"She-ee-it.''

The mention of Harrington reminded Altman of why he needed to talk to Percy. Not wanting to seem too interested in the bars coming up from the *Edinburgh*, he asked, "How far along is the current bell run?''

Percy glanced at his watch. "They're almost three and a half hours into it. The divers'll be switching soon.''

"And is that when they send the gold up?''

"Yeah. You keep finding so many bars that it's easier just to pile 'em and send 'em all up at once at the end of your turn on the wreck.''

"Oh," Altman answered. "I was wondering because I saw one of the mates by the starboard winch on my way over here.''

"The crane's not manned most of the time. The crew doesn't like standing around out in the cold. When they figure it's getting close, they send some stiff out to wait for the signal. Then he goes and gets the crane operator, who hoists up the booty.''

"Makes sense." Altman thought that Percy had done a pretty careful job of checking out the process. "Is the procedure pretty regular?''

"Like clockwork.''

"I'll talk to Jones," Altman said, "and see if I can get the next run stopped." He turned as if he were going to leave and then, looking back, said, "Try to keep a lid on the rumors." He laughed as though he intended his next state-

ment to be something of a joke. "Mathewson told me that
you were the source of some of his info."

"What?" Percy appeared confused.

"He said he got some of the scuttlebutt from you."

Percy frowned. "He's barely spoken to me since I got on
him about his jabbering while he was sedated. He's on the
intercom with the other divers a lot, but he avoids me like
I've got the clap."

Altman hoped that the surprise did not show in his face.
"Well," he said, "I'd better find Jones before it's too
late."

▽ **Twenty-three** ▽

When Altman returned to *Seerauber*'s small starboard crane, the operator was already working the winch controls. The young sailor, his back hunched against the wind, leaned against the railing. Spindrift blew from the twelve-foot waves heaping around the ship. Altman approached the operator in what he hoped was a nonchalant manner, and, spray whipping in his face, asked, "How's it going?"

The crane operator, a huge man wearing a dark slicker, answered in broken English, "The night is . . . *nicht* so good."

"Many bars coming up?" Altman asked.

The operator held up five fingers as he said, "Much. *Fünf* sack."

Altman glanced at the canvas and steel-mesh bags next to the steel trolley near the bulkhead. "I'll give you a hand," he said.

"*Danke. Kein Russe* this night."

Altman nodded and watched as the first bag rose from the sea and was swung over the railing. It landed with a dull thud on the deck, icy water still pouring through the mesh. As if on cue, the sailor bent over, unshackled and opened the bag, lifted out an oil-smeared bar, and slid it onto the trolley. Although there was no one to clean the bar or read the serial number or log it in a notebook, the bars would, Altman realized, nevertheless continue to rise, bag by bag, from the depths.

The crane operator shackled the second bag to the cable's steel eye, swung the crane's boom over the water, and pressed the winch's switch. The sailor shook his hands and wiped them on his pants. Altman reached into the bag and felt the cold, slimy metal of the second bar. He lifted the bar and slid it onto the trolley. He then watched the sailor, who grabbed another bar and slipped it carelessly onto the trolley as though the bar was an iron ingot. Still hunching his shoulders against the cold, he paid scant attention to what he was doing.

When they had emptied the bag of its five bars, they silently waited four minutes for the next one. The sailor slouched against the railing, pulled a pack of cigarettes from his pocket, and shook one free. He then tried to light a match, but it barely flared before going out. He turned his back to the wind and cupped his bare, shivering hands, but he still couldn't keep a match going long enough to light the cigarette. Finally, he swore to himself and threw the cigarette over the railing. The crane operator glanced at Altman, laughed gruffly, and watched the cable wind around the drum.

They repeated the unloading process for the second and third bags, which, between them, held nine more bars. When they finished emptying the fourth bag of its five bars, the sailor slid the bag against the bulkhead. His fingers numb, Altman folded his hands into his armpits and hoped there would be five bars in the fifth bag. When the bag finally landed on the deck, Altman let the sailor take the first bar. Altman then reached into the bag, touched each of the remaining four bars, and exhaled. He lifted a bar and placed it onto the trolley.

When it was Altman's turn to take the fourth bar from the

bag, he glanced at the crane operator, who was busy shackling off the cable. Altman then lifted the bar, handed it to the sailor, and slid the bag still holding the fifth bar over next to the other bags against the bulkhead. "Good, we're finished," he said as he straightened up.

The operator checked the crane's toggle switches; the sailor wiped his hands on the back of his pants. Neither man had noticed that one bar still remained in the bag. The operator grabbed the trolley's handle, took a deep breath, and began to pull as the sailor pushed the trolley from the rear. Altman took a few steps with them and then stood watching them as they headed toward the hatchway near the bridge. "Good luck," he shouted after them.

"*Auf Wiedersehen*," the operator shouted over the wind.

Altman scanned the deck. He stood still, drenched by the ocean spray, until he was sure that he was alone. He then hurried back to the bag and lifted out the bar. He wiped silt and oil from the bar with his coat sleeve, unbuttoned his coat, and slipped the bar under it. By holding the bar on top of his belt buckle with one hand and steadying it with his other hand in his pocket, he was able to carry the bar out of sight. He slinked around by the moonpool and along the ship's port railing to the forward hatchway. The bar was even heavier than he had expected, and he was both shivering and sweating by the time he reached the stairwell.

He slipped into Harrington's stateroom and, as he shut the door, realized that he was panting. He laid the bar on the writing table, took off his coat, and hung it on the hook on the back of the door. He then grabbed a towel from the washbasin rack, wiped the bar clean, and stood back to look at the gold.

Long and rectangular, the bar glistened in the light.

Still standing, he dragged his finger along the bar's surface, which was ice-cold and smooth except for the serial numbers. What had Harrington discovered? he wondered again as he took the style from his pocket and sat down. If the bars really were lead covered with a thin veneer of gold, that might explain both the KGB patrol boats and Strinivitch's possessiveness about the *Edinburgh*'s cargo. And if Harrington had confronted Strinivitch, or even Petrosky, with damning evidence, they certainly might have killed him to keep him quiet. But how could they expect to get the cargo off *Seerauber* without causing an international crisis?

Holding the style as he would a pen, Altman tentatively made his first stroke along the length of the bar. The surface barely scratched, and only fine grains of gold stuck to his fingers as he went over the bar with his hand. Drenched by ocean spray and sweat, he could not control his breathing. He wrapped his hand around the style's wooden handle, his thumb providing pressure at the top, held his breath, and pulled the style toward him along the bar's surface. He scored the bar a sixteenth of an inch deep, gold filings marking the style's path.

He exhaled and, wiping the slit with his finger, saw it gleam in the light. His whole body began to shake. He gripped the style even more tightly and placed its point in the slit he had already made. As he pressed and dragged, he felt—or thought he felt—the style catch on some harder metal. He blew the filings from the slit and peered down into it. Leaning over and partially blocking the light, he saw nothing but gold.

As he scored the bar a fourth time, he was so intent on what he was doing that for a moment he did not notice the wisps of pale smoke twisting behind the point of his style.

"Oh, God," he muttered, dropping the style, jumping to his feet, and knocking the chair over backward. He almost tripped on the chair as he backed away from acrid smoke swirling from the slit in the bar. His fists clenched and his mouth agape, he stood staring at the bar. In his mind, he was again a boy of ten. He was out prospecting with his father in the rugged foothills south of Cheyenne along the Colorado–Wyoming border on a bright, hot morning before the thunderheads moved in from the Rockies towering to the west. His father was, as usual, providing him with a running commentary as he worked his way around an outcropping.

For a time, his father grew silent. He had chipped away a section of rock to find dark, crumbling rock beneath it. His father took a chunk of the black rock the size of a baseball and held it up. "This is pitchblende," his father said, his tone somber. "It's not all that scarce—many times more abundant than gold, for example—but the whole world is looking for it."

His father placed the pitchblende on a flat rock between them. "You see, Will," he continued, "it is two-thirds to three-quarters uranium." His father, always the teacher, went on to tell him about the Manhattan Project and Hiroshima and Nagasaki, which Altman had already heard about in school, and about the Rosenbergs and how the Russians had stolen atomic secrets from the United States.

His father then took his smallest, sharpest pick from his belt loop and said to Altman, "Uranium is strange and deadly, Will. But its oddest characteristic is that it is sometimes pyrophoric." He raised the pick and split the chunk of pitchblende. "That's Greek, Will, meaning that it can burn spontaneously."

They both watched wide-eyed as pale smoke whirled above the crumbled black rock.

▽ Twenty-four ▽

When Altman examined the smoking bar, nickel-white metal was visible at the bottom of the eighth-inch-deep slit. Mesmerized by the twirling smoke, he had all of the empirical evidence he needed but was still unable to accept the fact that the gold encased pure uranium. There was no way, he thought, that the Russians could have processed uranium in 1942. Only the United States and Germany had possessed the expertise to do so, and the Germans had lagged far behind the Americans.

Who already knew about the bars? he wondered. Petrosky must know, and perhaps Strinivitch had known. Certainly Harrington had known—at least for a short time. Jones could not know—or could he? Sold to the government, the uranium was worth much less than the gold; but offered on the open market to the highest bidder, the uranium was almost priceless. Jones liked to project the image of a pirate, but could the man be secretly planning such a flagrant act of piracy? Whoever else knew about the uranium, Altman had to pretend that he did not. He had been duped throughout the salvage mission, and now feigned ignorance would provide him with what little protection he had.

He picked up the chair and slid it in front of the writing table. He then wrapped the bar tightly in the towel with which he had cleaned it. When the smoking did not stop completely, he dampened the towel, rewrapped the bar, and left it on the sink. He brushed all of the gold filings he could find into an envelope, sealed it, folded it, and put it in his shirt pocket with the style.

He lifted the wrapped bar, which had finally stopped smoking, and was about to take his coat from the hook when he realized that he would almost certainly be safer if the bar was in Harrington's stateroom rather than in his own. Someone, or more likely a number of people, had already searched Harrington's cabin and would have no reason to do so again. Stooping, he groped under the sink for the spot where the pipe curved toward the bulkhead. Then, lying on his back, he stuck the bar between the pipe and the base of the sink. The damp towel enabled him to wedge the bar completely out of sight.

He took the envelope from his pocket and, as he was jamming it between the bar and the basin, heard footsteps in the passageway. He rolled over against the bulkhead, rose to a crouch, scurried to the switch, and turned off the light. He pressed against the bulkhead behind the door and listened as the footfalls halted.

His heart pounding, he heard knocking on the door of his stateroom and Jones saying, "Are you in there, mate? Wake up, Altman, dammit." The captain's voice was strained, but his words were less slurred than they had been earlier that night. Half a minute of silence was followed by the clicking of a door being opened. Silence again, and then the door shut. The sound of Jones's footsteps echoed above his muttering as he headed back along the passageway.

Altman waited almost five minutes before he grabbed his coat, cracked the door, and slipped across the passageway into his own stateroom. Sitting on the bed for a moment, he wondered what time it was. Days might have passed since he had found Strinivitch's body. Exhausted, he smelled of sweat and fear; his head throbbed. He took off his shirt, rolled it so that the stains did not show, and stuffed it into the bottom of his laundry bag. He then changed into a clean shirt, corduroys, and socks. While putting on dry boat shoes, he decided what he had to do first.

When Altman entered the radio room, the operator on duty, a stocky, blond-haired youth who was dozing in front of the receiver, jumped to his feet. "Morning," Altman said, glancing at the clock. It was six-fifteen: less than ten hours had passed since he had called Elizabeth. That thought turned the world upside down for a moment, and the room seemed to spin away from him. When he regained his bearings, he said, "I need to make a call . . . to London . . . immediately."

While Altman waited for the call to go through, he attempted to separate what he knew as fact from what he had merely surmised. He was getting nowhere, his mind unable to focus on a jumbled mess of interlocking images, when the radio operator told him that the London operator was on the line. Altman gave the number and listened to the ringing of the phone.

When Elizabeth answered on the fourth ring, her voice was fuzzy with sleep.

"Elizabeth," he said, "this is Will again." He heard the rustling of sheets.

"Yes, Will," she said; then, suddenly wide-awake, she asked breathlessly, "What is it? Do you have news about my father?"

"No, Elizabeth, I don't." The only information he had seemed too complicated and too dangerous to share. "Actually, I need your help."

"Yes," she answered, her voice deflated.

"I need you to find a man in London. It's very important. He's a retired navy man by the name of Frank Swanson. I don't know where he lives, but he frequents a pub . . ." His mind went blank for a moment. "... The, uh, Dove and Star." He adjusted the earphones. "He was an acquaintance of your father's."

"Okay."

"Today, this morning if possible. Bring him back to your place and put a call through to the ship."

"Okay," she repeated. "Will, is there really a chance that my father is still alive?"

He leaned against the transmitter console and rubbed his eye with the back of his hand. "Elizabeth . . . it's not likely. And I don't want to give you false hope."

"I need any hope I can get," she said, beginning to cry.

"Did Trevor contact you in any way in the last week or so?" he asked. "A call? Cable? Letters?"

"No," she said, still sobbing. "I haven't received any mail from him in four or five days." Her tone became slightly less despondent as she added, "There could be a letter en route."

Altman looked over at the mailbag next to the photocopier. *A letter,* he thought, recalling the stationery and envelopes in the drawer. He tried to remember when the supply helicopter had made the last mail pickup. "Yes," he said, "there's probably a letter in the mail."

As soon as he and Elizabeth were finished talking, Altman turned to the radio operator and asked, "When was the last mail delivery?"

"Three days ago," the operator answered, rolling his chair back to the receiver console. He spoke English clearly, with only a hint of a German accent.

"So no mail has gone out in three days?"

"None." The operator put on and adjusted the earphones.

"May I look for a letter?" Altman picked up the canvas mailbag by its nylon draw line.

"It is not allowed," the operator answered.

"Neither is sleeping on the job," Altman said.

The operator turned toward the transmitter and adjusted

one of the dials. "Maybe I did not see you do it," he said without looking back.

Altman opened the bag and slid its contents onto the top of the photocopier. As he rooted through the letters destined for Germany and various parts of the United Kingdom, his palms began to sweat. Elizabeth, Altman knew, was a woman a man could confide in, and Harrington seemed like the sort of man who might have unburdened himself to his daughter, especially after he had been unable to tell Altman what was on his mind. Altman stacked the letters in piles of ten or so until he had six piles but no letter to Elizabeth. As he stuffed the envelopes back into the bag, he mumbled, "Damn it."

"It is none of my business," the radio operator said, still not looking at Altman, "but are you looking for a letter from the Englishman, Harrington?"

Altman, his hand on the bag's draw line, froze. He stared at the operator's back and said, "Yes, I am."

"The letter is not there." The operator's voice suggested neither interest nor emotion.

"But there is a letter?"

"Yes. The Englishman brought it in the night he disappeared."

"Where the hell is it?"

The operator, his back still toward Altman, pushed himself a few inches farther away from the console. "I was not sleeping when you came in," he said.

Altman played the game. "Not that I saw."

"Captain Jones . . ." The operator searched for the correct English word. ". . . Confiscated the letter."

"Jones?" Altman let the mailbag slip to the floor.

"Yes." The operator turned toward Altman. "You see, everyone looks for the letter at night, when I am on duty."

"Everyone?" The draw line hung loosely in his hand.

"Yes." The operator's pale blue eyes gleamed. "The

Russian came looking for the letter earlier tonight, but Jones had already taken it.''

Altman's mind reeled. He dropped the bag's draw line. As usual, the others were way ahead of him.

Altman found Jones sitting at the chart table in the bridge. The calipers and rulers on the table suggested that Jones had been charting a course. The wind roared outside, and the rain beat against the expanse of windows. The storm having finally hit with full fury, visibility was reduced so much that *Seerauber*'s bow was obscured by thrashing waves and whipping spray.

"Morning, Will," Jones said, turning to Altman. The captain's face was puffy and his eyes were swollen. He was wearing a dirty turtleneck sweater with the sleeves pulled up. "I couldn't find you in your cabin 'alf an hour ago." His voice was strained, as though he was teetering on the edge of some emotional cliff.

Altman rested his hand on the ship's wheel. "I couldn't sleep," he answered. It looked to him as though Jones had not slept either. "I was over at the DDC. Talked to a couple of the divers."

Jones tapped the chart with the pencil he had been using. "What the 'ell does that mean?"

"They're worried about . . ."

"I'm stopping the bloody bell runs," Jones said. "This'll be the last run." He stood up, tossed the pencil onto the table, and went over to the windows. "One good thing," he said, laughing bitterly, "our Soviet shadows must be 'aving a 'ell of a time of it. I'd 'ate to be aboard one of those pint-sized gunboats in this blow."

Altman leaned against the wheel and said nothing. The telescope's teak case lay closed on the ledge below the windows.

"You can't see shit in this soup." Jones turned around.

"But the goddamned *Thorn* is out there circling us, coming a little closer on each tack, like a noose tightening."

"The *Thorn*? Why?"

"That's what I wanted to ask you," Jones answered, his tone almost taunting.

"Look, Mick," Altman said, his head throbbing. "I've told you before I'm just a rep on this salvage. I don't have any control over what the U.S. government is doing—any more than you do over what the British government does."

"Yeah. Yeah." Jones's shoulders slumped as he went over and sat in the chair. "Yeah, I know you don't." His voice was lower, almost devoid of emotion. "I'd just like to know what the Yanks are doing. And what those Russian bastards are up to." He dug his fingers into his scalp and then ground the heel of his hand against his forehead. "Trevor's the key to this whole bloody mess." He was staring at the base of the scar on his arm.

Your damned right, Altman thought, *but do you know why? What did the letter to Elizabeth tell you? Did it mention Harrington's cutting into the bar? Or what the* Edinburgh's *treasure really was?* Too tired to think clearly, Altman hooked his arm around the top of the wheel, glanced at the teak case and asked, "What do you mean?"

"I mean . . . old Trevor was either onto the commies or he was their bloody accomplice, their comrade. You know, a fellow traveler."

"Then Trevor must have been onto them," Altman answered, again wondering what the letter had said to make Jones doubt Harrington, "because he sure as hell wasn't their accomplice."

"Yeah, well think about it, mate." Jones sat up straighter in the chair. "Trevor is . . . was . . ." He waved his arm. "He's a typical upper-crust Oxford type. They're all a bit pink, those blokes. He was always taking the Russians' side when there was an argument."

"What the hell are you talking about?" Altman's headache was spreading down the back of his neck. "He was trying to keep everything calm. To keep the salvage operation from blowing up in our faces."

Jones shook his head and said, bitterness creeping back into his voice, "If that's the case, he did a pretty shitty job."

Altman turned and looked at the rain spattering against the windows.

"He could 'ave been keeping the salvage going until the commies 'ad what they wanted," Jones growled.

The man's gone insane, Altman thought.

His head cocked, Jones stared at Altman and repeated, "Trevor's in on it with 'em, those Russian bastards. Think about it."

"I'll do that," Altman answered. Jones had gone mad; his distrust of and animosity toward the Soviets had driven him over the edge. Harrington could not have been in collusion with the Soviets. Altman wanted to have it out with Jones then and there. He wanted to bring up the letter and the fact that Harrington had known that the gold bars were not gold, but he clung to the idea that his own safety depended on his seeming not to know much of anything. "I'll do that," he repeated as he walked out of the bridge.

▽ **Twenty-five** ▽

Lost in a dreamless sleep, Altman lay in his clothes on his bunk. The knocking on the door, for a time seemingly distant, abruptly charged toward him like some hell-bent brigade. He started awake, sat up quickly, and yelled, "What is it?"

Gunter Schmidt opened the stateroom door and said, "Herr Altman, you must come immediately." Schmidt's expression was even more dour than usual.

For a moment, Altman felt as though he were repeating in a nightmare something that had already occurred. The stateroom seemed to be swaying. He was sweating, and his head ached. "Why?" he asked. "What's happened?"

"The American destroyer," Schmidt said, "it is heading for *Seerauber*. Captain Jones has tried to raise it on the radio, but it does not respond."

"What time is it?" Altman asked, wondering how long he had slept.

Schmidt looked at his watch and said, "Almost 0800."

Altman had been asleep for less than an hour. "Tell Jones I'll be right there," he said. He got up, wobbled over to the sink, splashed cold water on his face, and rubbed his eyes and scalp with a towel. As he grabbed his foul-weather gear and headed out of his stateroom, he realized that the swaying he had noticed was the ship pulling at anchor. Either *Seerauber*'s stabilizing equipment had been turned off or the storm had wreaked havoc with the ship's electronics. In either case, the bell runs must have finally stopped.

Jones stood next to *Seerauber*'s wheel, staring through the spyglass out the port windows. Fourteen-foot waves crashed against the hull, and rain beat against the windows, but visibility was not quite as limited as it had been earlier. "They 'ave made radio contact," he said without turning toward Altman. "They want to put a bloke aboard."

"The *Thorn*?"

"The bloody *Thorn*." Jones lowered the spyglass and turned around. He hadn't shaved, and he still wore the dirty turtleneck; the dark rings under his puffy eyes made the fierce look he flashed Altman seem almost diabolic.

"The *Thorn* wants to send a man over in this weather?" Altman rubbed his face with his shirt sleeve. "How? It's too messy for a chopper."

Not bothering to answer Altman's question, Jones glanced over at the radar screen. "Where the 'ell is it?" he muttered to himself as he raised the spyglass again.

Altman went over and looked at the chart on the table. Jones had plotted a course that ran back toward Scotland along the northern rim of Europe. The course skirted Norway's myriad islands and fjords almost all the way to Stavanger before running due west to Britain's Orkney Islands and then south to Aberdeen. Jones seemed to have been preoccupied with staying in relatively shallow water and within sight of land whenever possible.

Schmidt entered the bridge and said, "There are no further messages, Captain Jones." He pulled off his rain slicker, hung it on a hook, and folded his arms across his chest. "The American ship should have already closed on us."

Jones glanced at the radar screen again and said, "Gunter, switch off the bridge lights."

The pale green light of the electronic screens cast eerie shadows around the three men as the gray-black world of the storm engulfed them. They stood in silence for a time, each man staring into the rain-splattered darkness. Jones scanned the expanse of windows with his spyglass and then, after compacting the spyglass, rubbed his eyes. Altman glanced at the teak spyglass case and then squinted into the storm.

"There it is," Schmidt said suddenly, pointing to a spot thirty degrees off the port bow.

The *Thorn* slid through the roiling sea. At first, the storm gave up the destroyer gradually—bow and forecastle, forward five-inch gun turret—and then the ship suddenly loomed almost on top of *Seerauber*. As the destroyer's bow, the number 988 painted on its hull, came abreast the bridge, the *Thorn*'s signal light began to flash.

Jones said to Schmidt, "Gunter, stay here. Keep track of the situation." He pulled his slicker off the back of the chair and, slipping it on, added, "I'll be on deck. You know what to do if things get out of 'and."

Pulling on his foul-weather gear, Altman followed Jones out into the storm. On deck, three sailors stood by the port railing forward of the bridge. The wind, blowing at thirty knots, drenched them with rain and salt-spray. The bellowing wind and water almost drowned the sound of the *Thorn*'s engines backing down as the ship edged closer to *Seerauber*. As the *Thorn* came to a complete stop, she rose and fell with the swells. Six men wearing standard naval rain gear stood on the deck just aft of the *Thorn*'s bridge.

One of the men on the *Thorn*'s deck shouted through an amplified megaphone, but his words were lost to the storm. A catapult then shot a grappling hook attached to a cable across *Seerauber*'s deck. As the crew members retrieved the hook and shackled the cable to a stanchion, Jones glared up at the men on the *Thorn*'s deck. Altman stood with his back to the wind and watched the sailors on the *Thorn* ready the jack seat.

As the officer again yelled through the megaphone, Petrosky rushed up to Altman and Jones. He was wearing a belted raincoat that did little to keep him dry. "What is the meaning of this?" he shouted in Altman's face.

"I have no idea," Altman yelled back.

"Mr. Jones, I demand . . ."

"I know nothing more than you do," Jones shouted, anger evident in his voice.

When the cables were set and the seat hooked up, a man of about Altman's size wearing hooded foul-weather gear and carrying a briefcase and folding travel bag, appeared on the destroyer's deck, harnessed himself in, raised his hand, thumb up, and began the forty-yard journey above the swells. When he passed over *Seerauber*'s railing, he unhooked the harness and slid almost gracefully to the deck. Approaching the three men, he said, "Hello, Mr. Jones. Nice weather you're having here." His voice was raised above the din, but he did not shout.

It was only as the man spoke that Altman recognized him as Richard Grey.

When Jones did not answer, Grey turned to Petrosky and said, his words barely audible, "The Soviet representative, I assume. Mr. Petrosky, is it?"

Grey shifted his briefcase into his left hand and extended his right hand toward the Russian. Looking incredulously at Grey, Petrosky shook the American's hand.

Grey then turned to Altman, nodded, and said, "Mr. Altman."

Altman was too dumbfounded to speak.

"A meeting of the principals of this salvage mission is necessary immediately," Grey said. "A representative of the ship's owners should be included. In the wardroom in twenty minutes." He looked at his wristwatch. "At 8:45. Is that acceptable, Mr. Jones?"

Jones continued to glower at Grey.

"Good," Grey said. "That's settled. I'll need quarters in which to change. Would you see to it, Mr. Jones?" He shook the water from his briefcase and folding bag. As he passed Altman, he said, his voice condescending, "You look a mess, man. At least shave before the meeting."

▽ **Twenty-six** ▽

Schmidt stood near the wardroom doorway. Jones, Petrosky, and Altman sat in their customary seats around the table. Jones slouched with his elbow hooked over the arm of the chair; Petrosky inspected his fingernails.

Leaning forward in Harrington's seat, Grey rubbed his index finger along the edge of a manila file folder and said, "I must apologize, gentlemen, for the nature of my arrival, but circumstances dictated it." He wore pressed flannel pants and a maroon cashmere sweater. His pale blue eyes gleamed in his deeply tanned face.

Altman crossed his legs away from Grey and looked at Strinivitch's empty chair. Standing in the shower fifteen minutes earlier, Altman had tried to figure out what Grey's arrival on board meant. He had no way of knowing if Grey was aware of the real nature of the *Edinburgh*'s cargo, but he suspected that Grey knew. Altman had turned the hot water off and let the cold water stream down on his chest and smother his anger.

"The recent reports Captain Jones has sent concerning events aboard this ship have caused grave concern in London and Washington," Grey said.

"What's it to you?" Jones asked, his voice strained.

Grey pulled at the sleeve of his sweater. "On a number of levels, it is of concern to London and Washington," he repeated. Reaching over, he lifted the coffee pot from the center of the table and poured coffee into his mug. "The diver's death, Mr. Harrington's disappearance, and most recently the death of the Soviet representative . . ."

"Murder of the Soviet citizen," Petrosky interrupted.

Grey glanced at the Russian, nodded, and then, his voice still smooth and even, said, "All of these events have raised serious doubts about the merit of continuing the salvage."

Jones sat up, cocked his head, glowered at Grey, and muttered, "What the 'ell does that mean?"

At first, Grey did not respond. He sipped his coffee, put down the mug, opened the file folder, and took from it two sheets of paper. "It means," he said, looking first at Altman and then at Jones, "that I have been authorized by the President of the United States to replace Mr. Altman as the American representative and to relieve him of all duties on board this ship." He slid one sheet of paper toward Jones and placed the other in front of Altman.

Wanting to crumple the paper and shove it in Grey's face, Altman stared at the man for a moment before reading the sheet. Below the letterhead of the Office of the President, the letter, one short paragraph, gave Grey full authorization to make all decisions concerning American interests on the *Edinburgh* salvage.

When Altman glanced up from the sheet, Jones was still reading the other copy and Grey was shuffling other papers in the folder. His face expressionless except for a hint of a smile, Petrosky gazed across the table. Altman pushed the paper away. *Fine*, he thought. It had all been some bizarre international game from the start—let Grey and Petrosky play it. Altman had never known the rules and only recently had learned the stakes. But he still intended to discover the whole truth about the *Edinburgh*'s cargo and to find out what had happened to Harrington. And, when he did, someone was going to pay. Not having to represent the U.S. might even free him to . . .

His face red, Jones hit the sheet of paper with the back of his hand. "Are you going to take this shit?" he asked.

Trying not to show his resentment, Altman shrugged and said, "It's been Grey's show from the start."

"Shit," Jones said, slapping the paper with his open hand. "Don't you have . . ." he began to say, but then he stopped and scowled at Grey.

"Mr. Altman will, of course," Grey said, his voice still even, "be allowed to provide input, especially in technical matters. The critical point, however, Mr. Jones, is that American interests are represented by me alone." He picked up the coffee mug but did not drink from it. "The first order of business is that I be apprised of what exactly . . ." He paused, looking Jones in the eye. ". . . Of what has occurred aboard this ship."

While Jones explained what had happened, Altman said nothing. Grey asked numerous questions, and Petrosky occasionally interjected comments. Schmidt paid little attention to what was said. As Jones began to describe Strinivitch's death, Grey asked, "Where was the gaff kept?"

"On the bridge, 'anging up," Jones answered.

"And who had access to it?" Grey asked.

"I did," Jones answered. "And Gunter. But neither of us were on the bridge. No one was seen on the bridge just before Altman found the body. The watch on duty 'ad been called to the radio room. Anybody could 'ave taken it." He waved his hand around the table. "Altman or Petrosky or anybody."

"Mr. Jones is covering up," Petrosky said. "He murdered Comrade Strinivitch with the gaff."

His gaze quizzical, Grey turned toward the Russian.

"The man should be arrested," Petrosky insisted. "He threatened a Soviet citizen and then killed him."

"Shut up, goddammit," Jones barked. He rubbed his left temple with his fingers. "Let me finish."

"He threatened Strinivitch," Petrosky repeated. "There are witnesses."

"Your statements will be taken under advisement," Grey said to Petrosky. "But Mr. Jones is correct. Let him continue."

"What the 'ell does that mean—taken under advisement?" The knuckles of Jones's clenched hands were white. "I'm the captain of this ship."

"Mr. Jones," Grey said, seeming to speak as much through his nose as his mouth, "there have been at least two, and probably three, murders aboard this ship. Order must be restored before any resolution of this salvage can occur." Grey opened the file folder.

"I'll keep order on my ship, mate," Jones said. His face was again red, and the veins in his neck protruded.

"As a matter of record, Mr. Jones, it is not your ship," Grey said. "As you well know, *Seerauber* has been leased to the salvage consortium by the Hamburg Shipping Line."

"To me, you mean, you . . ." Jones gripped the edge of the table. Saliva beaded at the corner of his mouth; his eyes glazed over.

"Not to you, to the salvage consortium," Grey repeated. He slid a sheet of paper in front of Jones. "Perhaps you should read this." Grey held a second copy up and added, "Herr Schmidt, you need to read this as well."

Schmidt lumbered over, took the sheet, scanned it, and said, "It is signed by my superior, but I do not read English good."

Grey said, "It states that . . ."

"This is bloody piracy," Jones yelled. He tore the paper and leaped to his feet. His eyes bulged, and the muscles in his jaw twitched.

Grey stood up and faced Jones. "It is perfectly legitimate. You can cable Hamburg if you want."

"It's fucking piracy." Jones clenched and unclenched his fists. "You can't take over a ship at sea."

"The intention is not to take over the ship." Grey stared into Jones's eyes. "It is simply to ensure the safety of the ship and its crew."

"You can't legally do anything until the ship reaches port."

Grey's temper flared. "Listen to me," he hissed. "That letter authorizes me to make decisions and to give orders relative to *Seerauber*'s safety only if I deem it necessary and in the best interests of the owner." He twisted the university ring on his finger so that the cut stone jutted out. "The quickest way for that to happen is for you to fly off the handle like this."

"You bloody fucking bastard," Jones sputtered.

"Jones," Grey said, "get control. The *Thorn* intercepted a message in Russian last night." He looked down at Petrosky. "When it was decoded, the message said, among other things, 'The time has come. Send the ship.' A Soviet destroyer off the coast of southern Norway changed course within minutes. A second destroyer left Murmansk an hour later."

Petrosky stood quickly and said, "I protest, Mr. Grey. The message I sent reported the murder of a Soviet citizen."

Grey leaned on the table and looked Petrosky in the eye. "You deny that two Russian destroyers are headed this way?"

"I would not know."

Altman's mind was clearing, and he was more calm than he had been in days. Feeling detached from the argument swirling above him, he realized that Grey, although ostensibly in control, had already blundered twice. The letter from the Hamburg Shipping Line had been dated prior to Harrington's disappearance and Strinivitch's death. Grey had, therefore, been planning to board *Seerauber* and, if necessary, take command even before Jones had cabled

London about the problems aboard the ship. Worse, Grey had tacitly admitted that the American navy possessed Soviet codes. Could the stakes be so high that Grey would risk that admission?

Grey turned to Jones and said, "You have a clear choice—the Soviets or me."

Jones dug his fingernails into the palms of his hands, glared at Grey and Petrosky, and then kicked his chair and turned away. Petrosky continued to stare across the table as he slid back into his chair. Grey pulled at the sleeves of his sweater and sat down. Schmidt, who had been gaping at the others, read the sheet of paper again and then laid it in front of Grey on the table.

Grey said, his voice once again calm, "Herr Schmidt, as I was about to tell you before, the letter states that, in certain situations, I may give you orders that contradict Mr. Jones's commands. The Hamburg Shipping Line directs you to obey my orders." He looked over Jones's back and added, "Is that a fair paraphrase of the letter, Mr. Jones?"

Schmidt glanced from Grey to Jones. "Captain Jones," he said, "what should I . . . ?"

Jones turned slowly. "Gunter, that is what the letter says." His eyes were clearer and his voice calmer. "But until that time . . ." He stared at Schmidt. ". . . You still work for me. Understand, Gunter?"

Schmidt stared back at Jones and nodded.

"Of course," Grey said, glancing at Schmidt. "I am glad we have that cleared up." He extended his hand. "Have a seat, Mr. Jones, we have one other order of business."

Schmidt moved back over toward the door, and Jones sat heavily in his chair. His expression sullen, he said nothing.

Grey took another packet of papers from the manila folder, removed the paper clip that held the sheets, and gave a copy to each of the three men seated at the table. "As you can see, the British Defense Ministry has also requested that I represent Her Majesty, not only in the *Edinburgh* salvage but also in the investigation of Trevor Harrington's disappearance.''

Altman skimmed the letter and dropped it on the table. Grey had done his homework. He was, Altman realized, attempting a legal act of piracy. As Grey and his cronies in Washington had no doubt planned it, Grey could, at least in theory, control *Seerauber* and the salvage mission. But the men now present were aboard a small ship in rough seas, and Grey did not know Jones as Altman did. The captain's sudden calm was, if anything, more dangerous than his anger.

Jones slid the sheet back to Grey without comment.

Petrosky folded the sheet carefully, stood up, and said, ''Very nicely done, Mr. Grey, very nice.'' His voice was like ice. ''But the salvage is not yet complete.'' He turned, and without saying anything more, walked from the room.

Jones put his elbows on the table. ''You bet right, Grey,'' he said. ''I'd rather have you than the Russians. But what you're doing here is still bloody piracy.'' He nodded his head and smiled maliciously. ''And I'll get you if you try anything with that gold I've brought up.''

▽ **Twenty-seven** ▽

As Altman opened the door to his stateroom, Grey called to him from the stairs at the other end of the passageway. Leaving the door open, Altman sat on his bunk.

Still holding the file folder, Grey stood in the doorway and said, "I'm glad that part of it's over, but I had to show the SOB who was in charge." When Altman did not answer, Grey sauntered over to the desk, unfolded the cheesecloth, and said, "I see that you're still working on the scrimshaw."

"Some," Altman answered. He wanted to see what Grey knew, and letting the man talk seemed like the best way to do it.

Grey pulled out the desk chair but did not sit down. "My baggage is being moved down to Harrington's cabin," he said.

Altman thought about the bar wedged up under the sink.

"Look," Grey said, his tone sharper, "for what has to be done, I'll need your assistance. If you're angry about my replacing you, get over it—fast."

"I'm not angry," Altman answered. "I thought you handled the situation well enough." He was beyond anger, but that was something he did not expect Grey to understand.

Grey rested his hands on the back of the chair and said, "I showed them that the Old Man means business here, huh." He scratched the side of his nose, patted the chair back, glanced quickly around the stateroom, and added, "I'll be needing whatever documentation you've already collected concerning the salvage operation."

Altman stood up and asked, "Why?"

"Why?" Grey's smile twisted. "I want to gather all relevant information before I act. Your documentation will likely prove invaluable."

Altman pointed to the desk. "My journal and the film I shot are in the second drawer, but there's nothing there that will help you understand what's really going on."

Grey glanced at Altman, opened the drawer, and took out the journal. He opened it, and, while flipping through the pages, said, "And I suppose you know what is really happening."

"I don't." Altman sat down on the bunk again. "I was hoping you'd fill me in."

Grey shut the journal and shrugged. "The Soviets want all the gold for themselves. That's what's going on."

"That's all?"

Not seeming to pay much attention to Altman's question, Grey reached into the drawer, picked up three rolls of film, and read the labels. "That's it," he said matter-of-factly. "Just a hundred and sixty-five million in gold—enough to keep the Soviet economy afloat for a few more hours."

Altman rubbed his hand along the wooden base of the bunk. "The other reps knew all about me, but you didn't provide me with information about them. When I called you from Aberdeen, all I got was some general BS. You had files, but you didn't bother to send them to me."

Grey juggled the film rolls in his hand and looked at Altman. "It wasn't necessary," he said, his voice cold.

Altman remained calm. He felt almost as though he were

outside himself viewing the situation. "Who is Petrosky?" he asked.

"You've been on board with him. You know him better than I do."

"Yeah," Altman answered. "I know that he's no fool. He's Westernized, polished, suave for a Russian, one of the new *glasnost* types. But I don't know who the hell he really is or what he's doing on this salvage."

"Vladimir Petrosky," Grey said, "has only vague ties to the KGB, but over the last decade he has appeared on the scene every time the Soviets had something up their sleeve. One could say that he is a diplomatic troubleshooter of sorts."

Altman did not believe that Grey was leveling with him. "Is he a killer?"

"It's difficult to say."

"Well, *try*."

Grey looked sharply at Altman and then raised the journal and pointed it at him. "Watch your . . ." he said. Then, as if reconsidering, he lowered the journal and continued, "He has never been directly linked to the death of any of our agents, but, as I said, he seems to be around when . . ."

A tall, thin sailor, wearing glasses, stood in the doorway. "Excuse me," he said, nodding to the two Americans. "There is a call for Mr. Altman in the radio room."

Grey frowned as Altman brushed by him and out the door. Climbing the steps, Altman wondered if Grey was already searching the stateroom. When Altman entered the radio room, the operator pointed to the earphones and moved his chair away from the receiver console.

"Yes, what is it?" Altman said into the microphone.

"Will, is that you?" Elizabeth's voice held a note of urgency.

Altman straightened the earphones on his head. "Yes."

"I've located Frank Swanson."

"Already?" Altman glanced at the clock. Less than three

and a half hours had passed since he had last spoken with her. "You're remarkable," he said.

"I took a holiday from work. I've been so worried. I wouldn't have been able to concentrate anyway." She paused. "Will, I . . . I'll . . . Here is Mr. Swanson."

"Frank Swanson, Royal Navy, retired, at your service, sir." Swanson's voice was stronger and more forceful than it had been in the pub.

"Frank, it's Will Altman." Remembering Swanson's partial deafness, Altman spoke loudly. "I'm the American you met in the Dove and Star with Trevor Harrington."

"Yes, yes. I remember." Swanson cleared his throat. "Miss Harrington tells me that her father's life is in danger." Swanson's tone was formal, as though Elizabeth's presence sobered him.

Altman adjusted the earphones. "It's probably too late to help Harrington, but you may be able to shed some light on his actions just before he disappeared."

"Yes, yes, I'll help if I can."

Altman rubbed his forehead, which was damp with sweat. "When we talked in the Dove and Star, you were pretty insistent that the gold was . . . You seemed to feel that the gold was evil."

"It was cursed, it was—straight from hell. That's what I told you and the other bloke."

"Yes, but I need to know why you felt it was cursed."

"Because it was."

Altman asked, "Are you sure that you actually saw the gold after the crates had broken?"

"Yes, sir, I did."

"Was there anything about it, anything at all, that made you think it was evil?" When Swanson did not answer immediately, Altman added, "Frank, it's important."

Swanson remained silent.

"Frank, was there anything bizarre—eerie—about the gold that you saw?"

Swanson sucked in his breath. "Something eerie, yes." His voice began to quiver. "Yes, there was. One of the bloody bars down at the bottom of the pile was smoking, it was."

Altman glanced around the room. The radio operator had turned around. When Altman caught his eye, he turned quickly back to the manual he was reading.

"Frank," Altman said, "who else have you told about the smoke?"

"Just the other bloke."

"Harrington?"

"No, the other American."

"What?" Altman's question stuck in his throat.

"The American. He said he was a mate of yours, he did."

"What was his name?"

"Robert White."

"What did he look like?"

"A handsome bloke, he was. Athletic. An ex-footballer, maybe."

Keeping his voice calm, Altman asked, "Anything special about him? Did he wear any jewelry? A ring or anything?"

"Yes. Yes, he did, at that. A ring with a large stone. Kept fiddling with it."

Altman rubbed the side of his face and thought, *that goddamned ring*. "When was this? When did you talk to him?"

"Almost a fortnight ago."

Adrenaline rushed to Altman's head. *Almost two weeks ago,* he thought, *long before the first gold bar had been recovered.* "And he asked you about the gold, about what you'd seen in the bomb room?"

"Aye, that he did." Swanson cleared his throat. "But he was more interested in what I remembered about the American."

"What?"

"The American that boarded the *Edinburgh*. I didn't recall much other than that he was a tall chap, young, sturdy. He was bundled up against the cold, he was, and I didn't get much of a look at him."

Altman could feel a vein in his temple pulsing. "Did this, ah, Mr. White, ask you about our meeting at the Dove and Star?"

"With you and Mr. Harrington? No. Can't say that he did. Just asked me about the news. Did I follow the news." Swanson's laugh was raspy. "Follow football mostly, I do. That's what I told him."

"And you told no one else, not even Harrington, about the smoking bar?"

"No. It sounds so daft, smoking gold and all. I haven't told a soul in all these years."

"It's not a bit crazy, Frank. The gold was smoking. You've been more helpful that you can know."

"Glad to be. No problem." Sounding relieved to have the conversation finished, Swanson added, "Miss Harrington would like to speak to you again."

Altman could feel his back and shoulders tightening up. He rolled his neck to relieve the tension.

"Did you find out what you wanted?" Elizabeth asked.

"Not exactly," Altman answered. "But enough. More than enough."

"Will," she asked, "is there any news about my father?"

"No, Elizabeth, there isn't."

"Yes. Well, I . . ." Her voice trailed off for a moment. "Keep me informed, Will. Please."

"I will." He leaned over the console and lowered his voice. "Take care, Elizabeth." He hesitated, unsure what else to say to her. "And, thanks for finding Swanson."

▽ **Twenty-eight** ▽

Altman looked into Harrington's stateroom, where Grey sat on the bunk reading through a stack of papers that included Altman's journal. Harrington's suitcase had been removed. Grey's shoes, which he had taken off, lay at the foot of the bunk. His briefcase was open on the desk. Altman entered the room, turned the desk chair around, and said, "The call was from London. From Frank Swanson, the *Edinburgh*'s petty officer I told you about when I called you from Aberdeen."

Grey's left hand twitched for a second, and then Grey glanced up from the papers and said, "Really?"

"Yes." Altman stared at Grey, who returned to perusing the papers. Altman crossed his legs and looked at the ceiling. "You didn't think it was necessary to fill me in on the backgrounds of the other reps, but I guess you had a thorough file on me."

Grey looked over at Altman again but did not answer.

"The file certainly must have included information about my parents. Right?"

Grey put down the papers and said, "So?"

"That's the funny thing about government files. They contain all sorts of information but sometimes miss what's

195

most important. Take my father, for instance. My file must have mentioned that he was a public school principal. It might even have mentioned how old he was when I was born, how much income tax he paid, his political affiliations, that sort of thing.'' Altman stood up and put his hands in his pants pockets. His tone remained conversational. ''But I can't imagine that the file mentioned his hobbies.'' Grey stared at him as he walked over, took his hands from his pockets, and tapped the sink with his fingers. ''I doubt you know that he was a prospector and an amateur minerologist. Damned good at it, too.'' He waved his hand expansively. ''He used to take me on prospecting trips with him. I learned a lot from him.'' He shrugged. ''Most of it hasn't been useful in my work, but occasionally something happens . . .'' He let his voice trail off.

Grey sat up stiffly on the bunk. His face did not appear quite so tan. ''What are you trying to say?'' he asked.

Altman stooped, felt around under the sink, and retrieved the bar wrapped in the towel. The envelope fell to the floor, but he did not pick it up.

Grey swung his feet onto the deck.

Without unwrapping the bar, Altman returned to the chair, sat down, and said, ''You're scum, Grey. Goddamned scum.''

''Wait just a minute,'' Grey said.

Altman unwrapped the towel. The bar glistened, and the gouge he had scored shone like a silver streak.

''You have the bar Harrington took?'' For the first time, Grey sounded baffled.

''No,'' Altman answered. ''This is a different bar, one on which, quite without intending to, I duplicated one of my father's lessons.''

Grey opened his mouth but did not say anything.

Altman turned the bar over in his hands. ''You've known all along that the *Edinburgh*'s cargo wasn't gold. Yet you've

kept this goddamned game going even though it has already
cost three men their lives."

At first, Grey said nothing. Then, his tone again confi-
dent, he said, "Look, Altman, you self-righteous fool..."
He pointed his finger in Altman's face. "Only one American has ever known exactly what the *Edinburgh*'s cargo
really was."

Altman scoffed. "Are you telling me that the Russians
just happened to be shipping processed uranium encased in
gold to the U.S.—years before they had the capability to
process the ore?"

Grey shook his head and lowered his hand. "You simply
don't have all the facts." Disdain was clear in his voice.
"You may have pieces, but you don't have the whole
picture."

"Try me."

Grey exhaled slowly. "You're familiar with the Manhattan
Project."

Altman nodded. "Somewhat."

"What you don't know," Grey said, "is that in the spring
of 1941 a bipartisan committee reported to President Roosevelt
that a nuclear explosion would probably not be possible
until late in 1945. The problem was that uranium 238 was
not fissionable, and it would take three to five years just to
separate enough uranium 235 to make one bomb. You can
imagine how FDR took the news. We weren't in the war
yet, of course, but he knew the Nazis were already starting
to develop the bomb." Grey began to toy with his ring.
"Most pitchblende," he went on, "is about one-third
uranium."

"Actually, pitchblende tends to be between 45 and 85
percent uranium," Altman said. He put the bar on the floor
by his feet and leaned forward, his forearms resting on his
knees.

"Whatever," Grey said. "The critical point is that,

although most uranium is less than one percent U-235, the composition varies from deposit to deposit."

"And a deposit rich in U-235 was discovered in Russia," Altman completed Grey's thought.

"Exactly. Near Lake Baikal in Siberia. The Soviets owed Uncle Sam huge war-debt payments. When Roosevelt's personal emissary asked for payment in processed uranium rather than gold, the Soviets were more than amenable. They had no use for the uranium anyway, and their gold reserves were fast being depleted." Grey lifted his hands. "It was quite a pragmatic solution for all concerned."

"And the gold would not only camouflage the uranium but also serve as an anticorrosive."

"You're a quick learner," Grey said sarcastically. "But that was only part of it." His smile was contentious. "The gold provided airtight security. It gave the Soviets an excuse for the heavy security measures that were necessary in transporting the cargo. And it also—and this was the real beauty of the plan—insured that, even if the Nazis captured the gold, they'd never suspect what they really had. Hitler, that greedy bastard, would have hidden the bars away in some secret vault."

"So U-235—highly radioactive uranium—was put aboard a British cruiser . . ."

Grey glanced for a moment at the shimmering bar. "In 1942, no one knew the dangers of radioactivity."

Altman sat back and said, "Americans must have been involved in the setting up and running of the heavy-water processing plant."

"Exactly. And that's the crux of the problem. Americans designed the plant. But Stalin used slave labor, so Roosevelt pulled out most of the American advisers when the plant became operational."

Although he knew he shouldn't be, Altman was amazed by the dubious morality that had enabled Americans to design a slave labor camp and accept the camp's finished product, but kept them from actually witnessing what occurred in the camp. "So no American actually saw the uranium processed or encased in gold?" he asked.

Grey shook his head. "One American did. Nobody wanted to remain in that frigid hellhole, but the junior member of Roosevelt's oversight team stayed on."

"But if you knew the *Edinburgh*'s cargo wasn't gold, why agree to the salvage? Why go through with this whole goddamned charade?"

Grey laughed spitefully. Slipping back into his bureaucratic voice, he repeated, "You simply don't understand. The President, the Old Man . . ."

"The President could have simply not agreed to the salvage in the first place," Altman interrupted.

"International agreements are never elementary." Grey made a clicking sound with his lips. "The Soviets were adamant about going through with the salvage. They had the Old Man by the short hairs."

Altman wrapped the bar in the towel and said, "Yeah. Damned straight, they did. They saw the chance to embarrass the hell out of the U.S. The President would be forced to admit that the U.S. provided the Soviets with the technology to produce fissionable uranium long before American atomic secrets were stolen."

Grey stared at Altman. The bureaucratic tone gone from his voice, he said, "The situation is far more critical than that."

Altman laid the wrapped bar on the deck and looked over at Grey. Swanson's final statements on the phone flooded his mind. "Jesus shit," he said, as much to himself as to Grey. "The President?"

Grey said nothing.

Altman rubbed the side of his face. "The President was the American who boarded the *Edinburgh* in Murmansk?"

Grey nodded. "The Old Man was the American left behind to oversee the project."

"Jesus shit," Altman repeated, his mind spinning.

"The Soviets want the Old Man out of office in the worst way, and they see the *Edinburgh*'s salvage as their best shot."

Altman's mind was still whirling through the President's past. "So our die-hard anticommunist gave atomic secrets to the Russians and later stood by as the Rosenbergs took the fall."

"That's the wrong way to look at it," Grey said, his tone again becoming quarrelsome. He sat up straighter. "The Nazis had to be stopped at any cost. War makes for strange alliances, and Roosevelt made the right decision—at least for the times. The Old Man was just doing his job, his duty. And there's no reason he should pay now for the country's past miscalculations."

"Miscalculations? But he . . . You can't possibly believe that . . ." Altman stammered. He looked over at the doorway and then down at the towel.

"The Old Man has always acted in the national interest."

"His own fucking self-interest, you mean."

Grey slammed the wooden base of the bunk. "No, goddammit," he said, deep anger in his voice for the first time. "Even now, with the salvage, his actions have been dictated solely by the Soviets. They've had an extremely narrow window of opportunity. They needed to raise the *Edinburgh*'s cargo this summer, before the election. When our efforts to stall the negotiations in London were thwarted, it became clear that the Old Man had to agree to the salvage. But he also had to make damned sure the salvage failed."

"Then why the hell am I here? Why not send some CIA flunky?"

"Because of the Soviets. The American representative had to be someone they would accept as legitimate. Your background was perfect." Grey smiled at Altman. "As long as they believed in you, they'd be lulled into thinking they were going to pull off the salvage and ruin the Old Man. Clandestine operations to slow the salvage have proved unsuccessful, so more drastic . . .''

"What the fuck?'' Altman interrupted. Grey's convoluted rationalization for murder made him irate. He picked up the bar again. "What're you going to do now? Blow the cargo up?''

Grey's smile twisted into an inimical grin as he said, "Exactly."

Suddenly, much of what Grey had in mind became clear to Altman. The *Edinburgh* salvage had been doomed even before it began. That good men had to die to enable the President to save his political career was incidental. Grey had deceived Altman from the start. The President had needed an American representative with credentials in undersea technology that the Russians would accept. Grey had not chosen some CIA flunky because he had the ultimate chump in Altman. And Grey certainly wouldn't let Altman live to talk about what had occurred aboard *Seerauber*. Altman had been playing Grey's fall guy perfectly—and there was no way out.

Altman looked at Grey, who sat on the edge of the bunk smiling rancorously, and then jerked the bar upward and swung it with all his might.

Grey had time only to raise his arm halfway from his side before the bar smashed squarely into his face, crushing his nose and tearing a gash in his left eyebrow. Staring blankly up at Altman, he arched backward for a moment and then toppled forward onto his knees on the deck. Blood flowed into his left eye and poured out of his nose and down his chin. Thick drops fell to the decking in splotches. Trying to get to his feet, he fell backward against the bunk. Blood stained his shirt and pants. His lips moved, but only garbled sounds came from his throat.

▽ **Twenty-nine** ▽

As Altman wrapped the bar more tightly in the dirty, blood-stained towel and rushed from Harrington's cabin, he glimpsed Grey rising and stumbling toward the briefcase on the desk. Altman raced along the passageway, and, as he reached the stairs, glanced back. Grey, hunched over and dripping blood, lurched out of the doorway with a blunt-nosed pistol in his right hand.

Altman scurried up the steps and then, looking over his shoulder to make sure that Grey wasn't following him, cut through the crew's mess toward the ship's stern. When he was aft of the wardroom and bridge, he climbed to the next deck and, panting, stopped by the exterior hatchway. He peered through the porthole at a surreal, half-lit world that seemed to be neither day nor night. The wind had slackened some, but the rain had turned to sleet and the twelve-foot waves still rolled into the clouds hovering low over the ship.

Figuring that Grey's injury might provide him with the opportunity to find Jones, show him the bar, and explain what was happening, Altman doubled back toward the bridge. When he reached the stairwell up to the bridge, he heard a door slam. He peeked around the corner of the bulkhead and saw Schmidt lumbering down the steps. No,

Schmidt wouldn't do. He'd speak only to Jones. Altman retreated to a storage closet along the passageway, shut himself into the dark cubicle, and listened to the clanging on the steps and the heavy footfalls echoing along the passageway. He began to sweat; the astringent odor of ammonia and disinfectant almost made him choke.

He waited until the footsteps were no longer audible, and then he slipped out of the closet, climbed the stairs, and entered the bridge. Neither Jones nor any of the crew were there. He stood by the wheel and looked out the expanse of windows at the twilight world. The sleet, mixed now with snow, splattered against the glass. *Seerauber* yawed in the tumbling sea. The *Thorn* and the Soviet patrol boats were cloaked by the torrent and swells, but he could feel their presence out in the storm.

He turned and walked through the narrow passageway leading to the captain's cabin. The door was ajar, and he squinted into the room. Dull light from the one porthole cast the cabin in shadows. The sheets and blanket on the bunk lay piled in a ball. Books and magazines protruded from a net bag hanging from the bulkhead above the bunk. Clothes were spread about on the chair in the corner. Listening for the sounds of anyone approaching, Altman stepped into the cabin and shut the door halfway. Manuals, telex printouts, memos, cables, and signed and unsigned vouchers were strewn on the top of the desk. For a moment he felt safer, but then the darkness and clutter began to close in on him.

When he placed the towel-covered bar on the desk, he noticed a torn beige envelope addressed to Elizabeth in London. He picked up the envelope, turned it over in his hand, and, seeing that the letter had been removed, began riffling the other papers on the desk. He then fanned a stack of file folders without finding the letter there either. Sliding the files back onto the desk, he saw the corner of a white handkerchief wadded up under some shipping and diving manuals. He grabbed the handkerchief and unfolded it to

find the sculptor's knife that Harrington had taken the night
he had disappeared.

Altman picked up the knife and then crumpled the handkerchief and put it back under the manuals. Starting to put
the knife in his pocket, he thought better of it, leaned over,
and slipped the knife into his sock. Sweat was dripping
down his back, and his saliva was gummy. He sat down in
the desk chair and tried again to piece together what had
happened. He could barely figure out what day it was, much
less make the events mesh in his mind. He remembered
Grey's statement that the United States had tried to abort the
salvage clandestinely. Forcing his mind to slow down, he
became aware of how tired he was. His head ached, and his
back and legs were sore.

Suddenly, Altman heard the bridge's outer door click
shut. Altman listened carefully. Papers rustled; a metallic
object scraped against a hard surface. He stooped, took the
knife from his sock, and crept into the passageway. Near the
entrance to the bridge, he stopped and crouched against the
bulkhead, his breath coming in short, fitful strokes. Sweat
beaded on his neck and forehead. Shutting his eyes, he tried
to control his breathing. Time seemed to stop. The ship's
ventilators whirred, and somewhere more distant an engine
hummed. And then the bridge's decking creaked. He peered
around the corner of the bulkhead.

Just to the right of the wheel, Mathewson stooped in front
of the fuse box below the depth finder. The diver wore blue
jeans and a gray sweatshirt with the sleeves cut off just
above the tattoos on his arms. He had a diver's watch on a
black rubber strap on his left wrist; a black-hafted diver's
knife, sheathed in plastic, hung from his belt. A blue Nike
athletic bag lay open on the deck beside him.

Altman exhaled, rubbed the back of his left hand across
his eyes, and stood up straighter. "Sam," he said, entering
the bridge.

Mathewson wheeled around. In his right hand he held a

detonator cap. "Altman," he said, "you startled the hell out of me," He glanced at the short, curved knife in Altman's hand. "I've been looking for you."

"I need your help," Altman said. "I've got to find Jones to tell him that Grey plans to blow . . ." He stared at the detonator cap in Mathewson's hand.

The diver slipped the cap back into the bag, stood, and casually wiped his hand along the knife's sheath.

"Goddamn it," Altman said. "Goddamn Grey."

"That's right," Mathewson said, "Grey's got control of the ship."

Altman's hands were sweating, and the knife handle was slippery. "And you're his saboteur?"

Mathewson's rancorous smile was lopsided. "Grey's leaving nothing to chance," he said. "I've already set the charges." He folded his muscular arms across his chest. His left shoulder was slightly lower than his right.

That bastard, Altman thought, *has every angle covered. Even before we sailed, he was planning to blow the ship if he needed to. And now . . .*

"In about forty minutes me and Grey'll be safe aboard the *Thorn*, and the *Edinburgh* salvage'll be history," Mathewson said as he looked first at his watch and then at the clock above the loran. It was 10:17. "But that's not your problem." His voice became low, almost matter of fact. His crooked smile broadened. "Because you're dead already."

Altman inched to the left to put the wheel between Mathewson and himself. Needing to keep the diver talking, he asked, "So your blowback was no accident?"

Mathewson's laugh was guttural. "A happy accident. My original orders were to sabotage the operation, to slow it down from inside the DDC and bell. The blowback gave me free run of the ship."

"And you killed Hall?" The knife in Altman's hand felt small, far too small.

Mathewson unfolded his arms and rolled his neck. "Percy heard me babbling under sedation. It was him I wanted to get rid of. Hall was unlucky."

Altman's eyes darted around the bridge. Hoping that nothing had been moved in the last few hours, he backed against the ledge below the forward windows. His breathing was becoming erratic. He could hear the blood surging in his ears but could not make out the sound of the sleet striking the windows. He did not turn to see if it had stopped. "And Harrington and Strinivitch?" he asked, buying himself a few more seconds.

"Not my doing. There's more shit going down here than you'll ever know." Mathewson pulled the stainless-steel diver's knife from its sheath. The serrated top of the seven-inch blade gleamed darkly.

Just as Mathewson tensed to lunge, Altman tossed the sculptor's knife at him. Mathewson stepped back, and the knife grazed his left ear and fell harmlessly to the deck. In the split second that the diver was distracted, Altman reached over his shoulder to the ledge and felt the corner of the teak spyglass case. As Mathewson began to lunge, Altman grabbed the case and swung it backhanded like a club.

The spyglass case caught Mathewson just above his right ear. His arm was jerked to the side by the case's momentum, and his knife blade slashed across Altman's left shoulder, slicing his shirt and skin and cutting into the muscle. Mathewson tumbled forward, his head struck the ledge, and the knife clattered to the deck. Dazed, the diver slumped next to the knife and rolled over onto his back. He lay there for a moment, his pupils dilated. His eyes then focused on Altman, and he suddenly slid his right hand along the deck and clenched the knife.

Altman stomped his foot on the diver's arm; Mathewson spun onto his side and drove his left fist against Altman's kneecap. Altman yelled in pain as his knee buckled. He swung the case as hard as he could with both hands. The hinges popped and the teak splintered as the case smashed across Mathewson's neck behind his left ear. As the shattered case fell from his grip, Altman fell backward and crashed into the wheel. The diver's hand went limp, and his body lay still. Altman stumbled forward before regaining his balance. The bent spyglass rolled out of the case and across the deck to the base of the ledge.

Wobbling, Altman leaned over, clutched his knees with his hands, and tried to catch his breath. It was almost a minute before he realized that the blood dripping onto the devil's-head tattoo on Mathewson's arm was not Mathewson's but his own. He pressed his torn shirt against his shoulder to staunch the bleeding and then knelt down next to the diver. Mathewson's body was flaccid, and his head was wrenched to the right, the blow from the spyglass case having broken his neck, severing his spinal cord. Altman knew he should finish Mathewson off, but the diver's breathing was already choked. His diaphragm, cut off from the sheared cervical nerves, twitched as he suffocated.

Altman considered the large diver's knife and then reached over, picked up the small sculptor's knife, and slipped it into his sock. He then took the diver's watch from Mathewson and strapped it on his own wrist. Time was critical now. The easy seafaring time of ship's bells and bell runs had vanished, and every minute mattered. He stood quickly, grabbed the Nike bag, and returned to Jones's cabin to retrieve the towel-covered bar, which he placed in the bag on top of the timer, detonator cap, and gray plastic explosives. Before leaving the cabin, he paused by the single porthole. The sleet had abated, and the morning looked a little less dark than it had earlier. His troubleshooting of complex mechanical and electronic problems had taught him not to rush. The searing pain in his shoulder focused his mind, and the rudiments of a plan began to form. If he had any chance at all of saving himself and *Seerauber*'s crew and divers, he

had to do everything in sequence. And he had to be certain
he had judged everyone—Grey and Petrosky and Jones—cor-
rectly.

Glancing at the diver's watch, he saw that it was 10:22.
Only five minutes had passed since Mathewson had told
him about the explosives, but he had less than thirty-five
minutes to locate and defuse the charges and to stop whatever iniquitous games Grey and Petrosky were still playing
with the lives of the men on board the salvage ship. It was
not, he understood with crushing clarity, nearly enough
time—unless he enlisted Jones's help. Despite the urgency
he felt, he realized he would have to deal with Jones
carefully. What he told Jones and how the captain reacted
were crucial if they were to survive. And, in a sense, he had
to manipulate Jones just as Grey and Petrosky had. With
pain rippling down his shoulder and that last thought gnaw-
ing at his mind, he hurried from the captain's cabin.

▽ **Thirty** ▽

When Altman entered the wardroom, Jones was pacing by the conference table. He wore an off-white turtleneck sweater. His hair was disheveled, and he was unshaven; dark rings protruded under his eyes. He held a bottle of rum by its neck. When he saw Altman, his hand pressed against the knife wound, he said, "What the bloody 'ell?"

Altman dropped the athletic bag on the table, picked up a cloth napkin, and unbuckled and removed his belt. "Figured I'd find you here," he said as he unfastened the top two buttons of his shirt, slid the napkin over the gash, and pressed hard.

"What the 'ell's going on?" Jones said. There was anger and mistrust in his voice. "You try to kill Grey, and now the bloody bugger's taken my ship. I'm going to get the son of a bitch if I 'ave to . . ."

"Mick," Altman interrupted, "tie this off for me." He looped the belt around his arm and slid it up to his shoulder.

Jones put the bottle on the table, set the belt around Altman's shoulder, and pulled the belt tight.

As Jones cinched the belt, Altman said, "Your salvage of the century is a goddamned hoax."

"What?" Jones sputtered. His breath smelled of rum. "You're bloody daft, mate."

"It's been nothing more than a power struggle between the Soviets and the President." Grimacing, Altman reached down and pulled the sculptor's knife from his sock.

"Where the . . . ? That's the knife Harrington had. You've been in my cabin."

Altman didn't answer. His shoulder was becoming stiff; the pain had begun to throb rather than burn. He took the bar from the bag, unfolded the towel, and pulled the knife's blade along the cut he had made earlier in the glittering bar.

"You're out of your bloody 'ead, you are," Jones said, his tone now more confused than angry.

Altman tried to spit on the knife blade, but his mouth was too dry. He licked his fingers and ran them along the blade.

As Altman gripped the knife more tightly and scored the bar again, Jones reached across to him and said, "Give me that . . ." Jones's hand stopped four inches from the bar.

Pale smoke swirled from the slit in the bar.

Jones dropped his hand and backed away from the table.

"The whole salvage has been nothing more than a Russian propaganda ploy," Altman said. "Petrosky's had you and me and everybody else set up from the beginning."

Jones hunched his shoulders, clenched his fists, and glowered at the smoking bar. "What the 'ell is it?" he asked.

"Uranium. Radioactive, fissionable uranium." Altman let the words sink in for a moment. "And Petrosky knew it all along. Why do you think the Russians were so god-damned willing to agree to an even split on the salvage?"

His face red, Jones looked from the bar to Altman and back to the bar. He kicked the table leg, lifted the bar with both hands, and stared into the slit at the nickel-white metal below the gleaming surface. His shoulders slumped for a moment, and then he hissed, "Goddamn it to 'ell," and heaved the bar against the bulkhead. The bar clanged against the steel wall and fell to the deck between the couch and one of the chairs. The deep ringing echoed around the two men.

"Grey came aboard because the Americans finally figured out what was going on," Altman lied. He wanted the full force of Jones's fury to remain focused on Petrosky as well as on Grey.

Jones's forehead furrowed. Running his hand under the collar of his sweater, he asked, "Then why'd you bust up Grey's face?"

His voice lower, Altman answered, "Because Grey's solution to the problem is not one I could live with."

Jones's eyes grew wide. "What?"

"Grey's prepared to do anything to make sure the Soviets never get their hands on the *Edinburgh*'s cargo."

Jones rubbed his face with his hand. "How the 'ell do you know all this?"

Altman held up the sculptor's knife. "I kept wondering why Harrington took this from my cabin. The only thing I could think of was that he needed to cut the bars." He did not tell Jones about the shavings he had found earlier in Harrington's stateroom.

"Trevor." Jones cleared his throat. "That bloke was a spy—a bloody double agent, at that."

"He was tricked by Petrosky just like you were."

"I . . ." Jones paused. "So you broke into my cabin to find the knife?"

Altman went over to the wet bar, ran water into a glass, and drained it in one gulp. "I was looking for you"—he pointed to the bar half-hidden next to the couch—"to show you that. Instead, I found the envelope Harrington had addressed to his daughter."

"How the 'ell do you know about that?" Saliva sprayed from Jones's mouth.

Refilling the glass, Altman answered, "When I was trying to find anything that might explain Harrington's disappearance, the radio operator told me that you had taken a letter from the mail bag."

Jones squinted at Altman and said, "You've been getting around, mate."

"Not as fast as Petrosky. He had been there before me, looking for the letter." Altman drank the second glass of water.

Jones clawed at the gray stubble on his chin. "I'm going to get that bastard," he growled as he kicked the leg of the table again.

Altman paused long enough to let Jones mull over that idea and then asked, "Where's Grey now?"

"Don't know. I got the 'ell out of the infirmary when 'e told Schmidt 'e 'ad taken command." Jones reached for the bottle of rum. "The son of a bitch's first order was to 'ave Schmidt arrest you." He swigged the rum and then wiped his mouth. "You messed up 'is face pretty good."

"Not well enough," Altman answered. "He already has a bomb planted—maybe two."

"What?" Jones stopped raising the rum bottle midway to his mouth. "Where? Why the fuck are you just standing 'ere?"

"Because I need your help. Mathewson said he'd planted 'charges.' There may be more than . . ."

"Mathewson's a bloody spy?"

"No. He's Grey's hired killer. He murdered Hall, but Petrosky killed Harrington and Strinivitch." Altman tried to make his guess sound like a fact.

"Shit." Jones slammed the rum bottle on the table. He looked again at Altman's torn, blood-stained shirt.

"Mathewson's out of the way." Altman glanced at the diver's watch. Speaking faster, he said, "I know his training. I don't know exactly how much time we have, something under half an hour, but I'm betting the charge'll be somewhere aft below the waterline, probably in the engine room. As long as Grey is still aboard I've got time, but I need you to check the fore hold in case there's a second charge. Start at the bow and work your way back. Check both the hold and the lower deck. Whether or not you find a charge, meet me back here. Petrosky is probably still going to make some sort of move, and we'll . . ."

"Don't worry about that, mate," Jones said. "I'll fix that bastard. And Grey, too, the bloody pirate." He turned, took two steps toward the door, reached into his back pocket, pulled out three sheets of folded beige stationery, and turned back around. "This won't tell you anything you 'aven't figured out, but 'ere you go," he said, tossing the letter to Altman. "Let's get to it, mate," he added as he left the room.

Without reading the letter, Altman shoved it into his pocket, took a deep breath, picked up the athletic bag, and rushed out of the wardroom toward the deck decompression chamber.

When Altman reached the DDC, he pressed the intercom button and peered through the porthole. Percy and a British diver, both of whom were sitting at the communications console, looked up.

"Jem," Altman said, even before the diver made it over to the viewing port, "get everybody into the emergency chamber."

"What?" Percy asked. He cocked his head. His eyes were bloodshot, and his beard was unkempt. "What the fuck is going on?"

Altman crouched so that his wounded shoulder was less visible through the porthole. "No time to explain. Just get in there."

"You better explain," Percy said. He leaned closer to the port and tried to look around Altman to see if anyone else was there. "Some serious shit is happening out there, and we're like fucking fish in a bowl . . ."

"Damned straight," Altman answered. He didn't have time to argue with the diver. "And the only thing you can do is sit tight."

"Some guy, a Commander Grey, has ordered us to . . ."

"Grey is no fucking commander."

"But . . ."

"Goddamn it, Jem," Altman shouted, "just get everybody the fuck into the emergency chamber—fast." He bit his cracking lip, glanced around the side of the DDC, and saw a sailor turn quickly through the forward hatchway.

Startled by Altman's tone, Percy gaped at him through the viewing port.

"And stay in the emergency chamber until you hear from Jones or me. Nobody else." He looked at the diver's watch. "And don't believe a fucking word Grey says." Leaving Percy standing at the porthole, Altman turned, jogged over to the ship's ladder, and clambered down to the lower deck.

Still carrying the athletic bag, Altman began his search in the compressor room, where he checked around the base of the Junkers high-pressure compressor and the compressed air tank. He tried to remain calm, to ignore the seconds ticking away, but his eyes burned and his arm ached, the belt having cut off the circulation. Not quite able to control his breathing, he worked his way aft into the engine room. He told the lone crewman he found there that Schmidt wanted him on deck immediately. When the crewman, looking befuddled, pointed to the intraship phone on the bulkhead, Altman shook his head, repeated Schmidt's name, and said, "*Schnell, schnell.*"

As soon as the crewman left, Altman ducked under a maze of pipe work and, moving from starboard to port and back, inspected the electric control transmitter, the 110-volt generator, the turbo-generator starting batteries, and the main engines. Although *Seerauber*'s main diesels were turned off, a jangling din from all of the other equipment echoed around the room. His throat was constricting, and his breathing was becoming more irregular. He was so dehydrated that he barely sweated despite the heat and noise. The skin on his back and legs prickled.

After checking the 20-kilowatt generator, he finally found the thick cylinder of gray malleable material wedged behind the centrifuge oil filter against the aft fuel-oil tank's bulkhead. He knelt down, wiped his hands on his pants, and examined the timer and detonator cap. Noting the time set on the timer, he took a long, deep breath. His hands were steady; the throbbing in his shoulder faded. His movements careful and precise, he deactivated the detonator cap and then disconnected the wiring between the cap and the timer. Still kneeling, he opened the athletic bag, separated most of the gray plastic material, and slipped it into the bag. Cautiously, almost gingerly, he molded the remaining material into a sphere a little smaller than a baseball and then also placed it and the timer and cap in the bag.

Altman stuck his head out of the engine room's hatch, saw no one in the passageway, and headed thirty feet aft to the ship's stern compartment. He shut the hatch and scanned the room, fixing his gaze on the A-frame lifting rig's electric panel. He opened the panel, took the small gray ball from the athletic bag, and flattened it inside the panel along the lower right-hand corner. As he placed the detonator cap and timer in the small explosive charge and reconnected the wiring, he heard distant shouting in German. He checked the diver's watch, reset the timer, and stood up. The German voices were louder, already in the passageway, moving closer.

He gripped the athletic bag in his right hand and mounted the ladder near the aft bulkhead. As he pushed open the hatch to the deck above, he felt the wound reopen; a damp warmth pooled below his shoulder. He climbed out into the blustery gray morning. The white foam from the ten- and twelve-foot waves blew in streaks along their crests. Icy spray whipped above the heaping sea and over *Seerauber*'s stern. The thick clouds were lifting, starting to break up. He crossed the slippery deck to the starboard railing and flung the athletic bag into the tumult.

▽ **Thirty-one** ▽

When Altman reached the wardroom again, Jones had not yet returned. Altman poured another glass of water, drank it quickly, and refilled the glass. His clothes were damp from the sea spray, and he shivered intermittently. He needed something to eat, but there was nothing on the table except for an empty coffee pot, two dirty mugs, and salt and pepper shakers. Jones had to find the second charge, if there was one, in the next few minutes, but there was nothing Altman could do but wait. If he went looking for Jones and the captain returned to the wardroom, they might miss each other entirely. Still, Altman could feel time fleeting with each throbbing beat of the pulse in his wounded shoulder. He drank more of the water and, pacing between the table and the wet bar, readjusted the dressing over his wound, which had continued to bleed.

He stopped by the couch, took the beige stationery from his pocket, and unfolded the letter quickly. Holding the letter to the light from the porthole, he began to read Harrington's small and meticulous handwriting.

My Dear Elizabeth,
    I am writing to you now, well past midnight, because

I do not know where the events of the next few hours will take me. I do know, however, that I have let this charade go on far too long. I had planned to speak with Will earlier about my suspicions concerning the cargo, but I decided that this path is one I must travel alone. I do not think that I can embroil him further in this affair in which, I have come to believe, he has no involvement whatever. He has no conception of what really is at stake here.

In a few minutes, I will accost the Soviet representative with my evidence. Although it is my hope that some rational solution can be negotiated, I can not predict what will happen. For reasons that you understand, I have attempted to be equitable in my dealings with all parties, but especially with my Soviet counterparts. I hope that this evenhandedness will now bear fruit.

You are a good woman, Elizabeth, and I wish that I had a more exemplary legacy to leave you. When you were young, I never told you about my work because I wanted to protect you from the baseness of the life I was leading. In retrospect, I realize that this was a blunder. Your imagination had to have made what is essentially a sordid business seem romantic and adventuresome.

When I saw you at dinner the other evening listening so intently to the stories that Will and I were exchanging, I understood that the real legacy that I am leaving you is a life of loneliness and isolation—a life not unlike the life I have led and that I unwittingly inflicted upon your mother and you. I have been worn down, depleted by the secrets I possess. Despite whatever you may think now, you will one day have to travel alone as well, and that path is a difficult one.

I am sorry that I did not raise you to discern the essential vacuity of a spy's life. I hope that one day you will not only understand but also forgive me. As for me now, I hope that what I am about to do will perhaps save lives that would otherwise inevitably be lost.

I love you more than you will ever know,
    Your Father

Altman stared at the letter. Jones had been wrong on two counts: Harrington was no double agent. And, the ending of the letter had told Altman something he had not known, something that he still could not quite believe. Folding the letter, he felt at first angry and confused. But those feelings soon gave way to a deep and pervasive sadness. He slipped the letter into his back pocket and finished the glass of water. The cool water trickling down his throat did little to prevent him from sinking into a dark mire of gloom and exhaustion. He put the glass on the wet bar, went over to the conference table, and, despite the fact that there would be no more meetings there, slumped into his usual seat.

The wardroom door's opening startled him. "Mick, I defused . . ." he said as he turned, but Schmidt, dressed in his starched white uniform, stood in the doorway.

Schmidt turned, shouted down the passageway in German, turned back, and walked into the room.

"Herr Altman," Schmidt said, his tone formal, "I must inform you that you are to be taken into custody." He came over and stood in front of Altman.

Altman did not move.

"I ask," Schmidt continued, "that you do not resist."

Altman looked up at the German. Although he no longer cared much what happened to him, he still felt the need to delay Schmidt until Jones returned. "What do you mean?" he asked.

"My orders are to take you into custody." Schmidt

glanced over his shoulder at the doorway. "You must come with me."

Altman stood up. Needing to know if Mathewson's body had been discovered yet, he asked, "Why, Gunter? What sort of crap has Grey come up with?"

"For the assault on Herr Grey." Schmidt paused, as though deciding what to say. "And for suspicion of the murder of Herr Harrington."

Altman breathed deeply. Apparently, Schmidt had been so busy tracking him down that he hadn't had time to return to the bridge.

Schmidt took hold of Altman's arm, but Altman jerked himself free.

"Get your hands off me," Altman said.

Avoiding Altman's stare, Schmidt answered, "These are my orders."

"I want to talk to Jones first."

"My orders . . ." Schmidt looked over his shoulder again as two burly crewmen, one of whom was the crane operator, entered the wardroom. "There is no point in resisting, Herr Altman," Schmidt said.

Altman stepped back, knocking into the chair, and said, "Get Jones. I need to talk to him."

"There is nothing to explain." Schmidt looked away from Altman at the two crewmen. "Herr Grey stated that you attacked him when he presented you evidence that you had murdered Herr Harrington." Schmidt looked back at Altman. "Herr Grey's nose and cheek are crushed. The medic had to sew . . ." He shook his head. ". . . Had to stitch the cut on his head." He looked away again. "Herr Grey said that you were to be taken into custody immediately."

Altman sank into the chair. "I need to talk to Jones," he repeated, wiping the side of his face with his right hand.

"It is not possible," Schmidt answered. "I do not know

where he is.'' He leaned over and took Altman's right arm.

"Let go of me,'' Altman said. He stood, glared at Schmidt, and stepped away from the German. "Where the hell is Grey?''

"He is on deck waiting for the Russian boat to remove Herr Petrosky.''

Why the hell is Grey letting Petrosky go free? Altman wondered. "What?'' he asked.

"The Russian patrol boat, it is already approaching,'' Schmidt answered as he once again took hold of Altman's right arm.

Schmidt led Altman from the wardroom, the two crewmen following close behind. When the four men reached the lower deck, Schmidt began heading down another flight of steps.

"Where are we going?'' Altman asked, stopping at the top of the stairs.

Turning to face Altman, Schmidt answered, "You are to be locked in the strong room with the gold.''

"That bastard,'' Altman muttered. Grey was going to leave him to die among the glittering radioactive bars. "Whose idea was that?''

Schmidt twisted the end of his mustache. "Herr Grey's. He insisted that you be placed in the strong room because he feared that you would attack him again.''

Altman tried to control his simmering panic. He felt the breath of one of the crewmen on the back of his neck. "Take me to Grey, Gunter.''

"It is not possible. My orders...''

With all his strength, Altman elbowed the man behind him in the throat, and, spinning around, swung at the crane operator. The crane operator blocked Altman's punch and hit him so hard in the stomach that Altman toppled over backward, fell against the railing, and tumbled down the stairs to Schmidt's feet. Unable to breathe, Altman clawed at the bulkhead for purchase. Schmidt stepped away, and Altman slipped down another step. His shirt was wet with blood where one of his ribs had punctured his skin. His lungs burned as he choked and gagged. As Schmidt and the crane operator pulled him up by his arms, he mumbled, "Take me to Grey, goddamn it, Gunter."

▽ Thirty-two ▽

Led by Schmidt, the two crewmen, one of whom was still coughing and clearing his throat, dragged Altman through the starboard hatchway to *Seerauber*'s foredeck and the blustery, half-lit arctic world. When they let go of him, he sagged to the dank deck. The deck's frigid dampness, seeping through his clothes, made him shiver. Pain knifed along his chest with each spasm, but the brisk wind cleared his mind. His breathing was labored, and his rib cage burned with each breath. His shirt was wet with blood, but as he moved his hand down along his chest he could not find the bone jutting through the skin. He reached for the bulkhead, braced himself, rose to one knee, and looked up.

Standing by the railing, Petrosky held an attaché case; a large black suitcase lay next to the railing's stanchion. He wore a raincoat open over a wool sweater. The coat's belt hung loosely at his sides. Grey stood three feet to the left of the Russian. His nose was completely bandaged. His left eye was purple and swollen shut, and a second bandage covered his eyebrow. He held a handkerchief in his left hand; his right hand was in the pocket of his coat.

"Herr Grey," Schmidt said, "I . . . Herr Altman asked that he could speak to . . ."

"It's all right, Schmidt," Grey interrupted. "Thank you. Mr. Altman and I have some unfinished business to conduct." His voice, though hoarse, was authoritative. "Go to the radio room and wait for my orders. Make sure that no messages are sent. Contact me immediately if a message arrives from either the Soviet or American ships." He turned toward Altman and, his voice raspy, almost a whisper, said, "Mr. Altman, I was wondering if I'd have the opportunity to see you again."

Altman stared at Grey but did not answer.

As Schmidt was about to follow the crewmen back through the hatchway, Grey said to him, "Give me your keys."

Schmidt turned and opened his mouth, but he did not say anything.

"I need your keys. Give them to me," Grey repeated.

Shaking his head, Schmidt unhooked the brass key ring from his belt, handed the keys to Grey, turned, and stomped through the hatchway. As Grey slipped the key ring into his left pocket, Altman, still bracing himself on the bulkhead, got to his feet. When he tried to stand straight, the pain took his breath away. Hunched over, he leaned against the wet bulkhead. Although his mouth was dry, he could taste blood in his throat. He wiped his cracked lips with the back of his right hand and glanced out to sea, where one of the Soviet patrol boats was four hundred yards from *Seerauber* and running at an angle so that it would soon close on the ship. Much farther away, the *Thorn*'s superstructure was visible only as a jagged scar on the horizon. Scraps of blue sky appeared through uneven tears in the clouds. "So you're going to destroy the cargo," Altman said, "and *Seerauber,* too."

"Yes," Grey answered. His smile twisted below the bandages. "And you with it." He cleared his throat and dabbed the bottom of his nose with the handkerchief.

"What about you?"

Grey looked at his watch. "The storm's died down just enough. In less than fifteen minutes, the *Thorn*'s helicopter will pick me up."

"So the Old Man has even enlisted the U.S. Navy in this fucking piracy?"

Grey's unbandaged eye twitched when Altman referred to the President as "the Old Man." "No," he said. "The *Thorn*'s captain knows nothing of the real purpose of my mission."

Altman nodded toward Petrosky. "And how do our Soviet friends fit into this scheme?"

"Mr. Petrosky understands that the only viable solution involves the destruction of the cargo," Grey answered. He coughed and spat blood into the handkerchief.

"But you're still letting him get away with murder."

"He would receive diplomatic immunity in any case," Grey answered.

As Altman turned toward Petrosky, a sharp pain shot across his chest. "But you did murder Harrington, didn't you?" He almost spat the words at the Russian.

Shrugging, Petrosky said, "Harrington acted foolishly. When he accosted me with the bar, I had to dispose of him. I do only what is necessary to ensure the success of an operation. No more." The lapels of his open raincoat flapped in the wind.

"But you murdered Strinivitch, your comrade." Altman made the last word sound like a curse.

"He did not know the true nature of the *Edinburgh*'s cargo. After he brought Harrington to me, he insisted on filing a report to Moscow that would have endangered the legitimate Soviet interests." There was no remorse in Petrosky's voice. "It was necessary."

"And it was also necessary to have me attacked in London?" Altman asked.

The Soviet patrol boat had closed to within two hundred yards of *Seerauber*. Three Soviet sailors, drenched by spray, stood by the twin forward 14.5-millimeter guns, but no one else was on deck. The sun broke between the clouds, igniting the wave crests and firing the spindrift blowing around the ships. The gray water turned to silver, and *Seerauber*'s wet deck and bulkheads glistened.

Petrosky put the attaché case down next to the suitcase, looked at Grey, and then turned back to Altman. "You were not attacked. My agents simply tested your tradecraft and informed you that it was not a good idea for you to board this ship." He pulled at his coat cuff and smiled grimly. "You reacted like a rank amateur, of course." His smile became hostile. "And, as you now understand, you would have been better off to have listened to the advice."

Altman glared at Petrosky. He then shook his head and said, "You're nothing but a fucking shark."

"No," Petrosky answered, waving his hand in the air. "I am a chess player." Anger began to rise in his voice. "A master plans for all contingencies, and I did not. I have been checked, and I must concede the game. My error, my only error, was in mistaking the nature of my opponent."

"You see, Altman," Grey said, his tone arrogant, "he didn't realize that you were just a pawn."

Shading his eyes with his right hand, Altman looked from Grey to Petrosky and said, "You two are both scum, the same goddamned scum."

"What you think is not important," Petrosky said.

Altman looked at each of the men again and asked, "What is this, honor among sharks?"

Petrosky waved his hand. "No, trust is not involved here," he said. "If it were, Mr. Grey's hand would not remain in his pocket. But I believe what Mr. Grey says. The Americans are willing to take any risk to prevent the *Edinburgh*'s cargo from reaching port. And I understand that the only reason I am alive is so that I can report this fact to my superiors." He rubbed his hands together almost daintily. "Mr. Grey is an excellent chess player. But per- haps I will succeed in the next gambit."

Altman's shivering caused the pain to ripple down his shoulder and across his chest. The sun slipped behind the clouds, the light left the waves, and the gloss vanished from the ship. Out of the corner of his eye, he noticed Jones darting along the starboard deck to the enclosed lifeboat twenty-five feet behind Grey and Petrosky. With surprising agility for a large man, Jones sprang through the lifeboat's hatch and disappeared.

Seventy yards from *Seerauber,* the Soviet patrol boat began to slow and turn so that it would come up broadside to the salvage vessel. A tall, gaunt man wearing a long black overcoat stood by the cockpit door. The three sailors remained standing by the forward guns.

Although he had no idea what Jones was up to, Altman knew he had to keep both Grey's and Petrosky's attention concentrated on himself. They had said that what he thought didn't matter, but they were wrong. That was really their critical error. He may have been a pawn in this clandestine game, but what he thought had already mattered—and would continue to matter—to its outcome. "Shit," he said, "Petrosky gets away with murder and you're home free, but the divers and *Seerauber*'s crew buy the ranch. That's fucking international relations at its finest."

Petrosky scowled at him but said nothing. Sunshine streamed between the clouds again, and the sea and ship were bathed in light.

Grey coughed, wiped his mouth with the handkerchief, and said, "You may think I'm scum, but at least I put the best interests of my country before my own."

"You son of a bitch," Altman said to Grey. "Don't lay that jingoistic bullshit on me. You're only trying to save the President's political ass."

Jones climbed out of the enclosed lifeboat. He strode deliberately across the slick deck toward the three men, two of whom had their backs to him as Altman argued with them. With the sun at his back, Jones looked like some dark, hulking apparition limned with light. His right hand was out of sight behind his hip; his left hand held a couple of red objects the size and shape of shotgun shells.

Stopping ten feet from them, Jones raised the orange and black flare gun. His dark, puffy eyes were like opaque holes; the sun caught the white scar heading up his forearm under the sleeve of his turtleneck. "Grey, Petrosky," he bellowed over the wind and waves. He set his feet on the deck; his hand wavered for a moment before becoming steady. As Altman ducked against the bulkhead and the other two men turned around and squinted into the sun, Jones fired.

The flare struck Petrosky in the neck above his collar bone and burst, crushing his trachea and knocking him backward onto the deck. The burning phosphorus splattered, bright orange flames seared his face and chest, and thick red smoke engulfed his upper body. The smoke swirled above him as he began to flail at his throat with his hands. His heels beat a staccato rhythm on the deck.

As the flare gun's report, like that of a shotgun, echoed away, Jones snapped the gun's barrel open and slipped in the second flare. Crouching behind the smoke, Grey fumbled in his pocket and drew the .22-caliber pistol. While Jones was snapping the barrel shut and raising the flare gun, Grey aimed and fired. Jones's head jerked back, a red dot appeared at the corner of his eyebrow, and the flare gun went off. Grey's second shot hit Jones in the center of his forehead. A perplexed expression on his face, Jones looked at Grey, took one step back, dropped the flare gun, and collapsed onto the deck. The flare, trailing a plume of red smoke, arced into the sky and vanished among the dispersing clouds.

During the twenty seconds it took the phosphorus to burn off, Petrosky writhed on the deck, thrashing at his neck and face. A high-pitched screech, part wheezing and part infernal wailing, rose from his scorched and gaping mouth. As the phosphorescent flames subsided, his clothing, skin, and hair still smoldered. His arms stiffened as he gasped for breath through his smashed windpipe, and his legs churned as though he were trying to march toward some indeterminable destination. The acrid odor of smoke mingled with the smell of burning skin and hair.

Grey looked down at the two men, one dead and the other dying, and then glanced out at the Soviet patrol boat forty yards away. "Damn," he said, under his breath.

Altman turned and looked out to sea. The three sailors on the patrol boat's deck had swung the twin 14.5-millimeter guns around so that they pointed at *Seerauber*'s bridge. The gaunt man in the black overcoat was yelling at six Soviet marines who lined the gunwale aft of the cockpit. Dressed in combat fatigues, they had their AKM assault rifles trained on the two men standing on the salvage vessel's deck.

Altman slid the sculptor's knife from his sock and, shaking with pain and cold, slinked toward the hatchway.

Grey turned, pointed the pistol at his face, and shouted, "Don't move."

Keeping the knife hidden in his palm, Altman said, "It seems your chess partner had one more gambit planned.

Grey did not turn to look at the patrol boat again. "They won't shoot," he said, his voice again calm and imperious.

▽ **Thirty-three** ▽

Stepping through the hatchway, Schmidt said, "Herr Grey, the flare . . ." He glanced down at Jones's pallid face crisscrossed with blood and then looked over at Petrosky's mutilated body. *"Mein Gott,"* he muttered. "Herr Grey, what has happened?" He stared at the pistol in Grey's hand. "You have shot Captain Jones?"

"Schmidt," Grey shouted, "push the bodies overboard."

Schmidt glanced at Altman before going tentatively out onto the deck.

The Soviet marines continued to aim their assault rifles at the three men on *Seerauber*'s deck. The skeletal man in the black overcoat stood half in and half out of the cockpit's hatch, staring across the waves at the salvage vessel.

Schmidt stepped forward, peered down at Petrosky's twitching mouth and sporadically heaving chest, and said, "But this man is not dead."

Raising the pistol, Grey repeated, "Push the body overboard. That's an order."

Schmidt glanced at Altman, stooped, grabbed Petrosky's ankles, and yanked the Russian's body around so that his head was near the railing.

"Do it," Grey rasped as he circled behind Schmidt to get out of the possible line of fire.

Looking over his shoulder, Schmidt frowned at Grey. He then turned and, still holding Petrosky's ankles, pushed the Russian's head under the railing's lower horizontal bar near where the suitcase and attaché case still stood. When Schmidt looked back again, Grey waved the pistol at him. Schmidt hunched his shoulders and shoved the body under the railing. Petrosky made no sound as he slipped over the edge and disappeared into the sea, leaving a trail of steaming blood and burnt phosphorus smeared across the deck.

Glaring at Grey, Schmidt said, "You should not have ordered me to do that. The man was not dead." He tried to brush the grime from Petrosky's shoes off his uniform.

Grey, the gun still in his hand, said, "Get rid of Jones."

Hesitating, Schmidt looked down at Jones's body.

Cocking the .22, Grey said, "If you don't obey orders, Schmidt, you'll be dead."

Schmidt knelt next to Jones for a moment before pushing the body under the railing. The man in the dark overcoat had disappeared, but the Soviet marines and gun crew stood rigidly on the deck as the spray whipped them with each roll of the idling patrol boat.

Altman glanced at the diver's watch: it was 10:50. He wrapped his fingers around the haft of the sculptor's knife and began to count silently.

Grey lowered the pistol and said, "Mr. Schmidt, return to the radio room."

"But the flare, Herr Grey," Schmidt said, his voice agitated. "I came to inform you that the Americans sent a message. It said the *Thorn* sighted the flare and is sending the helicopter immediately. I do not understand what . . ."

"That's fine, Schmidt, I understand." Grey raised the pistol a fraction of an inch. "Now get back to the radio room."

As Schmidt trudged across the deck, a young sailor

wearing an unbuttoned watch coat appeared in the hatchway and spoke urgently to him in German.

Scowling, Schmidt turned back around and said to Grey, "It is the Russians. They have radioed that they will . . ." He paused, trying to find the correct English word. ". . . Board the ship."

Grey looked at the United States Navy SH-60 helicopter flying low over the running waves toward *Seerauber*. Its rotor blade flashed in the sunlight, and a rapid thumping carried across the water. "Let them," he said.

When Schmidt stood there uncomprehending, Grey nodded in an exaggerated manner and shouted, "Get to the goddamned radio room and tell them to go ahead and board the ship." Still holding the bloody handkerchief, he waved his left arm at the helicopter circling above *Seerauber;* his right hand remained at his side.

When Schmidt and the sailor were out of sight, Grey looked again at the Soviet patrol boat. Although the boat had come about and was heading directly at *Seerauber,* the marines still lined the gunwale and the gun crew still had the twin guns trained on the ship. Grey turned to Altman and said, "I told you they wouldn't shoot. Jones did me a favor, blowing Petrosky away." He checked his watch. "The timing's perfect. The Soviets'll be aboard when the fireworks start. It'll look like they tried to sabotage the ship but screwed up."

The helicopter hovered above *Seerauber*'s deck. A cable with a jack seat attached began to descend, swinging in the wind. Spray from the helicopter's backwash blew across the deck.

Still counting in his head, Altman stared at the gun in Grey's hand. Needing just a few more seconds, seconds he was not sure he had, he leaned against the bulkhead and asked, "What about Mathewson?"

Grey started for a second. "Good guess. He's going overboard in a wet suit. The *Thorn*'ll pick him up. He'll be the only survivor." He smiled, his voice becoming spiteful. "The *Edinburgh*'s cargo'll be scattered so far across the ocean floor that no one'll ever find it."

Altman did not say anything. Grey had finally told him the last piece of information about *Seerauber*'s destruction, the scrap of information that Jones had likely known when he died. But there was nothing Altman could do now except count off the final few seconds.

The jack seat was only eight feet above their heads. Still smiling malevolently, Grey began to raise the pistol, cocking the hammer as he aimed it at Altman.

Seerauber's stern suddenly heaved upward; the blast of the explosion was followed a second later by a deep rumbling. Falling against the ship's railing, Grey barely kept himself from plunging overboard. He nearly dropped the gun as he grabbed the railing. Altman was knocked into the bulkhead, and a warm dampness spread again behind the dressing and down his chest. Black and gray smoke billowed up through *Seerauber*'s stern hatches and ventilation shafts. The helicopter swerved and then began to rise away from the ship. The cable and jack seat trailed after the helicopter like the tail of a kite.

Grey regained his balance, looked back at the cloud of smoke shrouding the stern, and said, "What the . . ."

Biting through his lip to staunch the pain, Altman planted his feet on the slippery deck and gripped the knife tightly.

Spinning around and raising the gun, Grey yelled at Altman, "You bas . . ."

Altman lunged at Grey's throat with the knife, but Grey turned just enough so that the blade caught him below his left ear and slit his skin to the collarbone. Blood oozed from the gash. His eyes widened, and he stammered, "You . . . you . . ."

Before Grey could get the pistol clear, Altman was on him, clamping his arm and trying to get another clear stroke with the knife. Grey took hold of Altman's wrist, and the two men tumbled over onto the deck. Altman pressed with all of his weight to keep Grey from turning the gun barrel, and Grey clenched Altman's hand. Oblivious to the thick smoke swirling above them and to the coughing and shouting of the men pouring out of the ship's hatchways, Altman and Grey struggled on the wet deck.

Pain swelled in Altman's chest; his breath came in short gasps. Slowly, the pressure he put on Grey's arm slackened, and his grip on the knife weakened. Grunting, Grey rolled him over and glared fiercely down at him. Blood from Grey's neck dripped onto Altman's forehead and into his eyes, partially blinding him. The feeling in his hand gone, he let the knife slip to the deck. Blinking to clear the blood from his eyes, he saw through a reddish haze Grey grinning down at him. His arm shook from the exertion of holding Grey back.

As Grey fought with Altman, the gun fired. Altman felt a hot stinging in his side between his ribs and hip. Though he still clutched Grey's arm, his strength was almost gone. With his free hand, he felt for the knife on the deck but couldn't find it.

Turning the gun so that its barrel pointed at Altman's face, Grey sneered. His voice raspy and strained, he said, "I should have killed you before."

Dread and desperation overwhelmed Altman. With the last burst of energy he could muster, he sucked in his breath, reached up, and grabbed the collar of Grey's coat. Pulling Grey downward, Altman swung his head upward. His forehead smashed into Grey's broken nose, driving the bone up into the man's brain. Grey's scream was choked as his head lurched backward. The pupil of his open eye dilated, his mouth contorted in unspeakable pain, and the white bandage across his face reddened. His back arched, his neck jerked forward, and, convulsing, he fell on top of Altman. The gun clanked to the deck beside them.

Altman squirmed out from under Grey and kicked at the

convulsing body to get it farther away. Then, on his hands
and knees, he pushed the body toward the railing. Grey's
arm hooked around the railing's post, and his body hung
there for a moment before dropping overboard.

Panting, Altman crawled over and slumped against the
bulkhead. His head throbbed, and his chest burned. He
trembled and shivered simultaneously. Blood and sea spray
dripped from his face. The taste of dread and death lingered
in his mouth. He barely noticed the Soviet marines clambering
aboard and dashing across the deck and into the hatchway.
The tall, gaunt man in the overcoat paused for a moment
and glanced over at Altman before disappearing into the
ship.

▽ Thirty-four ▽

With one hand, Altman covered the hot, prickling dampness in his side; with his other hand, he wiped his face. He gasped the dank sea air. With his clothes soaked from the wet deck, he could not stop shaking. He had set the charges inside the A-frame's electrical panel as a diversion to cause a lot of smoke but no structural damage to the ship's hull. The smoke not only would drive most of *Seerauber*'s crew to the relative safety of the open deck but would also attract the *Thorn*'s rescue teams. He had less than seven minutes, barely enough time to defuse the second charge, but at least he now knew where it was. Petrosky and Grey were dead. Jones had died also, but Altman still had a chance to save the divers and the crew.

He pressed his hand more firmly against the bullet wound, almost stopping the bleeding, but his side still felt as though it were on fire. Above him, the helicopter circled in and out of the twisting smoke. He pulled himself up so that his back was against the bulkhead, stood still for a moment as waves of nausea and dizziness washed over him, and then stumbled toward the hatchway.

Inside the ship, as he staggered along the passageway toward the stairwell leading down to the strong room, a

short burst of machine-gun fire echoed from the deck below.
Jesus shit, what the hell is that? he wondered, but he kept
moving. The pungent smell of smoke hung in the air. When
he reached the head of the stairs, Schmidt was plodding up
them toward him. When Schmidt saw him, he recoiled;
taking a step back, he gaped at Altman's matted hair,
blood-streaked face, and blood-stained shirt.

"Gunter," Altman gasped. His shortness of breath made
it difficult for him to speak. "I need the key to the strong
room. There's a bomb hidden in it."

Schmidt shook his head. "*Nein.* There was an explosion
aft . . . where you were seen before."

Altman climbed down toward the German. "Give it to
me, goddammit." He was still gasping for breath, and he
had no time to explain.

Schmidt tugged at the collar of his white uniform shirt
and then began to pull at the corner of his mustache. "I do
not have a key. Herr Grey took my key. Captain Jones had
the other." He continued to gape wide-eyed at Altman. "It
would do no good even . . ."

Altman propped his good shoulder against the bulkhead
and said, "Come on. We'll break in." He started past the
German.

"*Nein,*" Schmidt said. He took hold of Altman's left
arm. "*Nein.* The Russian soldiers, they have already shot
the door open. They are in the room loading the gold into
boxes."

Altman pulled himself free from Schmidt's grip and
stared at the German.

"Their commander stated that any person approaching
the strong room would be shot," Schmidt added.

Altman could feel his last reserves of energy and strength
sapping. "God-fucking-dammit," he said, looking at the
diver's watch. He had less than five minutes. "Gunter,
sound the order to abandon ship. Get your crew . . ."

"But Herr Grey ordered . . ."

"Grey is gone," Altman said. "You're in charge. Save your crew, goddammit. Abandon ship." He made the last statement as emphatic as his irregular breathing would allow. His voice then became low, almost pleading. "You've got four minutes at most." He passed the German on the stairwell, turned, and repeated, "Abandon ship, Gunter. Your whole crew'll die otherwise."

As Altman crept down the stairs, Schmidt stamped up toward the deck. At the bottom of the stairs, Altman peered around the bulkhead. Halfway along the corridor, a Soviet marine standing in front of the strong room's doorway held an AKM assault rifle at an angle across his chest. Altman certainly couldn't storm the Soviets, and he couldn't wait for them to leave. They'd all be dead in less than four minutes. His only hope was one last shot at reason. He knew no Russian, but the commander had apparently known German and might also know English.

His arms raised as high as the pain would allow, Altman stepped into the passageway. The marine, a young, round-faced man, turned and aimed his AKM.

"Don't shoot," Altman said. He trembled from the pain in his chest and side, but he kept his quivering arms raised. Amorphous red spots weaved in front of his eyes as he and the marine stared at each other for a moment.

The marine called out over his shoulder in Russian, and the man in the overcoat stepped out of the open doorway and gazed at Altman. His narrow face was pock-marked, and his skin was sallow, almost gray. His dark eyes gleamed.

"There's a bo . . ." Altman began to say, but there was something in those eyes, a cold disdain he had seen before, that caused him to leap back into the stairwell just as the man ordered the marine to fire.

The bullets slammed into the bulkhead behind Altman as he scuttled up the stairs. He crawled into the passageway, raised his head, and, gulping the air he could not get enough of, listened. There was no sound of footsteps following him.

Apparently the Soviet commander needed every available hand to load the *Edinburgh*'s baneful cargo—or he didn't consider Altman worth the effort to kill.

Altman let his face slip to the deck, his cheek against the cool steel. He lay there for almost a minute. Somewhere above him the ship's siren was blasting the signal to abandon ship, but he had no idea how long it had been blaring. He knew he had to get out on deck, as far away as possible from the strong room and the hidden explosives, but he could not shake the dismal feeling that Grey had ultimately succeeded in doing the Old Man's bidding. Even dead, even as his body sank through the frigid water into darker and darker depths, Grey had won. Just as the Soviets' mania had been the President's ally a half century before, it now, in the form of this final misguided attempt to ruin the Old Man by stealing the cargo, would save his political career.

Altman rose, careened through a haze of pain and dizziness along the passageway, and pitched out the starboard hatchway. The dazzling sunlight dimmed his vision. As he swerved blindly toward the enclosed lifeboat, an orange sheet of flame flashed from the forward hatches. *Seerauber*'s bow rose sharply, and the bridge buckled outward. Altman bounced against the bulkhead and lay bewildered on his stomach, his ears ringing from the explosion. Shattered glass and steel shards showered around him. Black smoke poured from the hatchways. The ship's bow settled lower in the water, and she began to list immediately to starboard. The forecastle had been blown apart; *Seerauber* was sinking fast under a cloud of dark smoke. Anyone inside the ship who hadn't been killed by the blast had little chance of making it to the deck before the ship went down.

Altman stood, and, dizzy and unable to get his bearings on the tilting deck, fell down again. He slipped into a whirling, excruciating fog. His ears ringing, he stood and tottered toward the enclosed lifeboat. More than a dozen figures were already aboard, chattering in some foreign tongue he could not hope to comprehend. Leaning against the lifeboat's forward davit, he tried to catch his breath. Dark smoke smothered the ship's bow; orange flames licked the hatchway he had come through a moment earlier.

His vision blurred and his breathing erratic, he fumbled for the base of the hatch. The lifeboat seemed to swing away from him, but a muscular arm in a white uniform shirt reached out and hooked his elbow. A large hand grabbed his collar. Barely audible above the clamor outside the lifeboat a vaguely familiar voice shouted, "*Schnell*, Herr Altman, *schnell*." Altman's feet were off the deck, the world spun, and he was inside. Shadows hovered above him, speaking incomprehensibly. An explosion rocked the lifeboat back and forth on its davits.

A final red flare of panic burst in Altman's mind. "The DDC," he choked. The fog thickened. "Jettison the divers' chamber, the DDC," he repeated. He had the sensation of falling, followed by a deep rocking that lulled him into darkness.

▽ **Thirty-five** ▽

Altman and Elizabeth stepped out of the black taxi by the Tower of London's stone fortifications. Silently, they followed the sidewalk that wound along the wall to the Tower Bridge. He glanced over his shoulder a couple of times, but he did not care much if they were being followed. Two and a half weeks had passed since *Seerauber* had sunk in the Barents Sea. Having almost died from internal bleeding in the lifeboat, he had spent the ensuing seventeen days in a hospital in Kirkenes. He had been operated on immediately to remove the .22-caliber bullet from his spleen, set his broken ribs, and stitch his shoulder. When the doctors were unable to stop the bleeding in his spleen, a second operation had been necessary to remove it. On his fifth day in the hospital, Elizabeth had called and offered to come to see him, but he had dissuaded her, saying that the authorities would not yet allow him to have visitors.

The investigators—American, British, German, Norwegian, Russian—had questioned him repeatedly whenever he was strong enough, but he had held to the story that he remembered little of *Seerauber*'s last hours. He had no explanation, he said, for the bullet wound or for the explosions that had wracked the ship. Lying in the hospital bed staring at the ceiling before the arrival of the first group of investigators, he had concluded that in some strange geopolitical sense Grey had been right. The *Edinburgh*'s cargo was best left scattered on the ocean floor; no government would ever use the cargo and its secrets sanely. The loss of the cargo served the President's ends, but the recovery of the cargo served no one's. Without the *Edinburgh*'s malignant cargo, the superpowers would keep lurching toward understanding, toward detente—and it really didn't matter all that much who the President was.

On Altman's eighth day in the hospital, Percy had visited him. He thanked Altman for saving the divers' lives and asked him what exactly had been happening aboard *Seerauber*. Although Altman trusted Percy as much as he did any man, he insisted that he had no idea. Telling anyone what he knew, he realized, would always be perilous.

Three days later, Schmidt had been allowed to visit him. During their fifteen-minute conversation, Schmidt explained to Altman what the investigators had failed to tell him. The arm that had reached out of the lifeboat to pull him aboard had been Schmidt's. Fourteen men of *Seerauber*'s crew as well as the six Soviet marines and their commander had been killed either in the second explosion or when the ship sank. The Soviet patrol boat, lying up next to *Seerauber*, had been damaged by the explosion but had been able to make it back to port under its own power. All of the divers, with the exception of Mathewson, had survived.

Schmidt had told the investigators only that the Soviets and the two Americans, Grey and Mathewson, had been fighting over the gold when both explosions occurred. Altman, whom Schmidt had stated had not been involved in the melee, must have been hit by a ricocheting bullet. The fact that, given Altman's wounds, no one believed Schmidt's story did not concern him; all of the evidence had sunk fifteen hundred feet to the ocean floor, and he had in *Seerauber*'s last horrific half hour come to despise both the

Americans and the Soviets who had murdered his captain, devastated his ship, and killed half his crew. Schmidt had ended his meeting with Altman by returning the blood-stained letter to him.

When the Norewegian doctors kept insisting that Altman's injuries could be causing his loss of memory, the investigators had finally stopped questioning him. He had been released four days later, after pledging to keep in close contact with the American authorities. His safety, he knew, still lay in his assumed ignorance. As long as the security officers, both Soviet and American, believed he thought the *Edinburgh*'s cargo was gold, they would leave him alone. He would learn to live with his secret about the *Edinburgh*'s cargo, those glittering bars that had caused so much death.

Now, as Altman and Elizabeth walked beneath the bridge's gothic North Tower, they still did not speak. It was early on a Saturday morning, and the clouds, like a layer of oatmeal, obscured the sun. When he reached the center of the bridge where the two bascules met, Altman stopped, rested his forearms on the blue and white steel railing, and gazed up the river at the *Belfast*.

Wearing a yellow cotton dress that rustled in the breeze, Elizabeth stood next to him. "So it's finally over for you?" she said.

Knowing that it would never quite be over, he looked down at the Thames, which was the color of pea soup. The tide was rising, carrying branches and wooden planking and other jetsam with it. When he had arrived in London the previous evening, he had called Elizabeth and told her only that he wanted to pick her up the next morning.

"Do you want to talk about it?" she asked, brushing wisps of hair from her face.

He smiled ironically and looked over again at the *Belfast*. The six-inch guns of the cruiser's stern turrets pointed at the bridge's high-level walkway ninety feet above the couple. A motorboat cut across the Thames from Hay's Wharf, where a dozen red and black barges were moored. The boat's wake rippled toward the bridge.

She put her hand on his arm and said, "It might help to talk about it."

A wooden launch with a green hull passed below them from under the bridge. Its wake created an inverted V that spread to the river's banks and seemed to slice a diagonal through the *Belfast*'s hull.

He turned to her and said, "You'd like me to talk about it, wouldn't you?"

"I think it would help," she answered, her tone confused. "What do you mean?"

Tourists strolling along the sidewalk behind them spoke a polyglot of languages. One German boy gleefully spat between the bascules into the river.

Without saying anything, he took the crumpled and blood-stained letter from his pocket and handed it to her.

She looked at the letter and then at him. Her hands shaking, she unfolded the letter and read it slowly.

He brushed his hand over the blue railing, where the initials MR and LM were scratched into it. The railing and sidewalk vibrated each time a heavy truck or double-decker bus crossed from one bascule to the other.

Elizabeth turned and leaned with her back against the railing. Crying, she let her hand holding the letter slip to her side.

"Captain Jones found the letter," he said, his voice just above a whisper, "but he misunderstood what your father said about traveling alone. Jones assumed all along that your father's attempts to be fair to the Russians suggested that he was a communist sympathizer." He rubbed his eye with his hand. "When I read the letter, I realized you were both British spies. And I've come to understand what your father meant about secrets wearing you down. I'm going to have to live with the *Edinburgh*'s legacy." Exhaling, he shook his head slowly. "But you've got to live with that and your father's death."

Tears ran down her cheeks.

"You used me from the start," he said, more sadness than anger in his voice. "Just like Grey and Petrosky and the others."

Her eyes glistening, she shook her head. "It wasn't like that, Will," she said.

He shook his head again.

"Really, it wasn't." She put her hand on his arm.

He looked down at the water, now more brown than green, that swirled around the bridge's stone and concrete foundation piers. "Your cover's good," he said. "Having your father in the service, too, helped, I'm sure."

"Stop it, Will," she said, her voice soft.

"There is one thing that still confuses me—what made your father suspicious about the *Edinburgh*'s cargo to begin with?"

"Our files pegged Grey as ex-CIA. We considered an ex-CIA agent turned NSC flunky an unlikely negotiator. That, and the Americans' uncharacteristic belligerence during the negotiations." She gazed at his scarred hand on the railing. "My father did not know what the cargo was, but he realized something about the salvage wasn't cricket. When Petrosky, whom he knew had previously directed Soviet covert operations in London, appeared aboard the ship, my father's fears were confirmed." She paused for a moment before adding in a low voice, "Your presence was the only thing that didn't fit. He could not figure out why Grey had you aboard instead of himself . . ." Her voice trailed off.

They stood silently for a moment. Altman looked again at the *Belfast*. The cruiser's superstructure seemed to him like some arcane religious symbol he could not fathom. "It's almost perfect," he said. "Your job allows you to travel freely on the continent . . . and throughout the world, for that matter." He pulled himself away from her. "I should have known when you told me a 'friend' found you a flat that looks out on the American embassy. While you're at work, the technicians can play in your apartment, no doubt. I wonder what sort of surveillance equipment an American team would find in the flat and how they would feel about the fact that even their closest ally, despite all the treaties and confidential agreements, was spying on the embassy?" He looked back at her. "You just *happened* to accompany your father to dinner that first night. You sure did a good job of feigning... attraction to me." He tapped the railing. "You really had me going."

She squeezed his wrist with her free hand and, crying again, said, "You don't have to believe me, Will, but..." She looked up at him. "The attraction was... is real... I..."

He pulled away from her again. "Frankly, Elizabeth," he answered, "I find that hard to believe. You and your father played me constantly, never once being straight about it. Your father came close the night he died, but even after his death you..." His voice faltered as he looked away. The sun was breaking through the clouds, turning them pink and blue. Three gulls swung and alighted on the river. A white tourist boat with a high prow headed down the river directly toward them.

"Will..." she said.

He turned back toward her, looked her in the eye, and said, "Don't worry. I'm not going to blow your cover. I don't give a damn about the wretched games you or anyone else is playing."

Her lips quivered.

"But remember your father's legacy to you. It's a sordid, worthless business, and ultimately a lonely one." Without another word he walked away, leaving her standing there, the letter in her hand fluttering in the breeze.